Little Triggers

Also by Martyn Waites

Mary's Prayer

Little Triggers

Martyn Waites

PIATKUS

Copyright © 1998 by Martyn Waites

First published in Great Britain in 1998 by
Judy Piatkus (Publishers) Ltd of
5 Windmill Street, London W1

This edition published 1998

The moral right of the author has been asserted

A catalogue record for this book
is available from the British Library

ISBN 0 7499 0455 0

Set in Times by
Wyvern 21 Ltd, Bristol

Printed and bound in Great Britain by
Biddles Ltd, Guildford and King's Lynn

For Hazel, Harry and Vera

Thanks once again to Caroline, Kate, Elenore, and, especially, Linda

And also a big thanks to Deb Howe for doing her day job in her spare time, and 'Sir' Robert Horwell for his invaluable contribution to the creative process.

The Highest Beauty

It had just gone eight when the boy finally died.

As he lay there, unmoving, the room was filled with a sudden stillness. But the naked man crouched over the body of the boy was oblivious to every sensation but the deafening rush of blood in his own head.

After the man had paid due homage to what he had done, he stood up and paced the room, flexing the fingers of both hands, then contracting them into hard balls of fist. He breathed steadily and deeply, pushing his diaphragm out to its limits, holding it until his windpipe and lungs started to ache, expelling the air in a slow, smooth stream until there was none left in his body.

He regarded the fragile masterpiece lying on the bare boards. The back of the child's head, where the initial knock-out blow had connected, was caked with dried blood; blue-black bruises, evidence of their earlier love-tussle, highlighted the skin wounds which decorated the delicate flesh. Streaked tears lay glistening on purple handprints: a final reminder that life had been choked out of him.

Looking steadily at the broken body, all the man saw was the beauty of innocence. The highest beauty. This wasn't a bad thing that had happened – quite the opposite. Now the child would never grow old, corrupted. The butterfly of his soul had been preserved forever in an amber of innocence. The world would lay no hand on him.

The man turned and smiled at the camera. Perfection.

1: Shot With His Own Gun

"Het, look a' her! Body of a sixteen-year-old, brain of a nine-year-old. Champion. Just what you want."

Larkin sighed and looked away. Another girl walked past.

"Hey, look at them baps! Wouldn't mind seein' them with the gloves off!"

Larkin stared resolutely across the road, promising himself that he would kill the man if he uttered another word. But Houchen, seemingly ignorant of his companion's dark thoughts, wasn't about to be put off.

"Wa's the time?"

The man must have a fear of silence, thought Larkin. "Haven't you got a watch?"

"Yeah."

"So why don't you look at it, then?"

Houchen seemed quite upset by Larkin's abrupt tone. "Just makin' conversation."

Larkin stared out of the window; Houchen looked at his watch.

"It's half ten. Funny that. It was half ten last time I looked."

Larkin ignored him.

Houchen nodded, as if that was what he had expected. He fidgeted his bulk in the passenger seat. There was silence again for a few minutes.

"You nervous, then?"

That's it, thought Larkin, mentally slipping the boxing gloves on. Houchen continued unabated.

"I am. I mean, when I say I'm nervous, I mean that I'm . . . you know, keyed-up like. Anxious. Aye, that's it, anxious."

Larkin said nothing.

Houchen gave a big elaborate sigh, conveying tension and boredom in equal measures. "It's just . . . you know . . . I mean, how long does it take to get a stiffy, for Christ's sake? Feels like we've been sat here for hours."

It was no good, thought Larkin: he was going to have to talk to him, if only to shut him up. "Well, you know how it is," he said, eyes fixed straight ahead on the hotel's upstairs front bay window, watching the weak light in the room faintly illuminate the shadowy figures behind the glass. "Some people take longer than others. Their erogenous zones are a bit more rarified. Their buttons take a bit more pushing."

"Aye, you're right, like," said Houchen, and settled back into his seat. Larkin turned to look at him. He was big, with an old quayside market leather jacket stretched tight across his flabby frame. His greasy, piggy face made his eyes resemble two raisins thumbed into soft white dough; his hair had the appearance of an ill-fitting black wig that had dropped onto his head from a great height. He wasn't the sort of man Larkin was used to working with.

Larkin turned back to the window, mainly to escape from Houchen's raging halitosis. Outside it was a clear August evening. Vehicles moved up and down Osbourne Road, oblivious to the occupants of the battered Volvo. People strolled along the pavement, enjoying the last of the day's sun. All the while they had sat there, Larkin had been treated to Houchen's opinion on every single girl who had walked past. That, combined with an almost endless stream of verbal punctuation accompanying his farts – "There you go"; "Have that one on me" – had almost moved Larkin to threaten violence on his new partner. If Houchen hadn't been so good at his job, Larkin would cheerfully have strangled him by now.

He wasn't all bad, though. At least he had opened the window. Eventually.

"So Ian," said Larkin curiously, "what did you do before this?" Houchen's past was cloaked in mystery; few were sufficiently interested to lift the veil.

"Well, you know. When I went freelance after *The Chronicle* I did a bit of everything. Weddin's, fetes, that sort of thing. I did a lot of children's parties for a while."

Larkin could just imagine screaming kids running for their lives as Houchen lumbered after them, grinning and breathing on them, waving his camera like a club. He smiled to himself at the thought.

4

"Hey," Houchen said suddenly, "there's the signal."

Larkin looked up. At the upstairs window stood a voluptuous silhouette, with big hair and a generous, hourglass shape. The figure made a surreptitious beckoning motion and then turned back into the room.

"That's us," said Larkin, and started to get out of the car. Houchen grabbed his camera from the floor between his legs, which was no mean feat, and began to prise himself out of the door.

They walked swiftly to the door of the hotel, an old converted Victorian mansion which looked like it had never seen better days, hurried up the steps and inside.

The ratty little moustachioed doorman's smile quickly vanished when he saw Houchen's camera. He tried to block their path, but Houchen swatted him out of the way without even breaking his stride. The doorman seemed about to protest, so Larkin pushed his left hand over the man's mouth and shoved him against the wall.

"One word," said Larkin, with his index finger so close to the man's nose that it was sending him crosseyed, "one word, and you'll be wearing your bollocks for earrings."

The man's face turned from indignation to fear. Larkin sensed he would be no more trouble. He let him go and followed Houchen upstairs.

Larkin found his colleague standing outside a door at the top of the landing.

"Number nine?"

"That's the one," said Larkin.

Houchen got his camera ready as Larkin opened the door for him and then stood aside. The photographer walked straight into the room, clicking away; the couple on the bed looked directly at him as his flashbulb popped.

"Lovely one, that," said Houchen. "Nice clear face shot. Big smile now." Off went the flashbulb again.

Larkin studied the man on the bed. His face was familiar from newspapers and the local news; he always seemed to have a response to every situation neatly encapsulated into a smooth, slick soundbite. But anything remotely resembling calmness and collection seemed to be well beyond him at the moment. His face resembled that of a rabbit caught in a car's headlights on the M1. It wasn't hard to see why he'd lost his composure. His well-fed, corpulent body was spread-eagled naked on the bed, secured at each corner by a different-coloured chiffon scarf, with a pastel yellow one around his throat and a pink one tied into a big bow round his rapidly deflating penis. The woman straddling him was wearing co-ordinated scarlet underwear, black stockings and fuck-me high heels. Her hair, immaculately long and dark, could only have been a wig, her perfectly made-up face was smiling at the camera.

"Get my good side, boys," she said in a husky voice and put on a teasing little pout.

Eventually, after a long struggle, the man found his voice: not his carefully modulated TV voice, the treacly one that he poured over all the ills of society, but an angry, aggressive whine that Larkin suspected was a truer reflection of his character.

"Who are you and what the fuck do you want?"

Houchen looked at Larkin. "There you go – fiver to me. The cliché king. Not very original, is he?"

"They never are," said Larkin.

The councillor seemed to be recovering a little of his professional demeanour. "Get out of here at once! Pauline, who are these people? Get my bloody hands loose, damn you!"

"Oh, Ian's just come to do my modelling portfolio – haven't you darling? D'you want me to strip off for you?" And so saying, she quickly whipped off her panties to show a perfectly formed set of male genitals. Pauline straddled the politician again. "Come on – get a good close up," she said, smiling seductively.

"Canny set of tackle you've got there, pet," Houchen said as his flashbulb popped yet again.

"Well," said Larkin, "this won't do much good for your reputation as family man and man of the people, will it?"

The councillor's face flushed so red, Larkin thought that steam was about to explode from his ears. He fully expected him to let off a high-pitched whistle.

"Get me untied *now*! You'll regret this!"

His tirade of clichés looked as if it might continue indefinitely.

"This is entrapment!"

"You wish."

"Why I—"

Larkin silenced him. "Shut up."

The councillor's mouth audibly snapped shut.

"Undo him, Pauline."

Pauline worked her way round the bed, starting with his feet, untying one scarf after another, with Houchen snapping away, catching every moment. As soon as she had finished the politician sat bolt upright, pulled the scarves from his neck and from his now totally shrivelled penis, and stumbled to his feet to start hunting for his clothes.

Pauline crossed to Larkin. "Am I done for the night, lover?"

"Yeah. Thanks, Pauline."

"Pleasure, love," the transvestite said, pulling her underwear back on and picking up her skimpy red dress from the floor. As she stepped into it Larkin spoke.

"Here," he said and handed her some bills. "Hundred."

"Smashing. One step closer to Denmark," she said, and turned around. "Could you do me up at the back? There's a darl."

Larkin zipped Pauline up. She stashed the money in her handbag and retrieved a fake leopardskin coat from where it was draped over an armchair. Larkin thought she couldn't have been less subtle about her status if she'd walked round with a neon sign over her head.

"Well, I'll be off then."

"Er . . . just a minute." It was Houchen.

Pauline sighed, rolled her eyes heavenward and delved into her bag, bringing out a pen and a scrap of paper.

"What'll I make it out for? Services rendered?"

"Anythin' you like. A receipt's a receipt."

She handed him the paper. "That all right for you?"

He looked at it, grunted, and put it in his pocket. "Cheers, Pauline."

"Don't mention it, sweetie." She turned to the politician. "I'd like to say it's been a pleasure. But I'd be a lyin' old cow. Ta ta. Bye, Stephen – Ian. Give me a ring if you need me."

They said goodbye and she swept out.

The councillor had managed to pull on his trousers; his shirt had defeated him. He sat hunched on the side of the bed, a sad sack of humanity.

Larkin moved to the armchair and sat down. "Well," he said, "party's died a death, hasn't it?"

"Just say what you have to say and then let me leave."

The man's self-pity was as strong as his sweat; Larkin caught a whiff and almost felt sorry for him. Almost.

"Tell me what you want."

Larkin sighed. "That's the trouble with you people. Money,

7

money, money." He leaned forward. "There are more important things, wouldn't you say?"

"Such as?"

Larkin reached into his leather jacket, drew out some folded pieces of paper and handed them to the politician.

"Look."

The councillor unfolded them and looked.

"Familiar?"

"Well, yes, but . . . I don't see how—"

"Then let me tell you. What you've got in your hot little hand is a list of all the companies that you and your cronies have some kind of stake in."

"That's a matter of public record. You can't—"

"Let me finish." Houchen handed him another sheaf of papers. The politician leafed through them, turning so pale it was as if the blood had been drained from his body.

"You led us a merry old paperchase. But we tracked you down. We got there in the end. The Rebirth of the Region, you lot call it. Your so-called grand scheme to rejuvenate the North East with lots of lovely lottery money. Don't get me wrong – it's a great idea." Larkin leaned into the councillor's face. "But let's look closer. It's all the schemes, all the urban renewal projects, that you're supposed to have been in charge of. And guess what. It's all your companies that have got the contracts. Look even closer and you can see where you've paid yourself consultancy fees to do the job the taxpayer already pays you to do."

The politician opened his mouth to speak, but Larkin was fully into his stride.

"Don't give me that competitive tendering crap. Don't tell me that you're just protecting the interests of your white-collar constituents. You can always find some bullshit to justify lining your own pockets. Didn't Nolan and Scott get through to you? Or was that just something to throw to the press on a slow news day?"

The politician remained silent. Larkin stood up and began pacing. "Now, I'm not naive. I know how you lot work." He moved closer to the bed, dwarfing the shrunken, defeated bundle where it sat. "All I'm saying is, if the people who elected you knew how much contempt you hold them in they'd tear you limb from limb."

Larkin stood still in contemplation. "I've got your whole future in my hands. Maybe I should treat you like you treat the voters –

just do what suits me and not give a fuck.''

The politician lifted his head. ''So what do you propose to do?''

''That's entirely up to you. I'm giving you a choice. Mend your ways, do your job properly and these photos won't find their way onto people's breakfast tables when they throw open their morning papers.''

''Marmalade droppers, I think they call them,'' chimed in Houchen.

''Thank you, Ian,'' said Larkin.

The councillor was stunned. ''What? But how can I . . .''

''Oh, I'm sure you can find a way. These photos could end your career, after all. I'm sure you could get yourself a nice comfy little directorship somewhere else – I know you've got friends in high places – but what about your wife? How will she cope when she's walking round Sainsbury's with people laughing and staring? What about your daughters? How would they manage at school? Children can be wicked, you know.''

''But what can I do? I don't understand why you're picking on me.'' He sounded like a kid himself.

''Think about it. Surprise yourself. And what makes you think you're the only one we've done this to?''

The politician was astonished. ''How many others?''

Larkin smiled. ''That would be telling.''

''So what's to stop me from finding out who the others are and making a stand against you?''

''Nothing at all. But d'you really see yourself going up to your esteemed colleagues and saying, 'Excuse me, but these two chaps burst into a hotel room that I was in last night and found me tied to the bed with a transvestite about to stick his knob into my mouth. Anything similar happen to you?' '' Larkin crouched down, eyeball to eyeball with the man. ''There's an old Chinese proverb: Steal your neighbour's wife. If you think you're strong enough.''

Their eyes were locked, a battle of wills. The politician flinched away first; he couldn't match Larkin's unblinking stare. He sat in silence for a while. Then he said, ''This is blackmail.''

Larkin almost laughted aloud; the clichés just kept on coming. Without his scriptwriter the man was nothing.

''Call it what you like. If it *is* blackmail, it's politically correct blackmail. It's a moral balancing of the books, if you like.''

''What if I go to the police?''

"They'll have a bloody good laugh. And we'll publish anyway."
He turned to face him. "And be damned."

"Christ, you're a shit."

"Ah," said Larkin lightly, "my secret is out."

The councillor sighed heavily. "So what do you want me to do?"

"What I've told you. Start working for the people who got you elected."

"And then?"

"The photos will be destroyed."

"And if I don't do what you say?"

"I'm not even going to dignify that question with an answer."

Larkin stood up and turned to go. Houchen did likewise. As they reached the door, Larkin turned.

"Oh, by the way," he said chattily, "I know you've got people, fixers and that, kept on your payroll for such an eventuality as this, but believe me, we've got this little operation sewn up tighter than a gnat's chuff. If anything happens to us, the photos get published. You won't be getting your hands on those negatives. If you think that's a bluff, go ahead and call it."

The politician had no strength left to fight. All the layers of security and power had been stripped away until his true self had been exposed: a fat, sad, middle-aged lech sitting half dressed on a semen-stained bed in a shabby hotel. A hollow white chocolate Buddha with no wisdom. Larkin gave it to him straight.

"You got where you are today by treating people as if they're stupid. Don't make that mistake with us."

Aware that that was a suitably dramatic exit line, Larkin swept out.

"See you then," said Houchen and lumbered after him.

Outside on the pavement, Larkin stood propping up Houchen's rusty Volvo, shaking a little as the tension ebbed away. Houchen came to join him. Taking a packet of Silk Cut from his jacket pocket he offered one to Larkin.

"Celebration fag?"

"I don't smoke, and you know it."

"Yeah." Houchen took one for himself, lit it, breathed it down to the pit of his lungs and exhaled slowly. "Well, that was an easy night's work."

"Yeah."

"Liked the bit about askin' his mates if they'd met us. Good one that."

"Yeah."

"What's up?"

Larkin sighed. "Oh ... I don't know. I thought I'd get a real kick out of it. You know, justice being done, seeing that bastard put in his place." He looked up at the room; the light was still on. Larkin imagined the politician would still be sitting in the same spot, huddled and abject. "I just feel ... sordid. Pathetic, really."

"Aye well," said Houchen, untouched, "it gets better as it goes on."

"Hope so."

"Aye." Houchen opened the car door and climbed in. "Wanna lift?"

"No thanks. I feel like a walk."

"Suit yourself." Houchen leaned out of the car window. "Oh, and I think I'm on to somethin' else. You'll like this one – it's a good 'un. Big an' all. I'll let you know when I know for definite, right?"

"Yeah, sure. Take care."

"Aye." Houchen laughed. "See you at work tomorrow."

And with that he sped off noisily, the car belching toxic fumes from its ruptured exhaust.

Larkin walked to the house, his feet becoming heavier the nearer he got. He stopped in front of it, searching his pockets for a key. The house loomed huge and dark against the clear night sky. Desolate.

An estate agent's board in the overgrown front garden had FOR SALE slapped across it in big red letters. No takers so far, though. No one to pour life into it; make it a home as Larkin never could.

He scanned the front of the house, his gaze focusing on what used to be her bedroom window. He scrutinised it, vainly looking for signs of life. But the void stared back, a dark, empty socket in a dead red brick skull.

"I'm doing what I can," he said. "I'm doing what I can."

He walked up the path, key in hand, feeling as hollow as the house. He opened the front door and entered. A light bulb flared briefly from deep inside the house, then all was darkness again.

2: Welcome To The Working Week

It was the incessant bleeping of Larkin's travel alarm that woke him. He opened his eyes, took a couple of deep breaths and sat up, mentally taking stock.

He was in bed, and his sleep had been undisturbed. Judging from his position he had hardly moved. And there had been no dreams. The ghosts had left him alone for another night.

While turning the alarm off, he noticed that his hand had a touch of the shakes: nothing new there. He flopped back on the bed, thirsty, his mouth dry. He should buy a teasmade, he thought, and smiled to himself, knowing full well that, like wife-swapping, such suburban banalities would never form part of his life.

He knew he would go back to sleep if he lay in bed much longer, so with a supreme effort of will, he groped for the remote on the bedside table and pointed it at the TV. The BBC breakfast programme came on. Larkin watched sober-suited men with sober expressions relating sober news. Politicians delivered pithy soundbites over the nation's muesli. A familiar face appeared; Blake Carrington's younger, more handsome brother, possessing teeth so white they must have been boiled. It was Alan Swanson, a charismatic local chancer who was now making waves nationally. Earnestly pontificating about something or other he looked, to Larkin, about as trustworthy as a basking shark. This man and his cheekbones were the driving force behind the "Rebirth of the Region" scheme – not to mention electing himself unofficial Minister of Youth – and it had won him more than votes.

"'And what smooth beast, his hour come round at last, goes slouching towards Westminster ...'" murmured Larkin, pleased that he could misquote poetry this early in the morning. He cocked his thumb and forefinger at the screen and fired his imaginary handgun until Swanson's image disappeared. *You're next*, thought Larkin, and yawned.

Switching off the television, he picked up the other remote and pointed it at the CD player. The melancholy, swooping pedal steel guitar and tinkling piano, followed by gruff vocals, announced itself as "Sweet Dreams", an old Patsy Cline song, covered by Elvis Costello and the Attractions. A soulful, lost start to the day. The song made him look at the empty Glenfiddich bottle sitting on his desk – and he remembered the night before.

Shaking down the politician hadn't given him the righteous kick he thought it would. Coming home to an empty house, he had opened the bottle, flirted with it, kissed it, made love to it, cried into it and, eventually, killed it. His sleep had been deathly, dreamless. The whisky had kept his subconscious in check, stopped the ghosts from haunting him. The bottle was proving to be a good jailer, and lately he had been relying on it more and more.

He flung back the duvet and swung his feet to the floor where they landed with a slapping plonk, as if they didn't belong to him. Standing up, he waited for the hangover to hit, but was pleasantly surprised to discover that it had decided not to put in an appearance this morning. Just the shakes, then. No problem. He padded around the attic, feeling the space. He hadn't long possessed the room and it still felt alien to him.

The attic was in Charlotte's house. After her death, it had been bequeathed to Larkin, but he couldn't bear to live in it. He had tried renting it out, but there were no takers, so he moved back in to the converted loft and left the rest of the house untouched. As long as he didn't spend too much time in the other rooms the place was fine, apart from the fact that his height prohibited him from deviating from the centre of the room.

Stretching, bleary-eyed, he headed off for a shower and some coffee.

He parked the car behind the Central Station, in front of a piece of Roman Wall tucked away between the Federation Brewery and a grim-looking pub, and just opposite a railway arch turned hot-dog-stand warehouse. After locking up, he walked the rest of the way, hoping that his soft-top VW Golf wouldn't be too conspicuous. God knows, he felt conspicuous enough driving it.

Rounding the corner he was confronted by Bolbec Hall, next to the library's old Lit and Phil building. On the corner of Mosely Street, situated on the fringe of the city's City district, it looked as though it had surrendered and was quietly dying in the middle of an uneasy truce between Victorian and Sixties architecture.

Larkin took the rickety iron lift up to the top floor, to where the sign on the door said THE NEWS AGENTS. He pushed the door open and entered. It was a newsroom in miniature, shortage of space determining depth of frenetic activity. The place consisted of three big rooms plus a kitchen-cum-toilet – or "restroom" as Bolland insisted on calling it – linked by a corridor. There was a rusted iron balcony on top of the fire escape, outside the main window, which the smokers had commandeered. If it wasn't bad enough that they had to risk their health to smoke, they had to risk their lives on a daily basis to do it.

The two largest rooms had been knocked through and contained the workstations: terminals, desks, faxes and phones. The third room had become Bolland's office. All the walls were painted a cool off-white grey, potted ferns were dotted strategically about the place. The decor tried hard to create the aura of an upmarket office space, but it still felt like a cheap lease in an old building.

"Mornin', Steve."

"Morning, Joyce," said Larkin, as cheerfully as he could manage given the hour. "How you doing?"

"Not so bad," Joyce replied. She was, possibly, in her mid-thirties; but ten years either side of that might have been equally accurate. Dark bottle-blonde hair, trim figure and a pretty face prematurely reddened by too many Happy Hours with the girls and not enough happy hours by herself. She hadn't been in the agency long, but had quickly established a niche for herself as an indispensable and lovable piece of office furniture.

"Good night, was it?" asked Larkin with a small-talk smile.

"Ee, Steve, I'll have to tell you all about it. You wouldn't believe it."

"You know, you shouldn't drink that much during the week. It's bad for you."

"Why? Cos it gives you a stinkin' hangover for work the next day?"

"No," said Larkin still smiling, "because it spoils it for the weekend."

14

"Ee, daft sod." Joyce laughed; Larkin joined in. After all, it cost nothing. He took off his jacket, hung it on the communal stand and sat at his bare desk – the only one in the room unadorned by gonks, family photos and other useless objects.

He shook his head in wry disbelief. For one thing he couldn't quite believe he had a regular job again; for another he couldn't believe how hard he was working at it. He supposed he needed something to occupy his mind – some mindless routine – and at least he was good at it. It was therapy, and he was getting paid for it.

As he sat down, other members of the staff filed in. Frankie Baker, solid, middle-aged. An old pro, always getting a round in after work. Mick O'Brien, young, eager to succeed. The type to get up early and write novels, thought Larkin. Then there was Carrie Brewer. Young, dark and fiercely ambitious. The kind of reporter who gave chequebook journalism an even worse name. She wouldn't sell her grandmother to get a good story, Larkin thought, because she'd done so already. A photo-journalist called Graham Rigby was hanging up his anorak as Dave Bolland made his entrance. Tall, splendidly coiffed and tailored, even with his jacket off and braces showing, Bolland both looked and acted as the ultimate Eighties revivalist. Larkin suspected that the much-vaunted image of Bolland masturbating at night over a picture of Michael Portillo might be a bit of a pisstake. He hoped so, anyway.

"OK, everyone, good morning," enunciated Bolland. There was a general mumble in return. Bolland smiled. "Lovely! To business." He swept his eyes round the room, headcounting. "Where's Houchen?"

Another mumble, this time negative. Larkin kept silent.

"No one know? Oh well, let's press on." Bolland referred to his clipboard. "Right then – unless there's something of staggering importance that you're working on, here's how I see today dividing up. Carrie, I take it there's no news on Jason Winship?"

Carrie sat forward on the edge of her desk, looking pure business. "Nothing, I'm still following up me leads and pestering the police, but no. Nothing new as yet."

"Well keep at it. Either the boy will turn up or his killer will. Either way it's a result for us and I want it covered. Right – Graham. Cobbler in Gateshead, retiring, local interest, that kind of thing. . ."

Bolland's voice droned on. Larkin looked at Carrie. She was lit from within by a fire that only showed in her eyes. With lizard's

15

blood and an actress's range, she was perfect for the job. Larkin wondered what it was that drove her.

"Stephen?"

"Yeah?"

"Graced us with your presence, for which we are eternally grateful. Now – Newton Aycliffe bypass, crusty protestors versus landowners. Head to head piece. How's that coming?"

"Well, I've got some tameish landowners ready to comment and I've got some Newbury veterans eager to talk. Which d'you want?" said Larkin.

"Does it matter?"

"Depends who wants the story."

"Well," said Bolland, "we've had some interest from the quality tabloids."

"Now there's an oxymoron," said Larkin, raising a half-hearted laugh. He checked Bolland's face; he was annoyed, but wouldn't admit it. He hated anyone else to be the centre of attention. Larkin ploughed on.

"OK, I'll visit the landowners. The *Daily Mail*'ll lap it up."

"If you're that bothered about balance you could also visit your veteran protestors and get a *Guardian* story from them."

More half-hearted laughter. Larkin, tactfully, joined in. Bolland, his authority restored, continued. "Take Houchen with you – when he eventually shows his face."

Larkin nodded; Bolland continued. "Anything else?"

"Yeah," said Larkin, "I'm still doing this local thing about people in the community. Bravery, not conforming to the accepted stereotype, that sort of thing."

"Oh – that. Yes. Any interest?"

"Colour sups. You know."

Larkin felt Carrie Brewer snigger behind him. He made a mental note to throw her down the lift shaft at the first possible opportunity.

Bolland appeared not to have noticed. But he allowed a sketch of a smile to appear on his lips. "Right. Onward and upward. . ."

Bolland rambled on, believing he was imbuing his troops with the power to accomplish superhuman feats. Finally he left the room. Larkin crossed to Rigby and pestered him into lending him a camera; Rigby, reluctantly, complied.

As Larkin was about to leave, Bolland unexpectedly beckoned him into his office. Sitting down behind his matt-black desk, he motioned Larkin to one of the pieces of black leather and twisted chrome trying to pass as a comfortable chair. Larkin managed to perch. Bolland leaned back and steepled his fingers, giving the impression of entrepreneurial pensiveness. After plenty of brow-furrowing, he spoke.

"How are you doing, Steve?"

"Fine, thanks." Larkin felt he should say something in return. "And you?"

"Oh, wonderful. Wonderful. The point is, Steve, I did have some initial misgivings when I offered you this job. I know we used to be friends way, way back, and that's why, as soon as I heard you were in Newcastle again, I rushed to see you."

Larkin felt the scar tissue on his right hand itch. "Aye. You heard what had happened and wanted an exclusive."

"Which you gave."

"In return for a job."

"And a handsome salary. Yes." Bolland allowed himself a smile. "That's why I want you to know that I'm very pleased with the progress you're making with us. Very pleased."

"Thank you. Sir."

Bolland reddened slightly but persevered. "I know you – have a reputation for – having – unorthodox working methods—"

"You mean, I'm a pain in the arse to work with?"

"Well, I wouldn't have put it quite like that. . ."

"Oh, that's OK. I've heard it that many times it doesn't bother me anymore."

"Mm. Well, what I mean is, you have a reputation for allowing . . . a higher sense of morality to creep in and inform your work."

Larkin attempted to stifle a smile as Bolland tried to dig himself out of his hole.

"Yes, well. What I'm trying to say is, I'm pleased you have adapted yourself to our work ethic so readily."

Larkin shook his head. "Needs must."

"I mean, if there are any prizewinners in this agency, you're the one."

"I think Ms Brewer would disagree with that."

Bolland smiled. "She probably would. But I just wanted to let you know. That's all."

"Thank you."

They both sat there for what seemed like a century. Eventually Larkin stood up.

"Well, I have to go now, *Dave*. I've got the prejudices of Middle England to confirm. Thanks for the chat." Larkin turned to go.

"Great, great. We must grab a beer sometime."

Grab a beer? "Yeah, *Dave*, smashing. I'll see if I've got a window. Sometime."

"Steve."

Larkin turned around.

"You are all right, aren't you? I mean . . . *all right*?"

Larkin looked at Bolland. The smug-bastard mask had slipped away, leaving an expression of genuine concern.

"Yeah. Yeah, I'm fine."

"Good. I know work can be a help, taking your mind off things and all that, but . . . well, if you're not, well, you know, old friends and everything. . ." He seemed to be having difficulty in finding the right words. Larkin was almost touched.

"Thanks, Dave. You're a good mate."

And he left the office and went to work.

3: Deep Pools Of Truth

Larkin drove down to Scotswood. If the Golf looked conspicuous behind the Central Station, then here it stood out like a Sunderland fan at a Newcastle game.

The area consisted of one dilapadated concrete monolith after another, with a few rows of two-storey houses thrown in: a half-hearted stab at community. But most of them had boarded up windows and doors sporting huge padlocks. That, and the blackened fronts, marked them out as easy, but pointless, targets for roaming gangs.

Brightly-coloured boards announced the imminence of urban renewal and promised a safe new future funded by EC money. But the glib declarations had the hollow and hopeless ring of a politician at election time. The Rebirth Of The Region didn't extend to here, noted Larkin.

Although the sky was a brilliant, cloudless blue, announcing the last burst of a dying summer, it couldn't make Scotswood look jovial. Larkin didn't know how Jane could bear to live here. He didn't know how anyone could. He rounded another corner, dodging the craters in the road, and thought back to his morning.

He'd just returned to the office from his conversation with the rabid landowning squire and found the message from Jane waiting. But before he could phone her, Bolland had asked him how the encounter had gone.

To describe the bloke as right-wing, Larkin had informed him, was to say that Hitler liked to start a bit of trouble. He had started off ranting about the bypass protesters; his diatribe had gone on to embrace the benefits of National Service, the wonders of capital punishment, the laxity of the immigration laws and the evils of homosexuality. In no particular order.

"Wonderful," Bolland had replied. "Extreme opinions, irrespective of the truth, make the best copy." He habitually spoke in epigrams.

"Yeah," said Larkin. "It was when he started on compulsory sterilisation for the poor and the unemployed that it got me."

Bolland smiled. "Not as bizarre a suggestion as you would think, Steve. Even that well-known vegetarian and left-wing intellectual George Bernard Shaw once vigorously championed the idea."

"Really?"

"Oh, yes. I've found that no one is ever fully good. And no one is ever fully bad. And nothing is black and white." He turned to go. "Oh, and Steve?"

"Yes?"

"Make it angry. The *Mail* will pay more."

He had hated writing the article; hated putting his name to something he patently didn't agree with. He had consoled himself by running over the events of the previous evening as the article took shape. The more he thought about it, the more justified he felt his actions had been. At least it was a way to make a difference, he thought, as he wrote. And he clung to that fact like a drowning man to a piece of driftwood.

And started to think about Jane Howell.

He had met her over six months ago, just after his return to Newcastle. It had been a boring party; she'd livened it up for him just by talking. Unmarried, living in a tower block in Scotswood with her young daughter, she ran a daycare centre for inner-city children and was trying to get a credit union going. She had established herself as a community activist despite disadvantages which would have turned most people into victims. They had gone out together a few times – drinking, the cinema, the odd meal – but it hadn't really taken off. Larkin was still shell-shocked after Charlotte's death and Jane was naturally wary of men in general. They had remained friends, however; Larkin was using her for one of his colour supplement features.

20

She knew he would be visiting her that afternoon. So why would she call?

Two and a half rings. Then the phone was picked up with such speed it left the bell echoing.

"Hello?" a voice said, too quickly.

"Jane?"

"Yeah?"

"Stephen. Larkin."

"Oh!" Relief, followed by silence. Larkin waited for her to speak. "You still comin' over today?"

"You know I am. What's up?"

"Nothing." There was a pause; Larkin could feel her tension. "Look – can you come a little bit earlier?"

"Why?"

"Can you?"

He told her he had some work to do but could make it by three.

"Come to the centre. That's where I'll be."

"OK."

"Right — " It was as if she wanted to say something, something important, but couldn't find the words.

"Are you all right, Jane?"

There was another pause. "Yeah. Look, I've got to go. I'll see you later, right?"

She put the phone down. And a puzzled Larkin held a dead receiver.

Larkin felt unseen eyes on him as he drove. He knew he was being watched; his car marked him out as not living in the area. They probably thought he was a DSS snoop. He remembered the torch he kept in the glove compartment: an American police model that could double as a truncheon, it was as effective as a baseball bat and twice as legal. Although he hadn't had to use it yet, he was definitely prepared to.

He pulled up beside another car: an anonymous, hermetically-sealed Nineties blob. Parking behind it, he noted it was a virtually brand-new Fiesta with a protective camouflage of inner-city dirt. He killed the Gold's engine, got out and locked it. Though if someone wanted to break in, all they had to do was slit the roof.

21

The daycare centre was a primary-coloured, single-storey, concrete-clad edifice. It had been enthusiastically, if not professionally, painted with a mural featuring huge daisies and smiling children. There was a cheerful optimism about the place that Larkin admired, as if it were refusing to be choked by the surrounding oppressiveness. He went in through the bright red double doors which opened onto a large room where children's paintings covered the walls. Care-used toys and games littered the floor, and a couple of shelves bearing well-worn storybooks and some over-loved stuffed toy animals completed the look of cheerful chaos.

He was expecting noise and he got it. Lots of small children were running around, shrieking with delight. They were supposed to be painting but from the looks of it the only thing they were painting was each other.

Suddenly, one of the children let out a shriek that wasn't due to pleasure. Larkin moved to where the noise was coming from, found a tiny boy with a clump of another boy's hair in his hand. The other boy was on the floor, his face red and wet from crying. The first child looked at the clump of hair in his hand almost in disbelief; then he started kicking the prone boy, rage in his eyes.

Larkin was wondering whether to intervene when a man who Larkin hadn't noticed before pulled them apart.

"Daniel! Stop that!"

The boy looked up at him and dropped the clump of hair, fear creeping into his eyes. The man pointed a finger at him sternly and the boy fell silent.

"Good," the man said. "Now apologise."

Hate and fear fought it out on the boy's face. The end result had an equal slice of both in it, as he muttered a sulky "Sorry."

The man nodded at him, and then turned his attention to the boy on the floor.

He examined the boy's head. It was bleeding. He picked him up, holding him close; he made comforting noises and the boy's crying gradually subsided. He was about to carry him out of the main room when he looked round and saw Larkin.

"Can I help you?" A clipped Scottish accent. His voice made the cradled boy flinch almost imperceptibly.

Larkin looked the man over. Under six foot, early thirties. Washed-out, dirty, thinning blond hair, glasses, shapeless jumper and trousers. Nondescript. Safe.

"I'm looking for Jane Howell. Is she here?"

"She is, yes. And who might you be?"

"It's all right, James. I'm here."

Both men turned to see Jane standing in the doorway. Blue jeans, boots, black T-shirt. Her dark hair in a long bob. She was attractive in an honest, intelligent way; though she carried the burden of a tough life, her big brown eyes lent her a fetching vulnerability. Today, though, they showed nothing but badly-concealed anxiety and trouble.

She saw the child in the man's arms and came dashing over. "What happened?"

"Daniel got a bit boisterous. Don't worry – it's all over. I'm just taking little Harry into the kitchen for a look at his head."

"I'll do that," she snapped, making both men start. Noticing their reaction, she forced a smile. "Go on then – you do it. Where's Carol?"

"In the loo."

At that moment another woman appeared and crossed over to them.

"Sort Daniel out, Carol. I'll be out in a while."

With that she crossed over to another red door and entered. Larkin looked round, smiled weakly at the woman called Carol, and followed.

When Larkin reached Jane's office he found her sitting behind an old paper-covered desk, delving into her bag for a Silk Cut and a lighter. She lit her cigarette and pulled a deep drag, her chest expanding. Larkin tried not to look at her breasts. After holding on for a few seconds she let go. Her tension ebbed along with the smoke.

"Fuck, I needed that."

Larkin walked round to her side of the desk. "Come on, then," he said, as reassuringly as he could manage. "What's up?"

"Nothing. Nothing."

"Bollocks. Tell me."

She took another deep drag and followed it up with a huge sigh.

"Oh, I don't know. It's just that. . . Everything was going so well, you know? This place was a success, the credit union was gettin'

23

taken seriously. I don't know. It just all seems to be turnin' to shit."

"In what way?"

"Well, for a start, the grant's up for renewal. If you'd have asked me a couple of weeks ago I'd have said sure, fine, we'll walk it – you know?"

"Why won't you now? What's gone wrong?"

"Oh . . . nothin'. It's just . . . I don't know." Another drag. "You don't want to listen to all this."

"Too late for that now. You called, I answered. So here I am."

She gave him a weak little smile. "Well . . . it's probably nothin', but I'm not so sure. Did you see what happened just now?"

"One kid fighting with another one. Nothing unusual in that."

"No, but . . . that boy, Daniel. He used to be such a good kid, but just recently he's started to behave . . . well, like you saw. Aggressive, arguin'. Startin' to hurt the other kids."

"What about his parents? Can't they do anything?"

The deepest drag of all. Then: "It's a classic abuse pattern he's developin'."

"Oh?"

"Yeah."

"You mean, his parents?"

"I don't think so. I mean, they're a rough lot, most people round here are, but they're not. . . I know them. No."

"What then?"

Her cigarette was down to a stub. She ground it out in an already overflowing ashtray, lit another one and settled herself, coming to decisions in her head. Larkin waited patiently for her to speak.

Finally: "No. It's not at home."

"Where, then?"

"Maybe . . . here."

"At the centre?"

She nodded her head, downcast, as if she didn't want to admit it even to herself.

"Who?"

She moved her face closer to his.

"You saw that guy when you came in here?" Her voice was low.

"The Scotsman with the charisma deficiency?"

She almost smiled. "Yeah."

"Him?"

She stood up, paced the room. "This place is a success. We've made it one. It's been hard fuckin' work, an uphill struggle, but we've done it. This place is open every weekday for kids under school age so their mothers can have a bit of time off. Try to get jobs, even." Another drag. "It's gone that well we've had to expand. We got a grant from the council and one of the other girls and me get paid to run the place. The rest work as volunteers."

"But?"

"About four months ago, this guy came to us. Said his name was James Noble and did we need any help. Said he used to work in Social Services with kids in Scotland until he was made redundant. Well, naturally we were interested. I mean, he had brilliant references and he sounded too good to be true. You know?"

She stopped talking again, took another drag. Larkin remained silent, letting her story unfold the way she wanted it to.

"Well, it was great for a while. But then. . . Well, we started to have doubts about him."

She stopped. Larkin sensed that she couldn't quite believe the enormity of what she was saying. He prompted her.

"What kind of doubts?"

"After he arrived, some of the kids began to behave – differently. Like you saw. I mean, at first he was left alone with them, but now . . . well, I can't be everywhere. When that happened just now I was on the phone, trying to get some sense out of the council about the grant."

"Why don't you just ask him to leave?"

"I've tried. He hasn't actually said anythin', but he's sort of made little intimations that if he goes our grant goes an' all."

"How can he do that?" asked Larkin.

Jane hesitated before answering. "He said he had friends in high places."

"Did he mention names?"

"No. And I don't want to know them."

"So what's he been doing, exactly?"

"Somethin' – physical. I think so, anyway. I haven't been able to examine any of the kids but. . ."

"So what are you going to do about it?"

She looked directly at him. "Stephen, I haven't a clue. . ." Her voice trailed off.

"Couldn't you get the wonderful Alan Swanson to help you?"

"What, our esteemed Minister for Youth? I wouldn't piss down

25

his throat if his heart was on fire – pardon my French. We'll get no help from that bastard.''

Larkin gave a grim smile. "Couldn't agree more.''

"Kids are too young to vote. Why would a politician wanna help them?''

"Yeah,'' said Larkin, "maybe he's just—'' He stopped suddenly, a terrible thought entering his head.

"What?''

"Paranoia city, this, but. . . What if Swanson is Noble's influential friend?''

The colour drained from Jane's face. "Then I'm fucked.'' She put her hands to her face, rubbing the skin as if to erase her worries. "Aw, hell, I've never felt so helpless before.'' She stared into her lap. "I'm sorry, I shouldn't have said all this.''

"Don't be daft. That's what friends are for.'' His voice took on a soothing, placating tone. "We don't know that it's Swanson. In all probability it isn't. So don't worry. Now listen. . .''

She looked at him, expectant.

"I've got a friend on the force. I'll ask him to check up on this Noble, see if anything turns up. I'll get him to check the referees on his CV as well, if you like.''

"Oh, Stephen, I hate doin' this! Creepin' around. Checkin' up.''

"Yeah, but what choice d'you have?''

She sighed. "I know. I've got to do it for the kids, haven't I?''

"Least you'll know one way or another. And no one's going to blame you. Or the centre.''

"But what if I'm right? And it makes the papers?''

He smiled at her. "If it does, who d'you think'll be writing it up?''

She returned his smile. Slowly the warmth was starting to seep back into her face; her soft, hurt, brown eyes were like pools of honesty and truth.

They talked for a while longer. Larkin got an address for Noble from Jane together with the names and addresses of his two referees. He got ready to go.

"You know,'' Jane said, her eyes shyly downcast, "we should go out again some time, shouldn't we?''

26

"Why not? Get a babysitter and I'll take you to the pictures one night. Go for a meal afterwards."

"I was hopin' we might just go out and get pissed."

They both laughed, then fell silent.

"Aren't you seeing anyone, then?" Larkin tried to make the question sound casual.

"You're kiddin', aren't you? As soon as men round here find out you run a children's centre, a credit union, that you're tryin' to start a woman's group and involved in politics, they take one look at you and think you're some kind of maniac lesbian."

"Mind you," said Larkin, "looking at most of the blokes round here, you're best off being a lesbian." They laughed again.

There was another pause.

"How's Alison, then?"

Jane smiled. "Ah, you want to see her, man! She's growin' up lovely. Really bright. And I'm goin' to make damn sure she doesn't make all the mistakes her mother did."

Larkin smiled at her. If Alison turned out anything like her mother, she wouldn't be doing so badly. Eventually he said: "Well, I'd best be off."

"OK. And – thank you."

"No problem. It's going to be all right."

"Yeah." She sounded unsure.

He hugged her and felt a hug in return. It wasn't a lover's hug, just a friendly one, but all the same Larkin felt an urge to kiss her. He looked down at her; she had her face buried in his leather jacket so he settled for a paternal peck on her forehead. He felt himself starting to stiffen. He was rapidly getting an erection, and that was the last thing he wanted her to know. He pulled apart from her suddenly, making her jump.

"I've got to go."

She seemed surprised at the speed with which he was making for the door.

"I'll see you out."

"No, no, it's fine. Look, I'll ring you. We'll do the article later in the week, yeah?"

"Yeah, OK."

And with that he left her standing alone in the room, looking bewildered and a little lost amongst office furniture that seemed deliberately oversized.

*   *   *

When he got outside he saw that providence had been kind and his car was still in one piece. He got behind the wheel and started the engine.

He got on well with Jane, he thought, as he turned the car round in a side street. There was definitely something there. He tried not to think too hard about the subject; he didn't want to push it. He wanted to get it right this time.

He was ready to depart. And as he drew away, he saw Noble come out of the centre and get into the Fiesta. Knowing he hadn't been seen gave Larkin an idea. He waited until Noble had started up and pulled away; then, as discreetly as he could manage, he followed him.

4: Bandits

The arcade was cavernous and dark; lit only, it seemed, by the blinking sequences of lights emanating from the machines. A stern warning over the door barred the entrance of under-eighteens. Larkin looked at the clientele: either the notice was being ignored, or the fountain of youth had been discovered in Clayton Street.

Kids were everywhere, dotted down the aisles of video games, fruit machines, the occasional ancient one-armed bandit, and cockpits that looked like they could be used for training astronauts. At the back of the hall was a raised area which had been turned into a gaudily lit cafe with the word DINER etched above it in depressingly cheap neon. At the tables sat a smattering of people staring listlessly at Cokes and coffees; behind them, lying on a counter, was a selection of 'food' that could have been mistaken for one of Quatermass's failed experiments.

Noble had parked his car and come straight into the arcade, Larkin following at a discreet distance. Larkin kept a linen jacket in the boot of the car in case he had to smarten himself up on an assignment; he'd swapped his leather for this, as a makeshift disguise, in case Noble should spot him. The gloom of the place was working in his favour. As his eyes adjusted, his ears were being battered by the machines' random cacophony of beeps, squeals, snatches of irritating tunes, electronic pulses. Thirty years ago the *avant garde* would have paid good money to listen to this, thought Larkin, but now it was no more than a soundtrack to squalid lives.

Larkin could remember when he was a kid: playing the nick from school and coming to the arcade for an afternoon. Donkey Kong and Space Invaders hadn't grabbed him the way it had some of his peer group and he'd eventually drifted off. The ones who stayed, who couldn't find anywhere else to go, soon developed an *idiot savant* mastery of the machines that they found they lacked in all other aspects of their lives. They began to live only to see their names on the screen in the Hall of Fame. This was the pinnacle of achievement, a standard by which all challengers would be judged; it made them heroes, the nearest thing to immortality they would ever grasp. It didn't last long. Someone else came along who was quicker and younger, and there they were: energy dissipated, burnt out at seventeen.

Larkin scanned the aisles. The machines had changed but the principles remained the same. Amongst the rapt teenagers, however, was a smattering of old, empty-eyed women, staring fixedly ahead. They shuffled from bandit to bandit, mug-punting the last of their pensions in desperate belief. Larkin knew they would turn up, week after week, to make their devotional offerings to an ungrateful, selfish god, living in hope until death released them from their slavery.

Larkin quickly ducked behind a fruit machine as he caught sight of Noble, who was prowling the aisles, scrutinising everyone like a film director waiting to pick a star from a bunch of unknowns. Noble's attention seemed to be drawn to a couple of teenagers who were becoming voluble over a video game; he stopped dead in his tracks and stared at them. His expression sent an involuntary shiver down Larkin's spine.

Larkin moved closer and looked at the two boys, trying to discover what it was about them that so interested Noble. One of them seemed to be a bit older than the other and affected a streetwise manner beyond his years; how much of this was assumed, Larkin couldn't tell. The other one was smaller, slighter, wearing glasses and a distracted air. They didn't strike Larkin as being distinctive in any way. Suddenly the bespectacled one spoke.

"Howah, man – gis a go."

"My turn. Fuck off," the cool one replied and shrugged. This annoyed the gauche one even more, and his voice raised in pitch. When he spoke, his words were loud, somehow slurred, as if his jaw and brain were running at different speeds. "Is it fuck your turn, you lyin' get! It was your turn last time, it's my turn now."

"Not finished."

"Aw, haway, man, it's my fuckin' fifty pee! Giz it."

And he grabbed hold of the other boy, momentarily distracting

30

him from the screen and allowing a ninja to jump out from behind a pile of cartons and ambush the heroically-proportioned Virtual Cop, kicking him to death with a series of synthetic grunts and sprays of cyber-blood. The two-dimensional dead body lay there covered in bright red globules as the machine played its obligatory, annoying signature tune and the screen flashed up: GAME OVER. The boy who had been playing turned and faced his distractor.

"Look what you done now! That's our last bit o' money."

The bespectacled boy immediately became defensive. "Whey, you shouldn't have taken over." He added sulkily, "That was my turn an' all, you knaw."

The cool boy shrugged. "Aw, Raymond, man, grow up."

Raymond flushed. "Don't tell me to grow up. Piss off, y' bastard."

The other boy smirked. Raymond's face turned redder.

"Go on, piss off, Kev!"

Heads turned sharply in their direction. Raymond turned beetroot and quickly looked at the floor; he hadn't intended to be so conspicuous. Kev, covering his embarrassment, smirked again.

Raymond began to gently rock backwards and forwards on the balls of his feet.

"I'm off," said Kev.

Raymond continued rocking and nodded, a big pout on his lips. He wouldn't make eye contact.

"Yeah, right," said Kev. "Later." And off he swaggered to the door. He was too young to remember James Dean, but he had the coded teen rebel hipswing off to a T, thought Larkin.

Raymond rocked faster, his mouth mumbling words that only he could hear. Then he allowed his momentum to decrease until he was still. When he finally looked up, Larkin was sure there were tears in the boy's eyes.

Raymond began to search his pockets frantically until he came up with more money. From the look on his face it wasn't the amount he was hoping for. Nevertheless he fed the coins into the machine, they fell, and the Virtual Cop was resurrected, alive and shooting.

The sight of the muscular cop, invincible in shades and kevlar vest, armed with a huge gun, seemed to cheer Raymond. As he became involved in keeping his hero alive and increasing the body-count of adversaries, Raymond seemed to forget all about his row with Kev. He didn't even notice when Noble arrived nonchalantly at the machine next to him.

31

One row back and out of Noble's direct line of vision, Larkin too placed coins in the slot of a fruit machine. But unlike Raymond he didn't notice how much he put in or what result he was getting; his attention was elsewhere.

For a time, the boy and the man played their respective games. Eventually Raymond's money ran out. As the Virtual Cop died for the last time, the boy reluctantly straightened up from the machine and stood there, confused and alone. He looked round the arcade in disbelief, as if he were seeing it for the first time. Perhaps the game seemed more real than the arcade to him: he looked like he didn't know how to cope with this alien environment. Vulnerable. For the first time, he saw Noble.

"Hello, Raymond. I thought that was you, there," said Noble, beaming.

"Hello," said Raymond, and smiled in return.

"Where's your mate? He not with you?"

"Naw. . . he's. . . er. . ."

"Never mind, eh?" Suddenly, Noble's machine died. "Aw, shit! Look at that!" Noble flung his arms in the air, shook his head, tutted. A bit of an over-reaction, thought Larkin, but it made Raymond giggle. Noble then let out an elaborate sigh and slumped his arms to his side. "Oh, well, there you go. You looking for a partner?"

"Eh?"

"The game."

"Aw. Naw, I've got no money left."

Noble took out a couple of pound coins and grinned again. The predatory look of a few minutes ago was well and truly gone, replaced by kindness and philanthropy. Larkin leaned forward, his heart quickening.

Raymond smiled. They agreed who would be player one and two, Noble stuck his money in; and off they went. As they started to play, Noble made small talk. He asked how Raymond had been since he last saw him, he asked how Kev was. Raymond talked to him easily, as if he were a favourite elder brother. Noble seemed to be the safest, most serene person in the place. No threat to anyone.

As the game progressed the two players developed a camaraderie. They seemed enclosed in a bubble of friendly competitiveness; Raymond was clearly enjoying himself hugely, high on his success, exasperated whenever he lost a point or a life. Noble, for his part, was joining in enthusiastically; his glee at the game was almost childlike.

In fact, Noble was having so much fun that Larkin began to doubt Jane's suspicions. Maybe she had it all wrong; maybe Noble was a genuine philanthropist with an unfortunate manner. Maybe. Larkin let the doubt linger at the back of his mind.

Eventually the game ended with Raymond the proud winner. Noble extended his hand in mock humility and deference; Raymond shook it, his face beaming. Noble shoved his hand in his pocket.

"Great! Another one?"

Raymond smiled, about to answer yes, when a memory rolled over his face and changed it, like a steamroller flattening a flowerbed.

"No, I'd. . ." Raymond nodded to the door and hesitated, unsure of his position. Noble jumped in.

"Not even one more game? It was good fun, wasn't it? One more won't matter much, will it?"

Conflicting emotions played over Raymond's face; his thought process was transparent. Duty – or pleasure?

Watching him, Larkin was hit by the sudden realisation that the boy was retarded. If Noble knew that and was exploiting it, then that made him one sick fucker. As Larkin observed the little scene, Raymond's face lit up in a big, trusting, happy smile.

"Go on then, eh?"

They both laughed and Noble started up the machine.

Larkin watched. *You bastard*, Noble, he thought – *you nearly had me fooled. You played that scene pitch-perfect.*

Noble and Raymond seemed at first to be having just as much fun as they had first time round; but on closer inspection, Larkin found that this wasn't the case. Noble's spontaneity had a forced quality to it, as if he were acting out the instructions from a manual on *How To Get On With Kids*. The movements and techniques that he had employed in the last game, once rumbled, didn't stand up to close scrutiny. Raymond, on the other hand, lost in his own world, didn't notice.

The game finished.

"Jeez, I'm knackered," said Noble. "Fancy a Coke?"

Raymond had completely forgotten his earlier appointment. "Aye, great!"

Noble bought a Coke and a portion of something approaching chips for Raymond and a coffee for himself. The two of them moved to a table in the cafe area at the back of the arcade, surrounded by the empty-eyed old women who had perfected the art of staring off into the middle distance while nursing the same cup of old tea for three hours. There they sat, Noble holding the coffee in front of him like a shield, Raymond dipping greasy strips of sickly yellow reconstituted potato into a pool of red sauce, swallowing them hungrily, then washing them down with large slurps of Coke. He seemed to be enjoying himself tremendously.

Larkin had positioned himself so he could hear as much as possible while remaining largely inconspicuous. In order to do this, he was standing with a pocketful of small change, pulling distractedly on an archaic bandit. So far he hadn't won anything; he hadn't heard much either, but short of donning an overall and wiping down the tables, he couldn't think how to get closer without looking shifty.

He had heard Raymond talk of home, but not in a conventional, familial sense, more as an institutional kind of place. *The* Home. In care? Perhaps. If Noble was the person Larkin suspected, it would fit the profile perfectly.

He fed another coin into the slot, craning his neck to listen, as he pulled on the machine's arm. Almost immediately the machine began to pump out coins with such force and clamour that he felt the avaricious eyes of all the old women being brought to bear on him. Even Noble glanced in his direction. Larkin quickly turned his back and dropped to his knees to avoid being seen while he collected his spewed jackpot from the floor.

As he stood up he glanced around. There was a free machine on the other side of the aisle nearer to Noble and Raymond; Larkin moved towards it, his body jangling with his pocketed winnings as he went. This one was a fruit machine, a modern one with so many different lights, rules and intricacies that it would have been easier to sort out the troubles in Northern Ireland than to have a decent game on it. Larkin stuck some coins in and focused on the conversation.

"Oh, listen," Noble was saying, as if the thought had just struck him, "what are you doing at the weekend?"

Raymond thought. "Er . . . just, yu'knaw. Just hangin' round, wi' Kev an' that . . ."

"Well, I was wondering," Noble began, his Scottish lilt like the purr of a hunting tiger, "I mean, your mate Kev might be interested as well — "

"Are you ganna just stand there?"

34

The voice was loud, indignant, and coming from right beside Larkin. He looked around. There stood an old woman, one of those who had witnessed Larkin's jackpot win, and had allowed it to put a crust on her bitterness in the process.

"Sorry?"

"Aye, so you should be. You're just standin' there like one o'clock half struck. Get out the way and let someone else have a go."

Larkin glanced over at Raymond; the child's face had spread into a grin and he was nodding. Noble too was smiling. A smile of triumph? Larkin looked back at the woman: she had the pinched, beady look of a constipated eagle.

"I'll be finished in a minute."

"You're not doin' anythin'. Look at you."

Larkin stuck another coin in. "There. You happy? Now shut up and wait your turn."

He turned back to the two in the cafe. They had stood up and were beginning to make their way out.

"That's disgraceful, that is. I'm callin' the manager."

"Look, one minute, and you can have this machine for as long as you want." He heard Raymond say, "Friday, then? Five thirty?" and saw Noble nod. The beaked woman was getting ready to squawk again.

"I'm goin' to tell the manager anyway. We don't like your sort in here."

At that moment, Raymond walked jauntily past the two of them, smiling to himself. Noble was also beginning to move in Larkin's direction. Trying to think fast, Larkin grabbed hold of the old woman by the arm and propelled her down the aisle.

"Get your hands off me, you — " she began to say, but Larkin silenced her.

"Shut it."

He ducked down a small side aisle with his back to the main aisle. He stared hard at the shocked woman as Noble walked past them, not even giving them a glance. Larkin watched him out of the door, and turned back to his female assistant.

She didn't look like an eagle anymore: just a frightened old woman in fear of her life. *Well done*, thought Larkin. *You're terrorising pensioners now.*

"I'm sorry, pet."

35

As a guilt-stricken attempt at restitution, he dug into his pockets – which caused her to flinch – and brought out his winnings.

"Here, take these," he said, stuffing the money into her rigid palms as she stood dumbfounded. "Take it. I'm sorry."

Before the woman had a chance to speak, scream or burst into tears, Larkin turned and rushed out of the door, squinting as the light hit his eyes. He looked up and down Clayton Street, but there was no sign of either Noble or Raymond.

"Aw, bollocks," he said out loud, and trudged off to look for his car.

5: Old Home Movies

Dusk was gathering and the city was changing from day to evening wear. Everywhere, one set of people ceased to be and another kind sprang to life, as if the clarity of order was giving way to the chaos of darkness.

Like the rest of the city, the Chinese restaurants in the mini-Chinatown of Stowell Street were gearing themselves up for another night: their gaudy signs offering "authentic Geordie" Cantonese food, their serving staff fixing on smiles, their kitchens frying up rice.

At the back of one restaurant, however, it was a different story. Inside a battered doorway ringed by overflowing dustbins full of discarded, rotting slop, and up a flight of bare, aged wooden stairs, was a room. It was small, dingy and cheap. The walls yellowed and stained with age, the windows painted and grimed shut, and the floor unvarnished boards. In the middle of the room sat an old, chipped desk, cluttered with piles of teetering papers and topped off by hardened, mould-encrusted coffee mugs. A kettle, a jar of Nescafé and an empty milk carton nestled round a plug socket in the corner; a virtually empty whisky bottle and a greasy glass perched on the edge of the desk. A single bare bulb hung from the ceiling, as if that alone could keep the darkness at bay.

On the far wall opposite the window was all the attendant paraphernalia of an ongoing police investigation in photocopied reproduction. There were photos, maps with areas circled, notes tacked up and, adjacent to that, an old blackboard. Chalked on it was a grisly family tree starting with one name – JASON WINSHIP. Branches led to events, incidents and suppositions, but as yet there was no final offspring: no kidnapper, or murderer.

DI Henry Moir sat with his feet up on the desk and his massive backside jammed into an old swivel chair, punishing the suspension. His ample stomach strained at his shirt buttons. He was a big man; judging from his shabby clothes and holed shoes, his unshaven face and unwashed hair, it seemed as if his appetite wasn't the only thing to have been given free rein. He looked, to the casual observer, to be a man who was only one step away from a wino. But behind the red-rimmed eyes, testament to too much whisky and not enough sleep, there was the camouflaged sparkle of a keen intelligence coupled with a wounded but as yet unbroken sense of humanity.

He preferred working alone and the comfortless room had become his private office, his *sanctum sanctorum*, his temporary home. He took another belt of whisky and thought about the case.

Jason Winship had disappeared nearly a week ago, abducted, as far as the police could tell, from a strip of waste ground in Byker while playing truant from school. The area was a demolition site between two warehouses sloping towards the river; about half a mile away, some Rebirth of the Region work was taking place. A pitted dirt track, invisible from the main road, ran down the side of one of the warehouses; this, Moir and his team had surmised, was the exact location of the abduction.

Moir had been put in charge of one of the biggest manhunt teams in the history of the region. The form that the investigation had taken had been dictated by his boss, Chief Superintendent McMahon. Part investigation, part high-profile PR stunt, it involved widespread door-to-door canvassing in the Byker area, with the results fed into a computer for cross-referencing. Since they didn't know precisely what they were cross-referencing for, they had reached no conclusive results. A hugely expensive waste of time, thought Moir.

The only thing that the exercise had yielded was the somewhat confused testimony of a middle-aged meths-drinker who *may* have seen a large car – make and colour unknown – driven by a smartly dressed, middle-aged man, in the area at around the time they thought Jason had disappeared. It wasn't much to go on.

All Moir had left was gut feeling. He knew that the kidnapper was a true predator, choosing his time and location carefully, making sure his prey was separated from the main herd before he struck. The official deadline of forty-eight hours had passed; Moir didn't hold out much hope now of finding Jason alive. He hoped that his passing had been brief and painless. But he doubted it.

The boy's parents had been informed of the disappearance. His mother still lived in Byker, her main purpose in life being to offer her bed – and, by way of consolation, herself – to whoever was too pissed to find his way home from The Rising Sun on a Friday night. Jason's father was currently serving seven years in Durham for a series of startlingly inept burglaries.

At the first appearance of the police at the front door of her Byker flat, Mandy Winship had given the expected response. Her eyes had slitted into suspicion and her mouth was readying the insults before her brain had kicked in. After Moir told her about Jason's disappearance, however, her mood immediately changed. Shock, then, gradually, anger took over, as she attempted to assuage her own guilt by screaming that the teachers should have watched him better, that the police – presumably by some massive act of clairvoyance – should never have allowed it to happen. Moir had stood impassively as she blamed everyone but herself and eventually collapsed into a heap of jagged, snotty sobs.

Since experience had taught the police that in cases of this nature it was usually someone either in the family or close to it that was the culprit, they had questioned her at length, but she was of no help. They asked her about Jason's schooling; his habits; friends; enemies. From the vagueness of her answers she might have been referring to a ghost that occasionally passed uninvited through her flat. They'd questioned her boyfriends and got the same response – basically, Jason was a nuisance when they were trying to get Mandy's kit off. They had then questioned Jason's contemporaries at school – a surly bunch of next-generation recidivists – and, again, got nowhere. The whole lot of them wore their inbred reluctance to talk to the police as a badge of honour, even if it meant leaving a possible murderer uncaught. No, nothing was bothering Jason. He'd just wandered off. No, he hadn't mentioned meeting anyone; no, he hadn't gone to the wasteground with a purpose. Another blank.

Moir and his team then hit the computers, linking up with the Paedophile and Child Sex Crimes Unit to target the paedophile networks. They started by contacting all the known abusers within a fifty-mile radius, paying particular attention to anyone who might fit the meths-drinker's hazy discription, and checking their alibis. Nothing.

They had hooked up with their tame contacts in the Paedophile Information Exchange to see if one of their number had recently requested a teenage boy. The thought of contacting this organisation in the first place repulsed Moir completely; he had even toyed with the idea of noting a few names and addresses and paying them an unofficial visit sometime. The only thing that stopped him was the need to follow the official line – by condoning and controlling a small evil it was possible to monitor and stifle a greater one. Allegedly. At any rate, that thin line of inquiry had yielded nothing. Moir found this both comforting and disturbing.

He had deduced that the kidnapper had taken Jason for his own uses and that he had no police record. If he was a peripatetic opportunist there was no way they could even put together a profile of him, let alone catch him. Not until he struck again. The other theory Moir had was that the abductor's identity was known and protected. That he had enough brain and muscle not to draw attention to himself. Whatever, they had a problem.

Moir slumped further back into his chair, kicked his shoes off and flexed his toes. He wasn't a natural team player and was surprised to have been put in charge of such a high-profile case. He had never been one to court popularity, and certainly wasn't one of McMahon's favourites.

He grunted and looked round the room. His private office contained duplicates of all the case notes so far; this was where he came to think when the rest of his team went to their homes at night. The trouble was, no matter how hard he tried to concentrate on Jason Winship, another lost child kept wandering into his head.

He could see her face in his mind's eye, coming towards him over and over again, spooling round his brain like an old home movie. Her face, at first innocent and trusting, became disappointed, then snide and sarcastic, finally consumed with bitterness and bile. There were no words to accompany this film. But Moir knew them off by heart.

He was reaching out for another shot of whisky to blur the image when there was a knock at the door. Moir's hand stopped in mid-pour. No one was supposed to know he was here. With a great effort he eased himself out of the chair. Irritated, he pulled open the door; the person behind it did nothing to improve his mood.

"What the hell are you doing here?"

"It's very nice to see you too, Henry," said Larkin.

"What d'you want? How did you find me?" grumbled Moir.

"Is this supposed to be your secret hideaway, then? Come on,

40

Henry – everyone knows about this place. It's about as secret as Fergie's Shag List. Can I come in?''

With a scowl Moir unblocked the door and resettled himself in his chair.

Larkin looked around. ''Well, it's not everyone's idea of home but it suits you.'' He pointed to a haphazard collection of files that were cluttering up one corner. ''I'll bet there's Japanese airmen living in there who don't know the Second World War's over yet.''

Moir's eyes turned into beady little dots. ''Tell me what you want then fuck off.''

''Charming. Aren't you going to offer me a drink?''

''Help your fuckin' self. You usually do.''

Larkin did so, topping up Moir's glass at the same time. Pleasantries concluded, they got down to business.

''I need your help,'' said Larkin.

''You do surprise me.''

''I think it might have a bearing on the case you're working on.''

Moir snorted; it wasn't an endearing sound. ''It better have.''

Larkin told him about his trip to see Jane and his encounter with Noble, and Moir listened with growing interest. Larkin concluded and sat back on the corner of the desk, fighting for space against the clutter of papers, and sipped his drink as Moir tapped an index finger against his chin and looked pensive. Just as the gesture was becoming irritating, he spoke.

''So you've no idea what he's up to this weekend?''

''None at all,'' said Larkin. ''I doubt it's going to be sweetness and light, though. From the way he spoke to this kid it looked like they knew each other. I got the impression he's been planning this a while.''

''Aye, that's how they work. Get into a position of friendship and trust, then make their move. Trouble is, he's done nothing that we can prove so far.''

''I know that,'' said Larkin. ''But I've got an idea. You get some background on him – you know, see if he's got any previous, if he's got an alibi for when that kid disappeared, that sort of thing – and I'll keep an eye on him. Let you know if he does anything that you need to arrest him for.''

''Are you a detective now?''

Larkin smiled. ''Just call me one of your Stowell Street Irregulars, Mister Holmes.''

"Fuck off!" said Moir, almost smiling. He drew in a deep breath. "I'll see what I can do, but I'm a bit busy at the moment."

"Yeah. How's it going?" asked Larkin.

"Don't you read the papers?"

"Not when Carrie Brewer's writing them."

Moir harrumphed in agreement. "Not the best advert for your lot."

"Or humanity, come to that," added Larkin.

Moir nodded. "But no. Nothing. Brick wall after brick wall." Moir shook his head and sighed; the escape of air from his body seemed to soften his attitude. "I've got a bad feeling about this one, son. Very bad."

"Yeah," said Larkin, "I think you're right."

There followed a lengthy, contemplative silence. Outside, the day had quietly slipped into a sodium- and neon-lit darkness and the city's denizens were beginning to embark on their nightly quest for comfort and confirmation. Inside the room, the single, unshaded bulb cast long, lonely shadows onto the far wall.

Eventually Larkin stood up. "Well, thanks for the drink and the cosy chat, Henry. My place next time?"

"Nobody asked you to drink my whisky."

"No, but it was very kind of you to offer." Larkin looked at his watch; it was later than he had expected. Not that he had anywhere to go, but he knew how the evening would end if he didn't knock it on the head now. He stood up, gave Moir a piece of paper with Noble's details and the names and addresses of his referees. Moir took it, looked at it and put it in his pocket. "I'd best be off," said Larkin.

The corners of Moir's mouth almost lifted. "I'll let you know if I come up with anything."

"Me too. See you later."

After Larkin left, Moir sat silently for a while, then reached for the bottle. Pouring himself a hefty measure, he settled back into his chair and cranked up his mental projector to let the old home movies run once more.

The whisky had given Larkin an appetite. An almost pathological hatred of supermarkets meant that he kept a virtually empty fridge so he decided to visit his local Indian takeaway on the way home, settling for a chicken dhansak with pilau rice and a keema nan. A trip to the off-licence next door gave him a six-pack of Stella. It was the kind of sustenance his body rarely needed, but always enjoyed.

As he opened the door and peered into the gloom, he noticed that the red light on his answerphone was flashing furiously, like a malevolently twitching one-eyed guard dog. He walked over and hit Play, shrugging off his jacket as he did so, then entered the kitchen to turn out his dinner onto a plate and crack open a Stella. But after hearing the first message he knew he wouldn't be eating for a while. He listened to another one, more frantic in its pitch, and picked up his recently discarded jacket.

As he slammed the front door behind him, he could still hear the voice on the machine, leaving a third message. Had he stayed a moment or two longer, he would have heard it being abruptly – and violently – silenced.

Iced Glass Memory

The man was powerful. In public and in private. He thrived on power, basked in its glow, mainlined it directly into his system like a class A drug. He needed power to survive.

The power had deserted him today, though. For once he felt unable to cope with what he was, what he had become. All he wanted to do was to sit alone and weep for what he had done.

He hadn't intended to kill the boy. But the more wilful the child had become – the more determined to refuse – the more the man had hit him. Eventually, he had come to enjoy it. Watching the skin change colour with each blow had been like taking a privileged walk round an exclusive gallery – each work of art strikingly similar yet with a myriad of subtle nuances.

When the boy had died the man had felt his powers reach their peak. But after the euphoria had died down and the mundanities of disposal had been attended to, another mood descended: black and morose. Try as he might, he couldn't shift it. It reduced him to a snivelling and helpless creature – just like his recent victim.

He had cried almost constantly; sometimes for the dead child, but mostly for the boy he himself had once been. Not the strong, confident cricket player and captain of the rugby team – the childhood he had invented for the powerful man he had become – but something quite different. He looked into his memories as if he were seeing them through an ice-frosted window in the depths of winter.

He came from a background that some would consider to be privileged. A moneyed family. Private education had furnished him with all the contacts he would ever need: a secure job with a golden future.

His mother was an alcoholic, his father cold and absent.

Following the birth of his elder brother and himself, his mother had withdrawn sexual favours from his father. Not that it had bothered him much; he had always sought his pleasure elsewhere and hadn't troubled to conceal the fact.

The boy's death had triggered these memories, dredging them up from the bottom of his mind like shit from a septic tank. He thought of his mother and the parties she would throw for a select group of her friends. He and his brother were always the entertainment. He remembered how she would dress them in her old underwear, paint their faces with rouge and lipstick, force them to kiss each other, touch each other. Her sexual thrill increased in proportion to the misery and humiliation her children suffered.

The one over-riding moment – the worst memory he could recall in a childhood chock-a-block with them – was when he had looked into his brother's eyes and implored him to find the strength to protect him. He had stared long and hard and found nothing. The eyes that met his were dull, flat, death-like. His brother had gone beyond all feeling. And with that realisation came a shock of recognition: his brother's eyes were a mirror of his own.

When his mother died, he and his brother, dutiful sons, had gone to the funeral and stared numbly and dumbly at the proceedings. The rest of the family, who knew nothing of the parties, assumed they were in shock. That night, they crept back to the graveyard intending to desecrate the grave, to spit and shout and scream their hatred at their tormentor, to dig up the cancerous husk of the body and rip it to shreds with their bare hands. As they reached the newly-turned oblong of earth they could only stand and gape helplessly. They looked at each other and knew. She was dead, it was done, but they didn't forgive; they wouldn't forget. Not ever.

Their father, who had long since faded out of their lives, died. The two boys were split up and farmed out to any relatives who would have them; then, in desperation, to a series of foster parents. His brother was eventually adopted: a new name, a new family. Safe. But he wasn't to be so lucky.

And now, as he had so often done in those far-off days, he sat alone and in tears. Re-examining his past had been like pouring pure alcohol into a deep festering wound: the agony excruciating, cleansing.

But he couldn't sit here all day. It was time to put on his mask of power and face the world again. No need to worry about the dead child: his people were taking care of that. All that was required of him was that he resume his everyday guise and act with complete conviction. He would return to his past again before too long; it was important to remember what he once was, what he had become. But life had to go on.

He had transcended pain and suffering; he had come through. And soon, no doubt, he would meet another wayward boy; a boy with no future, a boy who would quickly learn the harsh but necessary lesson of his past.

6: Burning Down The House

From a distance the red glow in the sky looked like Gateshead's entry into the space programme. Close up it was a different story.

The house was old and, like all the others in the street, built of sturdy Edwardian stone and redbrick. Although it had been cheaply converted into flats and bedsits it had always looked to Larkin like the kind of clement-defying edifice that would endure forever. He was currently having to amend his opinion.

The voice on the answerphone had belonged to Houchen. In the first message he was excited; there was something he had discovered that couldn't wait and Larkin would be very interested. In the next, his voice was tense; where was Larkin and why didn't he have his fucking mobile turned on? Larkin had left the house before hearing the third message reach its involuntary end. But he had heard enough to fear the worst and the closer he got to Bensham, the more he knew his fears were justified.

Houchen's house was ablaze. The whole street had been cordoned off and there were two fire engines blocking the road. The firemen were moving into place with well-drilled precision: hustling people back behind hastily-erected barriers, evacuating neighbouring houses, unpacking equipment, getting suited and tooled up to enter the burning building. There was an enormous crowd staring, as if it were a spectator sport and they had wangled free admission. Just down the street, the first TV crew had appeared on the scene, unloading cameras, scoping out the most dramatic angle.

As Larkin hastily parked his car, an ambulance sped past him, its klaxon clearing a path through the growing mass of onlookers. A fireman pulled aside a section of the temporary roadblock so it could pass through, and Larkin seized his chance to sneak in behind it, staying on the opposite side of the ambulance so that the fireman wouldn't see him.

As soon as he was inside the restricted area he stopped, dumbfounded. The fire was huge, a massive orange, red and yellow force of nature reaching about thirty feet into the air. The heat from it was so intense that Larkin felt sweat burst onto his skin spontaneously. The noise – big whooms of rushing air, explosive bursts as something combustible fed the fire's appetite, crackles and crashes as the structure of the house began to char and disintegrate – was deafening. He could smell people's belongings, their *lives*, both acrid and sweet, melting and being subsumed in the fire's hunger. For all he knew he might have been smelling burning people as well. He stared at the fire, hypnotised with fear and wonder, knowing if he stood there long enough the flames would consume him too. Any closer and his leather jacket would start to bubble.

He was startled back to self-awareness by a figure running towards him: the fireman from the barricade.

"What the fuck are you doin'? Get behind the line, you daft bastard!"

The fireman grabbed Larkin and started to force him back. Larkin reluctantly did as he was told, allowing himself to be pushed behind the line. He still had a ringside view of the whole operation.

The firemen, lit by portable arc lamps, uncoiled hoses and pulled on breathing apparatus. One of the engines had been positioned with its ladder extended to an upstairs window; through billows of smoke, a gesticulating figure could just about be glimpsed. A fireman at the top of the ladder was beckoning to the figure, urging it to step out. Instead of doing so, the figure – a woman, Larkin assumed – handed out a small bundle. A baby. The fireman took the baby and hurried down the ladder, handing the fragile package to a waiting paramedic who walked briskly to the ambulance with it. From his calm expression Larkin guessed the baby wasn't in any danger.

The fireman climbed back up the ladder and entered the building through the window; the crowd gasped and muttered. Simultaneously, firemen entered through the front door of the house, pulling hoses with them. All the while, another contingent of firemen kept up a steady bombardment of the house with high-pressure hoses.

The firemen at the upstairs window appeared with the woman in front of him. He gestured to her to step onto the ladder, which she

50

gingerly did. A fireman was waiting on the ladder to escort her down to the ambulance. She didn't appear to have been burned, but from her blackened skin and dazed expression, it seemed as if smoke and shock had got to her.

Larkin looked at the ambulance. So far the woman and the baby had been the only people Larkin saw being brought out. There was no sign of Houchen. *Knowing that crafty bastard*, thought Larkin, *he'll have his camera out looking for the best angle. Getting an exclusive. Or . . .* Larkin ducked under the barricade and ran towards the nearest fire engine, encountering the angry, crop-headed fireman who had forced him back before.

"Have I got to tell you again?" the fireman barked, his gloved hand pushing into Larkin's chest.

"Just listen a minute," Larkin said. Something in his tone made the fireman stop in his tracks.

"What?" It was a statement rather than a question.

"I'm looking for someone. Houchen. Ian Houchen? He lives in that house," Larkin indicated the burning building, "in the top flat. He was probably the first out. Where is he?"

The fireman looked straight into Larkin's eyes. "Top flat?"

They both looked up at the top of the house. The fire had virtually eaten away the roof slates and was now persuading the roofing beams to collapse.

"You know this for definite, do you?" asked the fireman.

"He phoned me earlier, asked me to come over quick as I could. When I got here, this was happening."

"Aw, fuck. . ." said the fireman.

As they stood looking at the house, the team of firemen who had recently entered by the front door hurried out. One separated himself from the others and began to stagger towards them, ripping off his facemask as he came. The crop-headed fireman moved towards him; Larkin, not wanting to be left out, did the same.

The fireman was in his early twenties, tall with dark hair. He was breathless and sweating and his uniform appeared to have been barbecued. The crop-headed fireman confronted him.

"What's the score?"

"Ground floor's cleared. Nobody there. Mother and baby son cleared from the first floor. The top floor's completely blocked."

"How?"

"Stairs have gone. No way we can get up there." He sighed and looked over his shoulder at the house. "I know it's a bit early to say, but it looks as if that's where it started."

The crop-haired fireman jerked his thumb towards Larkin. "This one says his mate lives up there."

The younger fireman looked towards Larkin and shook his head. "Sorry, mate. If he's there I wouldn't hold out much hope."

"Yeah," Larkin said.

"We'll have to calm it down a bit with the hoses before we can get a proper look in there. Sorry."

"Yeah," Larkin said again.

The three of them turned to gaze at the house. The blaze seemed to have been caught in time; it wasn't doing much damage to the houses on either side. As they watched, there was an almighty crack, like vicious thunder, and the roof of the house, its timbers devoured by fire, collapsed.

The firemen at the front of the house instinctively scurried out of the way. Even Larkin took a couple of steps back. The crowd oohed and ahhed as if they were watching a fireworks display. The hoses kept up a constant stream. After a while they were the only noise. Everyone else was staring in silence.

The younger fireman was the first one to speak. "We're sorry, mate." He looked genuinely upset.

"Yeah," Larkin said for the third time. He glanced over to the ambulance which was closing up its doors, getting ready to take the mother and child to hospital. The crop-headed fireman spoke.

"You'd better hang around, son. I reckon the police'll want a word with you."

"Yeah," said Larkin. He was starting to irritate even himself with his newly-discovered monosyllabic tendencies. "Tell you what, I'll just make a quick phone call."

And with that he turned towards the cordon, skipped underneath it and jostled his way through the dispersing crowd which, after seeing the roof fall in, had decided that anything else would be an anti-climax. Then he made it back to his badly parked Golf. The TV crew were rushing forward for an interview with the firefighters as Larkin turned the ignition over, reversed, and was off. He wouldn't stay and talk to the police. He had a feeling he'd said too much already.

7: Carte Blanche

The journalists stood huddled together in the main office of The News Agents. They were muted, downcast, shuffling from foot to foot. They already knew why they had been summoned.

Bolland swept in. For once, thought Larkin, he really did resemble Michael Portillo; not the smug, arrogant-bastard, leader-in-waiting demeanour, but the constipated look he'd worn when he lost his seat at the election. Bolland took up his customary position in front of the group, and addressed them in unusually halting tones.

"Now ... erm ... All right, everyone. All right ..." Bolland gave a half-hearted knock on the nearest desk to quiet the non-existent noise. Larkin looked around. Knifeblades of sunlight penetrated the vertical blinds fronting the windows, but failed to pierce the mood of the silent group.

Everyone in the office had heard about Houchen, either from the TV or from Larkin. And everybody's response had been the same; initial disbelief, then excitement that one of their own was actually making the news, then a kind of numbness as they realised that someone they knew – irrespective of whether they liked him or not – had died an horrific death.

After leaving the blaze, Larkin had phoned Bolland, filling him in on what had happened. Once Bolland had recovered from the shock (which hadn't taken long) he had suggested that Larkin might want to write a first-hand account and sell it to *The Journal*, before their own reporters produced second-hand eyewitness accounts. Larkin had put forward a token argument on ethical grounds but Bolland smoothly countered with, "I'm sure it's what Ian would have wanted," finally adding, without a trace of irony, "If the positions had been reversed, it's what he would have done."

Larkin had given in and written it. He had treated it as an opportunity to get the events straight in his head, make sure he hadn't missed anything. Of course, he didn't tell the whole story: the answerphone messages he kept to himself.

Now Bolland had his staff's full attention. Joyce's eyes were red-rimmed and her face puffy from crying; without doubting the sincerity of her grief, Larkin reckoned there was something of the professional wailer about her. He could imagine her crying on cue when coffins appeared and brides floated down aisles; he didn't know what that said about her life. Carrie Brewer, on the other hand, occasionally darted glances of a sort in Larkin's direction which made him think she would happily set fire to a building with a friend of hers in it if it meant she ended up with an eyewitness story.

Bolland had finished relating the facts of Houchen's death; he was now gearing up to deliver a eulogy that would give full rein to his effusive vocabulary. Larkin tuned out, his mind replaying the inevitable visit he had received earlier that morning.

He had just faxed his piece to *The Journal* and crashed out on the bed when the doorbell rang. He ignored it and turned over. It rang again. And again. The insistency gave him a fair idea of who it was. He got up, shrugged himself into his dressing gown and went down to answer it.

As expected, it was the police: two of them. The older one, who looked to be in his early forties, spoke first.

"Mr Larkin?" The man brandished his warrant card. "We're — "

"The Sweeney, and you haven't had any dinner?" Larkin interjected.

The older man's lips briefly flicked into a pained expression that could have passed for a smile. "Detective Inspector Umpleby. This is Detective Sergeant Grice." The younger one bobbed his head. "May we come in?" he said, not waiting to be invited.

They all moved into the front room and sat down as Larkin sized his two guests up. Umpleby wore a black and white checked jacket, crisp shirt and tie and razor-creased black trousers, with thinning hair cut short and combed back and a neatly-clipped moustache sitting on his top lip. He reminded Larkin of a retired professional footballer, poured into his Sunday best and begging to be a pundit for Sky TV. A slight paunch was beginning to make its presence felt just above his belt. Just like a striker turned commentator, it looked like his glory days were behind him. And he carried the air of never having made it to the Premier League.

Grice was younger, rigged out in a smart three-button charcoal grey suit, black polo shirt, highly polished black boots. Hair cropped close to his skull. He resembled a pampered Rottweiler, or perhaps a failed Darwinian experiment into species regression: intelligent enough not to go looking for trouble, neanderthal enough to be in the thick if something kicked off.

The two policemen stared at Larkin, unsmiling, waiting for him to betray something. Anything. Larkin, knowing an interrogation technique when he saw one, stared right back.

Eventually Umpleby sniffed and looked round the room. "Nice place you've got here. Scandal and sensationalism must pay well."

"I wouldn't know," Larkin quickly replied. "Not my style."

"No," said Grice, "we know what your style is. We know all about you."

"My reputation precedes me, then." Larkin held Grice's look, allowed himself a small grin. He didn't know these two or what their game was, but he wouldn't rise to the occasion. "But never mind – it's always a pleasure to be visited by the boys in blue. Tea, gentlemen?"

Umpleby and Grice were clearly taken aback, but managed to nod. Larkin excused himself politely and went into the kitchen. *One nil to the home team*, he thought.

Considering he was one man living alone, and all he'd done the night before was tip out an Indian takeaway onto a plate and open a four-pack of lager, the kitchen looked like a Russian nuclear reactor gone into meltdown. Globs of bright orange goo coated the sink and other surfaces; unnaturally radiant flakes of uneaten pilau rice and crimson stripes of keema nan added additional decoration. The air smelled of sour hops. He ignored it, boiled the kettle, filled the tea pot, put three mugs, milk and sugar on a tray, and returned to the front room.

"Out of biscuits, I'm afraid," he said as he entered. The policemen didn't seem to know whether to take him seriously or not. Good, thought Larkin: that's what I wanted. He sat down.

Grice spoke first. "I presume you know why we're here, Mr Larkin?"

"A new community policing initiative?"

Umpleby's expression grew murderous, but his voice remained calm. "Ian Houchen, a colleague of yours, is dead. We've informed Mrs Houchen of her ex-husband's demise – always a painful task. She couldn't be of any help. We understand you were at the scene of the incident. Is there anything you can tell us?"

"I suggest you read my *Journal* article. Milk and sugar?"

They grunted affirmatively; Larkin handed them their mugs.

Umpleby took up the conversational duties while Grice gave his tea a suspicious stare, as if it had been poisoned. "I'm afraid I haven't seen your article yet," he said. "Perhaps you'd like to ...?"

"OK," said Larkin. "I got a call from Houchen. He asked me to go over to his place. I went. When I got there it was on fire. The fire brigade reckoned he was dead. That's it."

Umpleby nodded. "And this call you received. How did he sound?"

"Well — " Larkin began.

"Did he seem distressed? Anxious? Was it a social call or was it work?"

"I ..." Larkin hesitated. *He sounded terrified. In fear for his life.* He opened his mouth to speak but stopped himself. These two hadn't done anything to earn his trust. Their confrontational, accusatory attitude had forfeited them their right to be told anything. "He just – called. Asked what I was doing. Asked me to come over. That was it."

"And you spoke to him personally?"

Larkin swallowed, eyes downcast. "Yes."

Grice leaned forward. "And he seemed all right, did he?"

"Fine. Had a bottle. Malt. Wondered if I fancied sharing it." Larkin kept his eyes down.

"And this was something you often did? A matey get-together?" Umpleby again: suspicion in his voice.

"Sometimes," said Larkin. He felt his mouth go dry; he cleared his throat.

"And he wasn't ... worried about anything? Nervous, like?" As Grice spoke, Umpleby turned to him: a coded message flashed from his eyes. Grice immediately fell silent. Larkin pretended not to notice, but it had the effect of a mild electric jolt. Suddenly, for some reason he didn't yet understand, lying felt like the right thing to do with these two.

"As I said, he seemed fine. Why? D'you think he killed himself, or something?"

"It's early days yet, Mr Larkin," said Umpleby, looking pointedly in Grice's direction, "but from what we can piece together so far, it seems as if the fire did indeed start in Mr Houchen's flat. Antiquated gas supply. Maybe that whisky you mentioned made him clumsy with lighting it. That's only a theory, of course, but it seems the most logical at the moment."

"Right."

They fell silent again. A question popped into Larkin's head; he decided not to ask it. Instead he slowly sipped his tea, trying to look relaxed.

"So there's nothing more you can tell us, Mr Larkin?" asked Umpleby.

"Nothing that's not in the article," he replied.

"Well, in that case . . ." Umpleby stood up, followed by Grice. He handed his mug back to Larkin – Grice's tea sat on the floor, untouched. "Thanks for the hospitality. We'll see ourselves out."

"Any time," said Larkin.

Grice sidled past him on his way to the door. As he went he curled his lip at Larkin. It could have been anything, a sneer, a smile or an Elvis Presley impersonation. Larkin gave a solemn wink in return.

As he reached the door, Umpleby paused and turned. "Mr Larkin?" There was a glint in his eye as he spoke. "Perhaps our remarks about your chosen profession were tactless. So if you think there's something we should know, something perhaps omitted from your article — " He produced a business card. "You know where to find us."

The door shut and Larkin stood alone in the hall. Something was going on, their manner told him that, but he didn't have a clue as to what it was. He was just glad he'd trusted his instincts and kept quiet.

He looked at his watch. It wasn't worth going to bed. With a sigh he padded back to the kitchen, to microwave the remains of his discarded supper for breakfast.

Bolland was wrapping up his eulogy. Prior to this morning, the office staff had believed Houchen to be just another overweight, sweaty photographer: Bolland's words left them wondering how they could have failed to notice the true Houchen; the crusading ambassador for truth and justice, blessed with a Gandhi-like wisdom. Larkin shook his head in disbelief.

The meeting broke up. Slowly, people drifted back to their work-stations. Bolland surveyed the office, accepted that applause would not be forthcoming, and motioned Larkin into his office.

"Twice in two days I've been in here, Dave," said Larkin, attempting to perch on the chrome and leather construction. "Tongues will wag."

"Tongues can do what they bloody well want."

"Like that, is it?"

"Yes it is," said Bolland, leaning forward. "I've had the police round here, asking questions."

"So have I," said Larkin.

"Then catch me up on the investigation, Stephen."

"Pardon?" said Larkin. Either Bolland had been picking up hip but obscure slang from American cop shows, or he was fighting a losing grammatical battle.

"Just tell me what's been going on," he demanded irritably. "Was Houchen into something he shouldn't have been?"

"I know as much as you, Dave," said Larkin, comfortably, finding it easier to lie to Bolland than to the police.

"What did you tell the police?"

"That he seemed perfectly normal. That he asked me round to his place to share a bottle of malt. They reckon he was pissed and playing with the gas fire."

Bolland nodded twice in succession, the corners of his mouth pulled down. "And what d'you think, Stephen?"

"I think Houchen must have been sharing his flat with Eskimos to want the fire on in the middle of July."

"Did you mention that to them?"

"No."

Bolland frowned. "Why not?"

"Why d'you think? If they reckon he wanted the fire on in this weather then they're either thicker than they look – which would be hard – or they're lying."

"So why would they lie, Stephen?"

"Why does anyone lie?" Larkin leaned forward. "Look. Houchen left a message on my answerphone. Actually he left

58

several. Said he'd discovered something, needed to see me. The last message ended really abruptly – too abruptly. Next thing Houchen's dead – and the police don't suspect foul play.''

"Perhaps they would have done if you'd told them this.''

"I didn't want to. Those two couldn't find their arses with both hands. And they pissed me off. The last thing I was going to do was confide in them.''

Bolland fell silent; Larkin could almost hear him thinking. When he eventually looked up, a flame had ignited behind his eyes. "D'you think there's a story here?''

"I don't know. But it's worth looking into.''

"I'm inclined to agree,'' said Bolland, the fire now dancing. "Stop whatever you're working on and do this instead. I'm giving you *carte blanche*. If you find something, I'm backing you to the hilt. If you don't, all you've been doing is misleading the police.''

Larkin shrugged. "There's a first for a journalist.''

"Exactly. But that's strictly your business. Fair enough?''

Larkin smiled. "You wouldn't be saying that if you didn't think there was something for me to find.''

Bolland gave a snort that could have been either a laugh or a fly trapped in his nostril. He sat back, put his hands behind his head and sighed. "Bloody shame, though. Waste of a good photographer.''

"I believe you mentioned that earlier. At some length.''

"Yes, well . . . I had to say something. It was expected.''

Larkin nodded, straight-faced.

"I suppose we'll need a replacement.''

"Yeah,'' said Larkin. Suddenly a smile spread across his features. "I know a photographer.''

"I know lots of photographers, Stephen.''

Larkin grinned. "Yeah, but this one's special. He's *good*. And – we've worked together in the past.''

Bolland furrowed his brow and looked at Larkin suspiciously. "I don't like the sound of this, Stephen. Who is it?''

"An old mate of mine. We've – been through a few scrapes.''

Bolland was looking decidedly dubious now. "And can we rely on him?''

Larkin gave a short, hard laugh. "Trust me. Dave.''

8: Old Friends

Larkin sat back on the bench and breathed in deeply. Leazes Park on a warm summer's day wasn't a bad place to be. His bench was directly in front of the lake where children larked about on pedal boats, laughing and pushing, fooling around, shoving each other: their hurt disappearing quicker than money on a Friday night.

Toddlers played with absorption, their mothers close by. Pre-coital couples indulged in surreptitious foreplay on the grass; horny puffed-up pigeons cooed each other on. Office workers – jackets off, collar buttons undone – ate pre-packed sandwiches and planned utopian futures for themselves – until their mental alarm clocks told them lunchtime was over, the mortgage had to be paid, and the desk was beckoning.

Larkin stretched out his arms along the back of the bench and crossed his legs. A city idyll. An idle city. Post-industrial Eden.

He didn't fully buy into the scene before him, though; he knew every garden had its predators. Wherever children gathered so did child abusers, and Peeping Toms cruised sunbathers; an innocent movement or gesture was often the trigger a potential rapist needed to put theory into practice.

It was the way Larkin viewed things – life glimpsed sidelong, from the corner of his eye, with darkness only a blink away. It didn't do much good to the inside of his head, but he couldn't help it. He knew what went on. The monsters didn't just come out at night; the brighter the sun, the darker the shadows.

It was now one o'clock in the afternoon and he still hadn't had any sleep since the night before last. The first thing he'd done after leaving Bolland's office was rifle through Houchen's desk. He didn't know what he was looking for in particular: some clue.

Something. An address book, a slip of paper with a phone number on it. A signed confession to be opened in the event of his death. If only. All he found was some photographic accessory junk, an ancient Robert Ludlum paperback and a collection of festering Mars Bar wrappers. Not a great deal to go on.

There was nothing left of Houchen's flat. And he hadn't spoken to his ex-wife for months. Dead end. Larkin couldn't even contact Pauline the tranny hooker – Houchen had been the one with her number.

Realising he was getting nowhere fast, Larkin had sat at his desk to formulate a plan of action. To get a result for Jane *and* look into Houchen's death was too much for one person to do effectively. He began to make notes, piecing together ideas, developing them, scheming. Twenty minutes later he looked at the lengthy scrawl on his notepad and knew what he had to do. It was time to work the phone and call in favours.

Phone calls made and the rest of the morning free, Larkin had decided to take a long shot. The transvestite-loving politician was due to open a new old people's home in Felling: it was the journalistic equivalent of a graveyard shift, but Larkin went along anyway. He found the man desperately trying to turn the opening into a major PR event: pressing flesh, dunking biscuits into cups of tea for the few cameras that were there, whooping with laughter at the feeblest of jokes. The meagre collection of local journalists that were trailing him couldn't have shown less enthusiasm if they'd been at a Yawning Festival.

As soon as the man saw Larkin at the back of the tiny crowd, his jaw – along with his mask of fake hilarity – dropped. Larkin beckoned him over. The politician attempted to excuse himself in a jocular manner, graciously detaching himself from the senile old woman he had been attempting to cosy up to (who apparently believed him to be her son) and then coming straight across to where Larkin stood, waiting.

"Read the papers this morning?" Larkin had asked before the man had a chance to speak.

The man nodded hastily, summoning up bluster. "Now if you think—"

"That you had anything to do with my partner's death?" Larkin

61

finished the sentence for him. "Then you'd better tell me. It's in your own interests."

The councillor began to shake. He turned his back on the crowd and spoke in an urgent whisper. "I had nothing to do with it! Nothing! I didn't even know his name until I saw it under the picture in the paper. I swear, I *swear* I had nothing to do with it. Honestly!"

Larkin doubted that the man had ever been honest in his life. "D'you know who did?"

"No! No, I don't. I haven't heard a thing, honestly."

"Don't keep saying that. You're a politician."

"But I *didn't*. I didn't. And I don't know who did."

The pleading of the man struck Larkin as desperately pathetic, but something in his voice rang true. Larkin wasn't quite ready to let him go, though.

"What about Pauline? She been in touch?"

The man actually turned white. "No. I doubt I'll ever see her again." His last statement echoed both relief and loss.

"OK," said Larkin, "I believe you. I think. But if you hear anything, I want to know about it."

"How will I find you?"

"Don't worry. I'll find you."

Larkin turned and faced the mass of people waiting, though not eagerly, for the politician's return. The bewildered old woman he had been sharing a custard cream with was drifting back towards him, calling out a name that wasn't his.

"Don't fancy yours much," said Larkin, and gave the politician a wink. "Keep fighting the good fight. I'll call you when I need you."

The politician had been a long shot, Larkin knew, but he had had to try. Now he sat in the park waiting for the first of his phone calls to come to something. Waiting to meet The Prof.

Larkin had been wary about asking his old mate for help; their last attempt at working together had left them both tortured and hospitalised – in The Prof's case, nearly dead. He had survived, thankfully, but with a laborious walk and a disfigured right hand to show for it. And those were just the visible scars.

In addition to his physical disabilities, his mind had taken a long time to heal. It was doubtful that The Prof's mind could have been

62

considered normal to begin with, but he was now left with a noticeable vagueness; stopping talking in mid-conversation, gazing into
the middle distance.

Yet The Prof's near-death experience had been a boon to him.
For years he had believed he was on a personal spiritual quest,
ingesting hallucinogens and other mind-altering chemicals by the
bucketful, performing arcane peyote-fuelled rituals in search of a
shamanistic wisdom. He now believed his emergence from the coma
had signified a spiritual rebirth: a reaffirmation of his personal purpose and destiny. Now all he had to discover was what that purpose
was.

As Larkin looked beyond the duck pond to the tennis courts, he
saw a figure making its tortuous way towards him. The Prof.
Although The Prof refused to let Larkin take any blame for his
predicament (he claimed he had known exactly what he was getting
into) Larkin still felt a pang of guilt as the figure moved up the hill.
The Prof spotted Larkin, smiled, and wandered over.

He was wearing small round glasses, with clip-on flip-up shades,
button-up long-john vest, old baggy Levis held up by red braces,
trainers and a huge overcoat. On his cropped head, for good measure, sat a white sunhat. He sat down next to Larkin.

"What's that on your head?" asked Larkin.

"A sunhat," replied The Prof, surprised he had to state the obvious. "It stops the rays from penetrating." And The Prof nodded to
himself, pleased with the wisdom of his statement.

"What about the coat? Is that for keeping the rays out too?"

"No. That's because it's cold in the library."

"But you're not in the library."

The Prof's brow creased in concentration. "Hmm. Always a flaw
in the argument."

Larkin shook his head. "So how are you, anyway?"

"Fine, Stephen. And yourself?"

"OK." They both sat back, enjoying the sun.

"I saw your name in the paper this morning," said The Prof
casually. "Bad news."

"Yeah," said Larkin, although he hadn't really had time to think
what Houchen's death meant to him. He didn't feel guilty – he
didn't think he was to blame. He certainly wasn't heartbroken –
apart from working out of the same office, and their little night-time
activity, he had hardly known the man. His death had been a blow,

true; but he would get over it, move forward. He had done so before, with people he'd cared far more for than he had for Houchen.

"Anyway," said Larkin, "it just seems to have been – one of those things. But that's not why I wanted to see you today. I need your help."

A shadow crossed The Prof's features. "Help?"

"No, don't worry – not you personally. I wouldn't ask anything like that of you again."

The Prof nodded sagely.

"I need to get in touch with Ezz. I haven't seen him around lately. D'you know where he is?"

The Prof pondered. "He's out now, so he should be around. When d'you want him for?"

"As soon as possible. Today. Tomorrow at the latest."

"I'll see what I can do." The Prof opened his mouth to speak again. He had a curious look on his face, as if he wanted to ask a question but didn't want to hear the answer. "What d'you want him for?"

Larkin smiled slightly. "I think it's best that you don't know."

"If it's Ezz I presume it's illegal and potentially dangerous."

Larkin didn't argue.

The Prof sat back. "There's a fish that lives in the Amazon," he began. Larkin stared at him, nonplussed. He had no way of knowing whether or not this might be relevant.

The Prof continued. "A fish which, if a tribesman urinates in the water, jumps up the stream of urine and lodges itself inside the penis by embedding sharp prongs inside the shaft. It's impossible to remove, at least without mutilation." The Prof subsided into silence; he seemed satisfied. Larkin looked puzzled.

"Is that true?"

"Yes."

"So why tell me?"

"It's obvious. A parable, if you like. I don't want to stop you – just make sure you know what you're exposing yourself to."

Larkin nodded doubtfully. Was it imagination, or did he feel a slight discomfort in his groin? Slowly they began to talk, two old friends shooting the breeze. They didn't mention Larkin's urgent need for Ezz. Eventually The Prof got to his feet.

"Well – must be off."

"Anywhere interesting?"

"Yes, Stephen. Endlessly interesting. They've opened a cyber cafe. I spend days in there, on the Internet."

"I bet you do."

The Prof became thoughtful. "Y'know, I think that's the next step. Slowly we'll lose the use of our bodies and end up as no more than brains plugged into machines. Wouldn't that be something? Man and machine combined to create a new life form. A higher being. Beautiful." A wistful smile spread across his features. "Beautiful."

"If you say so, Prof."

"Oh, I do." He case an unconcious glance down the length of his maimed body. "Believe me, it is a union devoutly to be wished."

After leaving The Prof, Larkin decided to kill the rest of the afternoon in a bar. He felt he'd earned it. The one he chose was carved out of the front of a shopping mall down from the Haymarket; it was open-fronted and afforded a good view of the street. The wooden decor and mismatched furnishings made it look like the shopping centre – if not the city centre – had been built around it. It was only on closer inspection that the computerised tills, electric pumps and CD jukebox gave it away. It also claimed to be genuine Irish – if old photographs of Cork and irritating diggly-diggly songs on the jukebox could be considered genuine.

He had phoned Jane from his mobile to tell her that he would hopefully soon have some news for her, but she hadn't been there. The phone had been answered by another woman; Larkin hadn't left a message.

It was while he was on his third beer that his mobile rang.

"Your fuckin' one way system! I've ended up in the loading bay of Marks and friggin' Sparks twice over now!"

Andy Brennan had arrived.

Larkin gave him directions to Bolbec Hall and went to meet him.

Andy Brennan was a mouthy South London photographer who had been sent to Newcastle with Larkin in order to cover a drug dealer's funeral. The situation had escalated out of all proportion and led to the murder of Larkin's ex-girlfriend, Charlotte, who had been involved with some very heavy stuff. Larkin and Andy hadn't got on well initially, but Andy had been a good friend and ally when

Larkin needed him. When the whole, nasty little affair was over, Larkin had stayed on in Newcastle while Andy had taken off: "Have camera, will travel." Larkin, strangely enough, found that he missed him.

It was Andy whom Larkin had phoned to ask him to take over Houchen's job. He had needed some persuading, but had eventually agreed to drop everything and head north. Perhaps he sensed that wherever Larkin was, things seemed to happen. He could be an annoying little bastard, but Larkin had to admit he was looking forward to seeing him again.

As Larkin stepped out of the rickety lift he heard a familiar voice issuing forth from the main office.

"Yeah, but it's all cosmetic, innit? I mean, Melinda's all right as far as it goes, but you should 'ave seen 'er before the op! Nothin' spesh. Same with The Spice Girls. I mean – be honest – you wouldn't look at most of 'em twice unless you'd 'ad a few, now would you? No, natural beauty's the thing. Some people 'ave it . . ."

Larkin rounded the corridor. Andy sat on the corner of Joyce's desk, eyes gazing straight into hers, a sexually self-confident smile on his lips. Joyce, for her part, was swinging one leg back and forwards sensually; the tip of her tongue was visible at the side of her mouth. Natural beauty or not, her arousal was visibly deepening.

"Can't you come up with any better chat up lines than that?" said Larkin.

Andy turned suddenly when he heard Larkin's voice and Larkin got his first good look at him. Andy's hair was now cropped in a George Clooney; his goatee was still intact though, and he was starting to look too old for his expensive trainers, baggy combat jeans, and full-on clubbing T-shirt. He jumped off the desk and ran to embrace Larkin.

"Hey-hey! The miserable bastard himself!" Andy shouted, flinging his arms around Larkin, who – surprising himself – hugged the man back. "Good to see you, mate!"

"And you, Andy. Wish it could have been in better circumstances."

"Yeah, well," said Andy, "not your fault. Well, now you're 'ere, we've got to see this Bolland bloke. He said to wait for you."

They moved off together, towards Bolland's office.

"See you later," called Joyce, waggling her fingers flirtatiously at Andy.

"You certainly will, darlin'."

The meeting with Bolland was a formality. He could have got a photographer locally, but since he knew the details of Larkin and Andy's previous work, he was inclined to bring them together as a team again. Once they had discussed terms and conditions – Andy staying firmly freelance – Bolland turfed the two of them out to get some work done. They had got as far as the "Eiresatz" shopping-mall pub when the afternoon sun and the promise of a pavement table proved too much for them.

"So what's the score, then?" asked Andy, settling down to his pint.

Larkin didn't know where to start. "Well ... how much did I tell you on the phone?"

"Your partner had died unexpected like and you wanted a replacement ASAP. So I dropped everythin' and up I came."

"And it's good to see you."

"You too, mate." They raised their glasses.

"So what we workin' on, then?" asked Andy.

Larkin filled him in on Jane's doubts concerning Noble, the subsequent trip to the amusement arcade and the fact that something was going down at five thirty on Friday.

"That's today," said Andy.

"Good to see your brain's not completely coke-addled," Larkin replied.

"Fuck off. So what we gonna do about it?"

"*We* aren't going to do anything. *I'm* going to take you to the arcade and put names to faces, then *you're* going to follow them with your trusty camera and find out what's happening. You brought your car, didn't you?"

"Yeah, but talk about in at the fuckin' deep end," said Andy, sulkily.

"Has this spoilt your plans for the evening?"

"Well, I thought we could go out, you know, even get that receptionist piece — "

"You mean Joyce."

"Yeah, whatever, get her out or somethin'."

"This could be a big story, Andy."

Andy looked wistfully at his pint. "Yeah, right." He brightened up a little. "Reckon I am the perfect man for the job, though."

"How d'you reckon?"

"This is what I've been doin' recently. Industrial espionage an' stuff. Private surveillance, that sort of thing. Big corporations wanna keep one step ahead of the game so they employ people to, A, spy on the opposition, and B, spy on people on their own side who may be selling trade secrets. That sort o' thing. Handsome money, too."

Larkin was genuinely surprised. "How d'you get into that?"

"Well, I was doin' this porn shoot — "

That was more like it. "You do surprise me."

"No, really, I'd been doin' some straight model work, fashion stuff, and they asked me to do this porn mag shoot. So I did a few and, I tell you, they nearly put me off for life. Gynaecological fuckin' nightmare. Fuckin' butcher's shop." He took a swig of his beer, relishing his role as sleazy raconteur. "Then this other bloke who was workin' on the mag – don't know what it was called, *Big Jugs And Fat Arses* I should think, judgin' from the picture content—"

"You were saying?"

"Oh, yeah. So this bloke said 'e could get me some surveillance work. An' 'e did."

"Good. I'm happy for you."

"So 'ow come you're not trailin' this Noble bloke?"

"Because he knows me by sight, because I'm going to be gathering stuff on him at this end, and also . . . ." Larkin scrutinised Andy, trying to gauge his likely reaction to what he was about to say. "I'm looking into Houchen's death. It might not have been an accident."

Andy shook his head and sighed. "I can't leave you alone for five fuckin' minutes, can I? What you been up to this time?"

"Well . . ." Larkin opened his mouth to speak. "Well . . . Get the drinks in and I'll tell you."

"Oh, fuckin' 'ell," said Andy. " 'Ere we go again . . ."

9: True Confessions

For Andy and Larkin, settled in the pub, the afternoon began to slip away. Larkin avoided explaining Houchen's death, knowing he couldn't go into it cold; there were things Andy had to know first. Once uncorked, the whole lot would come pouring out. Instead, he kept the conversation general: reminiscing about mutual friends and old work colleagues, trading insults – getting acquainted with each other all over again.

But inevitably they drifted towards specifics. And Larkin, feeling more comfortable than he had done in ages, was able to speak freely.

"It goes back to when you left," Larkin began. "I sat around the house – Charlotte's house – in a right old state. Hated being there, couldn't bear the thought of moving out . . ." His eyes misted over at the recollection. For whole days he'd just lain on the bed, sobbing, inarticulate with grief. "I tried to get up, to do things, but every time I tried, this black cloud would pass over me and remind me of what had happened. Back to square one."

He took a long gulp of beer. Andy knew better than to interrupt.

"One day, Dave Bolland turned up. He was an old mate from way back. We studied journalism together. He asked if I fancied writing about my side of what happened. Needless to say, I told him to fuck off. He kept on at me. He saw the state I was in, said it would be cathartic. A means of getting it all out of the way, starting again. Eventually I told him I'd give it a try – to get him off my back more than anything.

"Once I'd started, well, it consumed me. It was difficult at first, taking myself back there, but once I got going I spent day after day reliving it, writing it down, sparing nothing . . . I gave it to Bolland

69

and he sold it to one of the broadsheets for a small fortune. He wanted me to turn it into a book – had offers there too – but I said no. I'd written it, it had done its job, and now it was time to move on. So he offered me a place with his agency. I took it; thought the routine might help to keep me sane, give me a bit of focus. It did.

"But at the same time, there was this little . . . kernel, I suppose – this seed of rage growing inside me. I was finished with the grief, but I couldn't get rid of the anger. I'd see Sir James Lascelles and his cronies grinning on TV, in the papers, everywhere. It made me feel sick. Everything I'd been through, and it was all for nothing. The bastards were still getting away with it! And I couldn't change things, because they're a fuck of a lot more powerful than me.

"Anyway, I got partnered with Houchen. To be honest, he didn't seem like my kind of guy. Then one day, we were talking about this Rebirth Of The Region thing – you heard about that?"

"No. Should I have?" asked Andy.

"Not really. But it's big up here. Like everywhere else, there's been a change of faces in charge and the new guy at the top in this area's called Alan Swanson. He got swept in to power on the strength of his Rebirth Of The Region idea. During the election he made it sound like he was going to turn Newcastle into some utopian vision where disease, poverty and inequality would be banished forever. Naturally, people went along with it. To be honest, right then they'd have voted for a fucking tuna fish sandwich if it had promised them change, but Swanson's bullshit was all they were offered."

Larkin took another swig of his beer. "Of course, it was all complete bollocks. Another jobs-for-the-boys stitch-up, playing on the gullibility of the electorate. So anyway, Houchen and me were talking, saying what a disgrace the whole thing was, and how people couldn't – or didn't want to – see through it. And he asked me what I would do if I had some dirt on one of the councillors involved with the project. Just a bit of relatively harmless sleaze, you understand. I told him I'd use it as a lever to make him keep his promises. He liked that answer, came back a week or so later with a proposition."

"And what was that?" asked Andy.

Larkin told him about setting the councillor up with the transvestite hooker. Andy's jaw just about hit the floor.

"You're a fuckin' nutter, you know that?"

"Had to be done, Andy."

70

"Why?"

"Because the wrong people keep on getting away with things," said Larkin. "You know that as well as me." He felt himself getting angry; this wasn't the response he had been expecting from Andy. He of all people should have understood.

"Yeah, but mate," started Andy, "you've got to know the difference between what you can and can't change." He shook his head, exasperated. "This other guy, Houchen. What exactly did he get out of it?"

"Don't know," said Larkin. "Maybe it just appealed to his sense of justice. Maybe it gave him some sort of kick. Perhaps it was just a way of filling in his evenings. I don't know – he was a hard guy to read."

Andy looked sceptical. "So – your moral crusade had any results yet? Done any good?"

"Dunno," said Larkin, huffily. "And as I said, we only did it once."

"And now Houchen's dead. Any connection?"

"There might be," said Larkin. And, finally, he told Andy about the answerphone messages.

"Oh, fuck."

"Exactly. And I've been to see our target, who swears he had nothing to do with it, and I believe him."

"So who does that leave, then?"

"Well," said Larkin, "I didn't tell you the full story about Noble."

"What's he got to do with this?" asked Andy, taken aback.

"Maybe nothing. Maybe a hell of a lot. Noble mentioned to Jane that he has friends in high places. Now because he reckons he's Minister for Youth, Swanson was the first one who sprung to mind. At first I thought the idea was ridiculous – a politician covering for a child abuser – but the more I thought about it, the more it made sense."

"To you, maybe," said Andy, sneering in disbelief.

"Just listen," said Larkin, his face grimly set. "Swanson's planning to create community centres for the young, after-school homework clubs, schemes for under-privileged kids – that sort of thing. He wants to take a hands-on approach. If he's using that as a front to get close to kids, he could be capable of anything. Even murder, if it meant saving his reputation and keeping his job."

"So how are the two things connected?"

"I don't know. Yet."

"But you do think they are? You think they all meet up each Tuesday to plot against you and Houchen? You haven't got any proof!"

"No," said Larkin, his eyes steely. "But I will have, eventually."

Andy laughed. "You've brought this one on yourself! Wasn't your fault last time, I grant you, but this – my giddy aunt . . ."

"I don't see the problem with what I'm saying!" Larkin was infuriated.

"No, you don't, do you? Why can't you accept that some things are never gonna change? For one thing, there's not a conspiracy round every corner – all right? If Swanson is dabblin' with kids and we find out, great. We'll get a good story out of it. But this councillor, now, that's different. Shake the bloke down, print some pics in the papers, he resigns, everyone pats themselves on the back for being fearless crusaders for the truth, you get another one in. Whole thing starts again." Andy leaned forward. "That's the way it is. They're politicians! You can't ask them to stop being that, any more than you can ask a rattlesnake to stop rattling. Some things are just the way they are. Accept it."

Larkin stared dead ahead. "We shouldn't have to accept it. I *won't* accept it."

Andy shrugged. They sat in silence for a while, slowly sipping their beer, until Larkin spoke, hesitantly.

"What if I got something on him? What if I prove that Swanson had Houchen murdered? You wouldn't think I was so naive then, would you?"

Andy sighed. "What time we got to be at this arcade?"

"*Would* you?"

"I said, what time?"

"Would you?"

"No!"

"All right! Good." Larkin allowed himself to relax a little, feeling that, in some way, he'd just won a little moral victory. "Now drink up. We'd better go."

Five fifteen, and Larkin and Andy were parked on a side street opposite the arcade on Clayton Street. The two of them had walked down from the pub to where Andy had parked behind the Central Station, Andy telling Larkin not to worry about the amount of alcohol he'd consumed; the drive would soon sober him up, he claimed. When they had reached the parking space, Larkin had done a double-take: Andy's vehicle was a gleaming, brand-new, purple and chrome soft-top Vitara jeep.

"What the fuck's *this*?" shouted Larkin. "I thought you'd done surveillance? I thought you'd been spying on people? Couldn't you have found something a bit more inconspicuous, like an ice cream van or a fucking Sherman tank?"

Andy shrugged, tried not to look hurt. "I like it."

Larkin sighed; it was too late to argue. "Oh well – you're the expert."

Now they waited, hopefully not too visibly, in the side street. Larkin prayed that the city-centre rush hour meant all the traffic wardens would be too busy to ticket them for parking on a yellow. Just before five thirty, Noble entered the arcade.

"That's him," hissed Larkin.

Andy sat up. All he saw was a mild, inoffensive-looking bloke. Then, a couple of minutes later, Noble emerged with two boys. They all seemed cheerful enough.

"Right, there you go, Andy. Best of luck," said Larkin, jumping out. He had already given Andy the gen on Noble's Fiesta.

"Now remember," said Larkin, "the first sign of anything untoward, you get the fuckin' law in, right?"

Andy nodded. "I'll be in touch," he said, and swung the Vitara out onto the main street.

Larkin turned and walked back in the other direction. He didn't want Noble to catch the slightest glimpse of him. At least he could trust Andy to do a professional job, he thought. Despite the pimp-mobile.

Larkin trudged slowly back to the Golf. Perhaps Andy was right. Perhaps it was merely bitterness combined with a misplaced idealism that was blinding him to some unalterable truths. Perhaps. Either way, it was good to see the old bastard again.

With nothing better to do, and nowhere else to go, Larkin headed the Golf towards Jesmond and home.

As he let himself into the house, he was immediately consumed, as always, by a feeling of entrapment. But what was trapping him?

Was it the house – his past? Or something inside himself he couldn't let go? He didn't know. He didn't want to know. So he took a can of beer from the fridge and made his way upstairs to his attic. He intended to lie on the bed, tune in the TV, and tune out his head to an alcoholic accompaniment. But when he was halfway up the stairs, he heard a noise.

Larkin froze. The noise came from above. From his room. He reached the half-landing and he quickly looked around. He didn't know whether to continue his ascent or run back down and out the front door. His heart was doing somersaults in his chest. His eyes caught on an ornamental, free-standing cast-iron candle holder; he put the beer can down and hefted the candle holder into his arms like a weapon. Taking courage from the weight, he decided to go on.

He climbed up the second set of stairs as quietly as he could. He reached the second landing and stood outside his door. His heart was pounding fit to burst; it filled his ears with rushing blood, blocking out any sound from the room.

With sudden force he kicked the door open, almost knocking it off its hinges, and stepped into the room, brandishing the candlestick, his breath ragged, adrenalin-fuelled.

At the far end of the room, on a chair in front of the window, sat a figure. Rays from the dying sunset cast an obscuring halo around its head. Apart from moving its arm to drag purposefully on a cigarette, the figure didn't move. Larkin too stood still. The silence was palpable.

Eventually the figure spoke. "I hear you've been lookin' for me."

Larkin lowered the weapon, in recognition of the voice. It wouldn't have helped him anyway.

"Hello, Ezz. How you doing?"

10: The Weekend Starts Here

Ezz. Larkin had known the man for about fifteen years, on and off, and was still no nearer to understanding him. Back in the early eighties, Ezz had been a contract burglar employed by Larkin (amongst others) to aid him in his work as an investigative journalist, both in Newcastle and London. Whenever there was a piece of evidence Larkin knew existed but couldn't access, Ezz was the man. He had a one hundred per cent success rate, and had been well rewarded for it, while Larkin had been supplied with some spectacularly incendiary information. When it came to burglary, Ezz was the expert's expert. He could enter a premises, do what he had to do, and leave, without the owners even noticing he'd been there. Years of practice had given him an unflappable serenity and mastery of physical movement that made him the best there was. While working he had perfect control: so light-fingered and nimble-footed he could have been a ninja. But he had a flipside: the need, outside working hours, to release his pent-up aggression.

It wasn't a simple matter of getting drunk and picking a fight; Ezz needed to be goaded. He waited for violence to find him, then used the consequences as a form of therapy. Larkin knew that Ezz went ballistic to relieve the stress of maintaining the rigorous control that Ezz's work demanded; but he suspected Ezz's need for aggro went much deeper than that. The violence Ezz sought didn't happen just for the sake of it; it was instinctive, emotional. It fulfilled a deep need, satisfied some sort of terrible anger. Larkin was amazed he'd never killed anyone; he'd come pretty close several times. He had never dared to ask Ezz about it, though. Ezz, Larkin had decided, was driven by some very deeply rooted and complex demons.

Of course, while Ezz didn't actively start trouble, he encouraged it to come to him. He loaded the dice in his favour. He had spent years searching for the most contentious image possible and, through trial and error, had honed it to the point of hostile perfection: the skinhead.

He now had the look just right: twenty-four-hole DMs, faded jeans, braces, white T-shirt and Union Jack tattoos all the way up his arms. Shaved head, crooked nose, broken teeth. He was a walking threat. A danger to society. And the uniform distracted attention from his curiously vulnerable eyes.

His fighting method was simple: go somewhere promising (usually one of the rougher pubs), find a target (or two, or usually three), send them intimidating looks and wait for it to kick-off. He was rarely disappointed; and he hardly ever lost the fight. Occasionally he attracted the notice of the police and had done time in Durham because of his leisure pursuit. But never for burglary. Never for his true calling.

And that was one thing Ezz was very insistent about; he was a *burglar*, not a common thief. A professional. He would break into an office, an institution, a home – and take only what he had come for. No unnecessary damage. Strictly business. Nothing personal. That, he felt, was a violation.

Now, though, Larkin's relief at discovering the identity of his intruder was turning quickly to irritation.

"How the fuck did you get in?"

Ezz shrugged, as if the question wasn't worthy of an answer.

"You scared the fuckin' life out of me! Couldn't you just ring the bell like normal people?"

"Sorry," Ezz said indifferently. "Habit."

Larkin sighed. He was beginning to regain his composure. "Anyway, you're here now."

"You wanted to see me," Ezz said again.

Same old Ezz, thought Larkin. No pleasantries, no small talk: just business, discussed in that same detached monotone he remembered so well. It was like conversing with a Dalek on methadone.

"Yeah, I did," said Larkin. "I've got a bit of work for you. Tomorrow night. Bit short notice, but I'll pay you."

Ezz nodded slightly, as if that were no more than his due.

Larkin outlined his plan; Ezz listened, motionless. After Larkin finished there was silence. Larkin was patient, waiting for Ezz to utter. Eventually, he was rewarded: "I always work alone."

"I know," said Larkin, "but I need to be with you. I have to be there. This is important."

There was silence again while Ezz thought.

"So what's he done?" asked Ezz presently.

"It looks like he might have been abusing children."

"You mean, sexually?" Was Larkin imagining it, or had Ezz's icy monotone become a little warmer?

"Yeah, I imagine so."

There was silence again. This time it seemed tense, menacing.

"All right," said Ezz. "But you're an amateur. And amateurs fuck up. You do exactly what I tell you."

"Absolutely," said Larkin.

Ezz stood up, and for the first time Larkin got a good look at him. He was still in prime condition; his arms and torso were like silk-wrapped rope. The sleeveless T-shirt emphasised his muscles. His arms were a picturebook of fascism: Union Jacks, bulldogs, home-made prison slogans crowding for space with Death Or Glory knives and hearts. No space for his mother's name. He didn't wear his heart on his sleeve, it was his guts as well: a whole political agenda, in fact. Larkin knew Ezz didn't subscribe to it, but that didn't stop it looking authentic.

Ezz repeated his instructions; Larkin nodded, in confirmation. Then Ezz was off. No goodbye, just straight out the door and soundlessly down the steps.

Larkin crossed to the window, opened it to disperse the thick cigarette smoke. He glanced down at the street. No trace of Ezz. He hadn't expected there to be.

He lay down on the bed. There was nothing else to be done till morning. He considered his options for the evening. Meet The Prof for a drink? No – he didn't want him involved in any way, not this time. Phone Jane? No. He didn't feel like talking to her at the moment. In fact, if he was honest, he didn't feel like talking to anyone at all.

He swung himself off the bed and went looking for the discarded can of beer. That would keep him company. That would be a start.

Beer in hand, he slapped an old Tom Waits tape – one with unerasable ghosts limpeted to the songs – into the machine and lay back on his bed nursing his beer. His mind ticked over, relentlessly.

Jane: where was the relationship (if it could be called that) headed? No idea. Houchen? He felt uncomfortable about the man's death, but not guilty. At least, not yet. He would try his damnedest to investigate it, though; he owed him that much.

Then after Houchen came Moir. Then Jason Winship, the missing child. Then Charlotte. Then he needed another beer. And so it went on, until the tape ran out.

Eventually, the hours were killed and the best part of another night had gone. Having successfully managed to stay this side of maudlin drunk, Larkin slept. And there were no dreams. At least, none he would admit to remembering.

Saturday morning. After getting up and shaking off his mini-hangover, Larkin felt his heart sink when the phone rang. He'd come to expect bad news.

It was Jane.

"Hiya." She sounded doubtful, as if she wasn't sure she should be calling. "How you doing?"

"Fine," Larkin replied. There was an uncomfortable silence down the line. "Or did you mean, how was my job for you going?"

She gave a small laugh of embarrassment. "Well, both, really."

"Well, as I said, I'm fine, and I may have something for you soon on that front."

There was a catch in Jane's voice. "Good or bad?"

"Depends how you mean. I think your suspicions were right, though. Don't worry – I'm on to it. I'll know for definite by tomorrow."

"Why? What you goin' to do?"

"I'll – just know, that's all."

No response.

"Look," said Larkin, "I'm sorry. I can't tell you how I'll know. But you'd better start thinking about your next step."

"Yeah . . ." Her voice trailed off. Larkin was just about to prompt her when she said, "Listen, d'you fancy meeting for lunch? I need to talk this through with somebody."

He did fancy it. They arranged a time and place and hung up. And Larkin went off to get a much-needed shower, looking with distaste en route at the debris of the night before. Empty bottles and cans; a pile of tapes; CDs full of lonely music. His Friday-night life, the melancholic's handbook.

In the shower he smiled to himself. It might just be a meeting to sort out damage limitation, he thought, but it was good to have something to look forward to.

Lunch actually turned out to be fun. They met in the Food Court of the Monument Mall, Jane having left Alison with another female worker from the centre, who had kids the same age. "They're all goin' to the park this afternoon. I doubt our Alison'll even know I'm not there," she said with a laugh.

Over jacket potatoes and cappuccino, they discussed the best way to approach the problem, so that the kids, the parents and the centre all came out of it as unscathed as possible. Larkin said he didn't know how much of the evidence he hoped to gather against Noble could be used in a court of law. "But I do have a sympathetic friend in the police force. He'll help us."

"Thanks, Stephen," Jane said. "I suppose we'll have to bring in Social Services for Daniel and his family. It might help if I have a word with them before we do that."

"It might."

Jane sighed. "I know it sounds selfish, but I'm really worried about the centre as well. I don't want it to close. We do good work. People need us."

Larkin was hit by an idea. "I think I've got a friend on the council who owes me a favour. Worst comes to the worst I'll have a word."

"Aw, would you? Thanks." She sighed again. "You know, we followed all the procedures with James . . . I dunno. You try and look out for them – the ones who get into these kind of jobs just to hurt kids – but they're so *convincing*. I mean, I reckon I can spot a bullshitter when I see one, but he had even me fooled at first. No record, great references — ."

"I'm getting those looked into too."

She smiled then; it lit up her face. "What a great guy you are!"

Larkin smiled, mock-modest. "I try."

A shadow came back into her eyes again. "His references . . . he once said, joking-like, if we ever tried to get rid of him . . ."

"I know," said Larkin. "And I shouldn't have to remind you, I'll be the one doing the media manipulation on this one. So don't worry."

Jane's smile was back in place. Larkin studied her. The anxious

79

frown that had been hardening her features had receded to allow a different range of emotions to take centre stage. She looked bright, positive, more like herself.

She was dressed in a long sleeveless denim dress with an open-necked collar, buttoned up the front, with stacked canvas sandals and small, round sunglasses perched on her head. And she was awakening in Larkin feelings long since repressed. Of course, it didn't hurt that she was showing obvious delight in what he had to say to her: a boost for the ego if nothing else, but it was still good to feel appreciated by such an attractive woman. She even smelled good. Larkin was feeling exhilarated – and scared.

"Hey," she said, "did you hear about that fire in Bensham the other night? He was a journalist, wasn't he?"

Larkin explained; Jane immediately apologised for her lack of tact.

"It's not your fault," said Larkin. "You weren't to know. He was my partner. We weren't close as it goes – but yeah, it is a loss."

She didn't mention Houchen again. Instead she looked at her watch and told him it was time for her to go and pick up Alison.

He walked her down to the bus stop on Grainger Street. Their conversation had slipped into a different gear since they'd stopped talking about Noble and Houchen: they were chatting easily, strolling along the pavement; to all intents and purposes like any other young couple. Larkin looked up. A perfect sun in a cloudless sky beamed down on Saturday-afternoon shoppers, busy buying merchandise to improve their homes and their lives. He smiled at Jane; she caught his glance and smiled back. Wordlessly, she slipped her arm through his. He didn't remove it.

They walked like that for a while. *Sometimes it all seems so easy,* thought Larkin.

Eventually, they reached the bus stop and stood in silence, somehow indecisive. Waiting not only for the bus, but for something else as well.

"Listen," said Jane, hesitantly, "what you doin' tonight?"

Larkin gave a sad smile. "I'm busy."

A light went out in Jane's eyes. "Right. Sorry."

"No, I mean it," he said. "I am busy. I'm working for you,

remember? Tonight's the only night I can do what I have to do.''

She perked up a little. ''Another night, then.''

''Yes,'' said Larkin. ''Another night.''

The bus, a bright yellow double-decker, chose that moment to arrive. But as Larkin prepared to say a matey goodbye, Jane turned to him, took his face in her hands, and kissed him full on the lips.

The kiss shocked Larkin's mouth open and he felt her tongue quickly dart inside. Then she pulled away from him and went to board the bus. She turned and gave him a last little wink, while the other people at the bus stop pretended not to notice.

''Give us a ring!'' she called.

''I will,'' said Larkin, grinning broadly.

The bus pulled away. And Larkin stood there, dumbfounded, smiling like an idiot. As he walked back up the hill towards Greys Monument, he made a conscious effort for once not to walk in the shadows cast by the tall, Georgian buildings, but to stroll in the sunlight.

He sighed. *Why*, he thought, *can't my life always be like this?*

Maxwell's House

The man breathed a sigh of relief. It was all under control. His earlier, dark mood had disappeared, evaporated like spit on a griddle. In its place was a kind of euphoria.

He had a lot to be euphoric about. For one thing, the boy's body still hadn't been discovered; the frisson he felt from knowing where it was while the search went on high and low was something to be savoured. In addition, chicken was on the menu for the weekend. During the last few days he'd had an almost permanent erection, thinking about the pleasures that lay ahead.

Safe in his cocoon of confidence and power, the man allowed his mind to wander again. Back to his life before power. Back to when he was the victim . . .

After their parents' death, his brother's name changed; and with it, his brother. His brother became soft, hugging his new parents, laughing with his new brother and sister, allowing himself to feel comfortable in his new home.

The man hated what his brother was becoming: safe, secure and, most of all, distant. The man wanted – needed – his brother, and deep down, underneath the layers of hate and rage, he wanted what his brother had. But he would never admit it.

Despite his mother's death, his life hadn't improved. Shunted from one unwilling relative to another, he had finally ended up at the thin end of the wedge, in foster care. His new 'parents' did their best but with three children of their own and a low income, fostering was a way of making ends meet rather than healing broken lives. In fact, they had already given a home to one foster child. Maxwell.

Right from the beginning, Maxwell had taken exception to the

*presence of the younger boy. Perhaps he thought he was being
usurped; that the new addition to the household would receive whatever limited share of their carers' attention had previously been
reserved for him. To retain his power, stamp his authority on the
situation, he became tormentor, torturer, and the younger boy his
victim. It started with sly kicks, pinches, blows that could almost
have been accidental. Then, as Maxwell grew in confidence, the
casual violence became more extreme, more deliberate. He would
beat the boy rigorously, scrupulously, being careful to leave marks
only where they wouldn't show. Beating became part of the boy's
daily routine. Maxwell knew by now that the boy was too scared of
retribution to carry tales. And, having reached an age when sex
governed every waking and sleeping moment, he took the next step.*

*He would wake the boy in the middle of the night, in the tiny,
claustrophobic bedroom they were forced to share, and force his
penis down the child's throat. The first few times the boy had
struggled, trying to pull his head away, unable to breathe; but his
frantic movements had simply driven Maxwell to a greater pitch of
sexual excitement and he had grabbed the boy and pumped all the
harder. Eventually the boy had learned that if he lay still and passive the pain and fear would diminish. It reached the point where he
was hardly frightened at all, even when Maxwell turned him over
and buggered him until he bled. He knew he was powerless, a natural victim. Why fight it?*

But one day, he snapped.

*He didn't have friends, playmates. Even the three children in the
family didn't want anything to do with the fostered boys. He did,
however, have some idea of how boys his age were supposed to
behave, and so he had been trying to make a swing. He had carried
a rope to an old oak tree in a nearby wood, had thrown it over the
sturdiest, highest branch he could reach, shinning up the tree to
secure it. As he pulled the knot fast, he suddenly stopped, gazing at
the rope as if seeing it for the first time. The rope wasn't just a
plaything – it could be an instrument of life and death. A hangman's
best friend.*

*Quickly, he turned his knot into a slipknot, testing it with his
hands to make sure it ran smoothly. Then he placed it over his head,
around his neck. He climbed on to the branch where the rope had
been tied and perched there, knot tight, arms outstretched. As he
prepared to launch himself into the air, into the unknown, a single*

thought ran round his head: would his brother do it like this?

But then, suddenly, he realised. If he killed himself, Maxwell had won. His power would be unlimited. As for his brother, he had his happy new family now. Would he even care?

A kernel of anger began to germinate inside him and he allowed it to grow. He tugged the rope from round his neck and threw it down, leaving the empty noose to dangle from the branch. He climbed down from the tree, tears on his cheeks; for the first time they were tears of rage, not terror and shame. He walked away deeper into the forest. From that moment he began to plot his revenge.

He wouldn't be the victim any more. Now he would be the master. He turned back and saw the rope hanging, swaying gently in the breeze. Through the tears, he could just make out the ghost of a boy swinging from side to side, head at a pathetic angle.

When he saw Maxwell again he would be ready.

That night, after the customary beating – which Maxwell seemed to use as a kind of foreplay – it was business as usual. Maxwell, as always, pulled his erect penis from his pyjamas and shoved it into the boy's mouth.

The boy took the swollen cock between his teeth and bit down, as hard as he could.

Maxwell screamed and tried to withdraw, but the boy held on, grinding his teeth backwards and forwards, deeper and deeper. He felt his mouth flood with blood. Still he didn't let go.

Eventually Maxwell, on the point of blacking out, stopped struggling and the boy released him. Maxwell stumbled off the bed, groaning and whimpering like an injured animal. He fled the room, pyjama bottoms round his ankles, his penis hanging flaccid and mangled between his legs, to tell his foster parents what the boy had done.

The boy rose from the bed also and went to the bedroom. Spat blood from his mouth into the sink. Looked in the mirror and saw his eyes. He didn't recognise them. They belonged to a different person, to the person he had become.

The incident was dealt with quietly. Maxwell was given urgent medical attention; the boy was removed from the household as soon as possible. No action was taken, but his case notes went with him. The authorities knew that he had savagely attacked an older boy, and that the attack had been of a sexual nature. Although the case notes stated that the boy may have been provoked – the foster carers' children backed him up on that one – they conferred a new status on him. No longer did people look at him with scorn or pity. The balance of power had shifted. Now they looked at him with fear.

This had been the man's first lesson.

Eventually he went away to university, left his past behind. He never saw Maxwell again.

At university he carried his new-found confidence before him. The pathetic victim had long since been left hanging on the old oak tree. He worked hard on his new persona: the rugby captain, the keen cricket player. He was tall, strong, charismatic. Even popular. People said he was a natural leader.

Over the years he perfected the precise science of human manipulation. And so successful was his new persona – his mask – that acting the part became effortless, requiring no thought. He was heading for the top and nothing could stop him.

But alone at night, in his dreams and fantasies, the scared, humiliated little boy he had once been came back to haunt him. He would wake bathed in sweat, trembling, robbed of the power he had fought so hard to achieve.

Soon he learned to be ready for the dreams. As the boy appeared, naked and vulnerable, the man was there to meet him. He would take hold of the boy, beat him till he huddled in the corner, utterly defenceless. And the the man would force himself upon the boy, repeating the unspeakable scenes he had enacted with Maxwell all those years ago. And then he would wake to find his heart pounding and his belly sticky with semen. Another small epiphany: one which convinced him he was now the powerful one.

After a while he would seek out these fantasies during the daytime. He told himself that he was merely keeping the past at bay, but he knew that wasn't true. He revelled in images of sexual torture, scenes in which his victims, however bloodied and battered, were nevertheless somehow liberated by their tormentor, just as he had been.

Yet, satisfying though they were, the realisation was growing within him that fantasies alone would not sustain him forever. The dreams had awoken needs in him which had to be fulfilled. Soon he had gained enough power for that to be possible. For his dreams to become reality.

11: Home Invasions

Larkin stood at the corner of the sodium-lit street, dressed entirely in what he hoped was inconspicuous black: Levis, long-sleeved T-shirt, rubber-soled canvas shoes. Staring out into the gloom, his face was a mask of inscrutability but his demeanour belied his true feelings. He was hyped up, adrenalin shooting down his body like pulses down a wire, readying him for fight or flight.

The street consisted of semi-detached maisonettes dating back to the twenties and thirties, two storeys tall. Overgrown gardens, rusted gates. Heaton Park to the right, Heaton Road to the left. Noble's home.

Larkin took deep breaths, trying to slow his heartbeat down. He knew he would be no use to Ezz in an excited state. He scoped the area, checking for observers. None. Good. He looked at his watch. Nine o'clock. Most of Noble's neighbours would be either inside their homes draining their minds into the TV, or out draining the dregs of Saturday. The street seemed to have a pall of thwarted ambition hanging over it.

Larkin looked down towards Heaton Park. The streetlights barely penetrated the deep lakes of darkness cast by the trees. As he watched, one of the shadows detached itself from the main clump and flowed along the street towards him. He blinked his eyes hard, not sure what he'd just seen. As he watched, the liquid shadow came nearer and began to assume human features. Zip-up bomber, tracksuit bottoms, kung-fu sandals, woolly hat pulled down hard. All black, absorbing the darkness. Ezz.

Larkin knew the burglar had cased the area earlier in the day: checking for hitherto unknown flatmates, identifying the make and strength of the lock, scrutinising the windows, noting any other security arrangements Noble might have in place, calculating the best odds for entry. He had observed the habits of the neighbours, seeing if anyone lived on the upper floor of Noble's building, at either side, opposite; and if they did, what potential trouble they could cause. He never left anything to chance. If there had been even the remotest chance of the situation going belly-up, Larkin knew Ezz wouldn't be here.

Ezz moved, feather-light, up the front path to the door and inserted something in the lock. He didn't acknowledge Larkin, standing on the corner. Within seconds the door was open. Ezz was in.

Larkin stood in silence, holding his breath. Nothing happened. Suddenly, he saw a small flash of light from Noble's window, fleeting; too brief for anyone else to have seen. The signal. He gave a surreptitious glance to either side, and thankfully found a deserted street with no walkers, cars, or twitching curtains. Taking a couple more controlling breaths, he crossed and entered.

With his surgically-gloved hand, Larkin carefully closed the front door behind him. He looked around, getting his bearings in the gloom. Off to the left he heard a swishing noise, then a thin beam of light clicked on.

"Couldn't we just put the light on now that you've drawn the curtains?" whispered Larkin.

"No," came the hushed monotone reply. "We don't know that that's his usual routine."

"Sorry." Larkin took out his own pocket flashlight, skimmed the area in front of him. White painted woodchip walls, bare to the dado, dark green from there to the skirting. Old, worn, brown check carpet covered the floor. A spring-shut flush door replaced the original panelled one. The hall alone screamed out Cheap Rent. He entered the front room.

The same white woodchip and brown checked carpet, complemented by a flecky, bobbly three-piece that had had its heyday long before Britain had embraced Thatcherism. Callaghanism, even. A charity-shop dining table and three chairs that looked like they wouldn't last through a single meal occupied the back of one wall. Directly opposite sat a TV and video combination. Given the age and condition of what he'd seen in the flat so far, he expected them to be steam-driven. On close inspection he was surprised to find they were both virtually brand-new.

90

Kneeling down, his penlight in his mouth, he carefully checked the videos, stacked in their sleeves at the side of the TV. All home-taped; neatly inscribed, crossed out after viewing with a neat line with the programme that presumably replaced its predecessor printed underneath. *Coronation Street*. A wildlife documentary. *Kavanagh QC*. Nothing out of the ordinary.

Larkin got to his feet and scanned the room with the penlight once more. His eyes fell on the bookcase. A few paperbacks: Agatha Christie, P D James, nothing interesting. On the next shelf down sat a small pile of textbooks. He picked them up and leafed through them. All on social work, particularly pertaining to the welfare of children. That was only to be expected.

He crossed again to the table, where there sat a portable word processor and an old box file, which he opened. Inside was a copy of the Jobs and Appointments section of last Wednesday's *Guardian*, the day on which social work jobs were advertised. He flicked through, clocking the ones Noble had ringed. All to do with children, most of them as care warden in various homes. Beneath that sat a second sheaf of folded-up newspaper. Larkin unfolded it and found the Lonely Hearts sections from all the local papers. He scanned the pages, again paying particular attention to the ads Noble had ringed. They had all been placed by women, most of them divorced. All of them mothers.

A frisson of disgust ran through Larkin as he read. As he replaced the papers, he realised that his hands were beginning to shake.

The box file also contained a transparent folder of photocopied CVs. He picked one out and glanced at it. It was identical to the one Jane had shown him, except it had recently been updated to include his work at the centre. He glanced again at the two named referees. One name stood out: Colin Harvey. Where had Larkin seen that name before?

Suddenly the penny dropped. Larkin scanned down the pile of books on the shelf – and there it was. *The Care And Rehabilitation Of Persistent Juvenile Offenders* by Colin Harvey. Larkin opened the book, reading paragraphs at random. As he read on, a shiver went down his spine; ice melted on his neck. Harvey was discussing childrens' allegations of abuse by carers:

Allegations of this nature should be treated with a healthy degree of scepticism. Workers in any environment can develop close attachments, whether it be in offices, factories, whatever. Either sex, any age. But it must be remembered here that the children are exploring their sexual potential and beginning to realise the power that lies in their bodies. They are frequently mature enough to embark on sexual relationships both with other children and with adults. This can, of course, be quite natural. The child is often fully aware of what it is doing in having sex with an adult. It is seldom without consent or encouragement. It is rarely passive. It is never wholly innocent.

Larkin couldn't believe what he was reading, *Kids are begging for it?* That was a paedophile's argument.

He closed the book and checked Colin Harvey's address on the CV. Northumberland. Significant, he thought, but he didn't know quite why, yet.

Larkin felt a flashlight on his face and turned; Ezz was silently beckoning him into another room. Larkin rearranged everything as he had found it, and followed him.

The bedroom. Again, cheaply anonymous: plain duvet over heavy wooden bed, old, mahogany wardrobe full of Noble's clothes, smelling faintly stale and sweaty. Ezz pointed to a locked door beside the wardrobe.

"I've been through everything in this room," he murmured. "Nothing. If there is something it'll be in there."

"Can you open it?" Larkin asked.

Ezz didn't even bother to answer. He turned to the door, clamped the torch in his teeth, drew something silver and glinting from his pocket and got to work. Within seconds the door was open.

The door led to what had once been a walk-in cupboard. Now, however, it was a shrine. The walls were plastered with pictures of children. Some had been clipped from catalogues and magazines: children in swimsuits and shorts, colour and monochrome, smiling for the camera. These were interspersed with pornography: children having sex with adults, fear in their eyes, tear-tracks down their faces. Blu-tacked over this collage were a number of polaroids. Children naked, vacant-eyed, staring numbly at the lens, a brick wall painted black as backdrop.

At the far end of the room was a table covered in a white cloth with a plastic recipe-book stand in the middle. Propped open on it was a kiddie porn mag, with two stumps of candle at either side. A

92

mirror rested on the table behind the lectern, its edges decorated with more cut-out pictures of children. On the floor in front of the table were several wadded-up paper tissues. Larkin's stomach turned over. He got the picture.

"Look," said Ezz from behind him.

Larkin turned, trembling, to see Ezz pointing towards a shelf of video tapes. Larkin played his flashlight over the spines. *Boys To Men. Special Love. Young Olympians.* It went on.

Larkin looked at Ezz. The skinhead was always quiet, but he seemed now to contain a perfect stillness. A dangerous calm. Like a dormant volcano: one wrong tectonic shift and all hell would break loose.

"Ezz?" whispered Larkin.

Nothing. Ezz stared straight ahead, eyes boring into the videos. Through the videos, past them, to something beyond.

"Ezz?" Larkin moved his hand out to touch him, and suddenly felt his fingers being bent right back. Ezz had barely moved, yet he had grabbed Larkin faster than a striking cobra. Slowly he turned to face Larkin, his grip not slackening. His eyes were fixed, rage-filled, homicidal.

"Ezz, man, it's me!" Larkin gasped. "What you doing?"

Ezz's eyes slowly came back into focus. His grip relaxed and Larkin snatched his hand away.

"Fuckin' hell!" said Larkin, flexing his fingers painfully. "You don't know your own strength."

"Have you seen what you came to see?" asked Ezz, his face unreadable in the shadow.

"I think so," said Larkin, staring at the man in bewilderment. "Let's go."

They left everything exactly as they found it. No one saw or heard them leave.

They walked down the street, not speaking. When they reached Heaton Park, Ezz stopped; Larkin, recognising his cue, dug his injured hand into his pocket and pulled out his wallet.

"Here," he said, drawing out the pre-arranged sum. It disappeared so fast, Larkin wasn't sure he'd ever held it. "Thanks. I think," he said.

Ezz nodded, once. "I want to know what happens to this bloke."

"I'll keep you informed," said Larkin, but Ezz had already disappeared into the darkness.

Larkin went home. He was shaking uncontrollably now; the relaxation of his controlled adrenalin rush combined with his disturbing discovery was taking its toll.

As he entered his attic room, the red eye of the answerphone was blinking. His heart flipped over as he remembered the last batch of messages. This machine was becoming synonymous with disaster. He hit Play. One message.

A long pause: bar noise in the background. Then, "I don't know if you'll get this." Moir. "I'm in Ruby's Arms. I'm drinking alone." Another pause. Larkin knew Moir would never be so straightforward, so transparent, as to ask him to come for a drink. But things must be serious – desperate even – for him to call. The final part of the message confirmed it. There was an Atlas-like sigh, then: "The boy – Jason. It's a murder inquiry now."

12: The Ghosts Of Saturday Night

Larkin made his way down the scuffed steps into Ruby's Arms. The place was an after-hours drinking club, unlicensed but officially tolerated, located in the basement of a big old house in the Gallowgate area of Newcastle. Ruby's was somewhere to go when there was nowhere else left. It had been there for years and harboured a mix of customers that appeared bizarre to an outsider but perfectly natural to an insider: gangsters and hard men doing done deals in darkened corners, actors and theatre people, a liberal sprinkling of career drinkers with no homes to go to. Or at least not a place they chose to recognise as such. This, Larkin knew, was the category that Moir fell into. And also, increasingly, himself.

He spotted the big man seated by himself at a corner table in the main room. Through a doorway to his left was the pool room; to his right the toilets. Straight in front of him, the bar. This was where Larkin headed. He ordered two Budvars and sat down opposite Moir, who grunted in acceptance of the beer.

"You found him, then," Larkin said. Not so much a question as a flat, hopeless statement. Moir nodded and gulped beer greedily from the neck of the bottle.

"Where?"

Moir took another swig, sighed. Then he started his story.

He had received a call from the force in Durham, they'd found a boy's body in Hamsterley Forest, a local beauty spot. A labrador belonging to a picnicking family, the Duncans, had started scrabbling at the fresh earth in a patch of recently-planted saplings. The eleven-year-old daughter of the family, Gemma, had gone to chastise the dog and found it licking a small white hand protruding from

95

the ground. Her screams had alerted the rest of the family; her father, Graham, had contacted the police.

By the time Moir and his team had turned up, the Duncan family had been sent home after giving anguished statements. The area had been cordoned off and was now swarming with white-suited Scenes of Crime officers. The body was in the final stages of disinterment as Moir strode up, flashing his warrant card at the officer in charge, Detective Inspector Brody.

"This look like your boy?" Brody had asked him.

Moir watched as the decomposing body was prised from its grave. He swallowed hard against the stench, forcing himself to look. The body was rank, black and bloated, entropy doing its inevitable, pitiless work. The height and hair colour looked about right, but until the lab boys could get to work there would be no way of knowing for definite. Except Moir knew. Instinctively. It was the moment he had been both expecting and dreading.

"Can't be certain," he replied, as business-like as possible, "but I reckon so."

"Hope so," Brody said sardonically, "otherwise we've got another one."

Moir nodded absently, then turned to his detective sergeant. "Get everything you can from the body here then get it shipped back to Newcastle for examination. Tell them to drop what they're doing – this has to take priority."

"They won't like that," the DS said.

"I don't give a fuck," said Moir, never taking his eyes from the small body.

Moir questioned Brody about the Duncan family statement. Shock first, then eagerness to help, anxiety in case they were implicated. Then, finally, once they realised they weren't suspects, the father had talked of suing the police for causing distress to his daughter. "I wished him all the best," Brody said.

Moir asked about the grave itself. It had apparently been dug after the saplings had been planted and recently enough for the fresh earth not yet to have drawn attention. Footprints? They were looking into it – nothing as yet. What about the tree planters themselves? Again, being looked into, but nothing much hoped for. Early indications were of an opportunist burial. A shallow grave.

Having retrieved all he could from the scene, Moir had then travelled back up to Newcastle to await the results of the forensic tests and the post mortem.

Preliminary results came through quickly: it was Jason. Next came the part Moir had been dreading even more than finding the body: informing Mandy Winship and asking her to make a positive ID of her dead son.

He drove around to her flat; he was hoping to postpone the moment, but unfortunately she was in. She seemed to have aged since he last saw her and the flat, not much to start with, had clearly been left to go to hell. As he was talking to her, an overweight, middle-aged man, wearing nothing but a pair of old, stained Y-fronts, appeared from the bedroom. She shouted at the man to leave; without protest he grabbed his clothes and slammed the door behind him.

Moir looked at Mandy perched in a cheap dessing-gown on the edge of her worn, old armchair beside the unlit gas fire, shaking, chain-smoking one Embassy after another, hunched into a self-protecting foetal ball. His heart went out to her. She wasn't the angry, ignorant person she had been on his last visit, the kind of person Moir came across and despised in a professional capacity every day on the other side of the wire; grief had changed her. He saw now that she was just an ordinary woman, poorly brought up, badly educated, with low self-esteem; ill-equipped to survive life's pitfalls. A woman created by her ancestry and environment, unable to move forward, stuck at the fag-end of society. But above all, a woman who had just lost her child.

He offered her official police condolences and led her away to identify the body. After that painful experience – wailing, sobbing, an unending fountain of grief – Moir had arranged for Mandy to receive some counselling. None for him, though.

"Every time you find a body, you lose part of yourself," Moir told Larkin.

A press conference had been hastily convened, Moir sharing the platform with Chief Inspector McMahon. Moir found the man eminently dislikeable: too much the politician, the pathological game-player. He was good with the media, though.

There they had sat, Moir his usual untelegenic self, McMahon resplendent in an expensively tailored dove-grey, double-breasted suit, well-cut dark hair receding at the temples, and a suitably mournful tie. After Moir's initial address, McMahon did most of the talking. "To hear him," said Moir to Larkin, "you'd think he'd bloody well done all the work himself."

97

When the press conference broke up, Moir had returned to the CID incident room. Despite having a body there was nothing concrete to follow up on yet. So Moir had returned to his solitary den, been unable to settle, and gone to Ruby's. There he'd sat all evening, alone with his thoughts and his alcohol.

Their bottles were empty. Moir went to the bar and bought them both another round with the addition of a very large whisky chaser for himself.

"So how was your day?" he asked Larkin, forcing himself back into the slender gap between chair and table.

"Rough. Not quite as bad as yours."

"What have you done?" Moir was beginning to slur.

"I've been gathering evidence against this Noble guy," said Larkin casually. "I broke into his flat."

Moir did a double-take that would have been comical in different circumstances. "You did *what*?"

"Before you start, just listen." Larkin went on to tell him about the discoveries he and Ezz had made, careful as always to keep Ezz's name out of it. As he talked, Moir's anger gradually abated.

"My hearing has become selective," Moir replied after Larkin finished.

"I'm glad to hear it. And I didn't get caught."

"Good for you. But that is categorically *not* the way to do things."

"Point taken. Did you manage to run a check on Noble?"

"Nothing," said Moir, knocking back his whisky in one fell gulp, barely pausing for breath. "Absolutely blank. Someone as involved as you say he might be should have shown up somewhere – but no."

"Maybe someone wiped him from the system."

"Don't talk crap." Moir's tone told Larkin he would brook no argument.

"Actually, I had a visit from a couple of your lot yesterday."

Moir raised his eyebrows quizzically.

"Umpleby and Grice? Questioning me about Houchen's sudden demise."

"Heard about that. My condolences," Moir muttered.

"Thank you," said Larkin. "I must say I didn't take to them. What's your opinion of them?"

"Fuck d'you care?"

"So the money you spent on that charm school wasn't wasted after all?"

Moir gave him an unnerving, half-cut stare.

"I just want to know," said Larkin. "They seemed a bit iffy to me."

"I don't like them," said Moir after some thought.

"You do surprise me."

Moir ignored him. "They're untrustworthy. Careerist. Not that I'm saying they're bent, mind you — "

"Heaven forbid!"

Moir didn't rise to Larkin's bait. "They just know which arses to lick. They know how to play the game. Surprised Umpleby didn't land the case I've been working on. Anything high-profile, he's in on it. Must've come in on his day off."

They sat in a silence which might have been described as ruminative as Larkin gave Ruby's the once-over. Linoleum-covered floor; mismatching pub furniture; brown walls that had, over the years, absorbed tobacco, alcohol, blood, and anything else that had been thrown at them. Yet they remained standing. Eventually, Moir broke the silence.

"I'll get someone from the Sex Crimes Unit to give your friend a ring. They'll be discreet. I reckon we'll have enough for a warrant, anyway."

"Thanks. It's much appreciated."

Moir shrugged and lapsed into wordless gloom. Larkin forced out a strained laugh. "We're not a barrel of laughs tonight, are we?"

A ghost of a smile passed over Moir's face. "Reckon not," he said, then sighed. "Fucked-up kids, fucked-up adults . . . I dunno. That's all I see. Human fuckin' garbage. And I'm the one who has to clean it up."

Larkin nodded, opened his mouth to offer a sympathetic comment, but Moir seemed suddenly to have found his voice. "Messed-up kids become messed-up adults. Fact. Then they have kids and take their own shitty lives out on them. Another fact. And on. And on. It's a vicious circle. And it doesn't look like it's goin' tae be broken . . ." Moir's slurring was becoming more pronounced. "You know how to do it?" He pointed accusingly at Larkin. "How to break the cycle? Eh? No, well, I don't either. I'm just here to clear up afterwards. Fuckin' road-sweeper. Get today's sorted – there'll be another tomorrow. And the next day. And the one after that. . ." His voice trailed off as he grabbed his bottle and upended it into his throat.

"You're drunk, Henry," said Larkin, stating the obvious.

The bottle was replaced on the table, probably harder than Moir had intended. The bang made several people glance across, then quickly back to their own business; they didn't want to get involved in someone else's misery. Larkin didn't blame them.

"Damn fuckin' right I'm drunk," Moir growled. "So would you be if you'd seen what I'd seen today. And you know what? I reckon that kid's better off out of it. Excuse me if that's offended you, but I couldn't give a fuck. I mean, what chance would he have? Slag mother – bless her – no father, fuckin' towerblock rat trap . . . Better off out of it." He drifted off again, shaking his head.

His words, drunkenly rambled, touched a chord in Larkin. He slowly nodded his head. "Triggers . . ."

Moir focused on him vaguely. "What?"

"Triggers. 'Little Triggers'. It's an old song I was listening to earlier. You could say that's what all abused, dysfunctional kids are – little triggers. The adults they become are loose cannons – you can either attempt to defuse them, or get out of the line of fire."

Moir nodded absently; Larkin didn't know whether he'd even heard him.

"Human garbage, and I'm the fuckin' dustman . . ." Moir mumbled, then fell into silent introspection, marked only by the lonely, hallow clack of pool balls, the muted, small victories and losses of the players.

"Your round," rumbled Moir. He had sat slumped and silent for so long, Larkin thought he had nodded off. He silently questioned the wisdom of making Moir even drunker than he was already, but he knew enough not to utter his thoughts aloud.

"And a chaser," Moir said grimly as Larkin stood up.

When Larkin returned to the table, Moir had made an effort to pull himself together. Larkin set the drinks down.

"All that – before . . ." Moir said, with an effort.

"It's OK," said Larkin.

"Sometimes, I just get—" He clenched his fists impotently.

"I know," said Larkin. He looked at Moir with compassion.

100

There were tears gathering at the corners of the big man's eyes. Moir sensed Larkin's inspection and dropped his head. He sat like that for a while, trying not to let the tears fall.

"I mean . . ." His voice, when it came, was thin and filled with pain. "I mean . . . how do you bury your own child . . .?"

Larkin knew now what was behind Moir's mood. Knew the reason for the fear and confusion in his eyes. And it wasn't just to do with Jason Winship.

Moir grabbed his chaser and guzzled it down as if his life depended on it. When he had recovered his composure, Larkin spoke.

"You OK?"

Moir stared at him furiously. The alcohol was fermenting his shame and embarrassment at exposing his emotions into anger. "Don't be so fuckin' patronisin', y' bastard!" He attempted to struggle out of his seat, make his way to Larkin.

"Henry, sit down," Larkin commanded.

Moir slumped back. "Bastard . . ." he mumbled. Then he was out of it, head on his chest, saliva drooling down his chin.

Larkin called across to the barmaid. "Could you phone for a cab please, pet?" he asked.

With a weary look that suggested she had seen it all and nothing now could phase her, she nodded soundlessly and shuffled down the bar to the phone.

Larkin regarded the collapsed body of his friend. Just another miserable, lonely drunk: someone who'd seen too much of the worst life had to offer and tried to escape for a while. Passed out, looking for the heart of Saturday night.

13: Home Invasions II

Larkin was on the long walk home. He had bundled Moir into a cab, paying the driver in advance and allaying the man's fears that the backseat upholstery – such as it was – wouldn't end up covered in vomit. As Larkin was manhandling eighteen-and-a-half stone of unco-operative bulk out of Ruby's, Moir suddenly roused himself, and with reddened eyes, began to mumble.

"Karen . . . Karen. All my fault . . . should never have left you . . ." His voice trailed off as his senses closed down again.

It was as Larkin had suspected.

Karen. Moir's daughter. Nineteen years old, heroin-addicted, HIV-positive. A history behind her for which Moir blamed himself. She was never far from his thoughts, Larkin knew; the Jason Winship case must have pushed her to the surface.

Larkin watched as the comatose Scotsman was driven away. He'd wake up alone and in pain, Larkin thought. Poor, sad bastard.

3.30am. Larkin walked. All around him, the city was starting to die. A few clubbers, failed Casanovas, headed for the taxi ranks, making one last desperate attempt to score in the queue, actions motivated more by fear of loneliness than genuine desire. Odd stragglers throwing up overpriced beer and undercooked kebabs down walls and in doorways. Occasional couples glimpsed fucking down alleyways, sodium-lit and silhouetted like Hiroshima lovers. Distant, whooping sirens circling in the air, like Indians laying siege to a stockade. Cop cars kerb-crawling, scrutinising walkers. City snap-shots from the corner of Larkin's eye.

As he walked, he thought about Moir. Was he right? Was Jason Winship better off dead? When life deals cruelty and unpleasantness to you first-hand, it can harden a person. But was there more to it than that?

The alternative was someone like Andy: accepting the world was shit and having as big a party as possible. When he thought about it, he realised Andy and Moir had both reached the same conclusions; it was only their methods of dealing with it that were different.

And what about himself? His experiences had led him to share their conclusions. His initial response had been – he thought – a genuine, pro-active attempt to improve matters. On the face of it, shaking down corrupt politicians had seemed like a good idea. But now he felt . . . Guilt? Doubt? He didn't know. In all honesty, would his actions actually make any difference? Or was he just seeking another sort of self-gratification, trying to turn today into tomorrow through hate and contempt? "You know how to do it? How to break the cycle?" Moir had asked; Larkin, once, had reckoned he did, but he wasn't so sure any more.

The whole thing was too much, too big, for his half-exhausted, half-cut mind to take in at that moment. His only course of action was to let his mind do what his feet were doing. Just keep on going.

As he approached the front door, he sensed something was wrong. When he entered, he knew it, immediately. The place had been ransacked.

The hallway had contained only an expensive vase filled with artfully displayed hazel twigs, a couple of rugs over polished boards and a phone on a wooden stand. It now contained smashed porcelain, broken twigs, ripped carpeting, and splinters.

The front room: slashed upholstery, broken picture frames and scattered glass, upended TV and VCR. Videotapes pulled from boxes, books flung from the shelves, CDs stamped on, cracked and broken.

Kitchen: drawers and cupboards pulled out and emptied, shattered china and cutlery decorating the floor. Fridge and freezer emptied, food and drink left congealing in soggy masses where they'd been hurled.

Back room: more of the same.

Larkin ran upstairs to Charlotte's bedroom and found similar carnage there. Her bed was stripped and upended, books were torn and CDs were scattered and smashed, her clothing – that he hadn't yet been able to part with – pulled out of wardrobes and drawers, shredded and discarded.

His heart had been racing since he stepped into the house, but now he felt his fear being replaced by anger. Some nameless bastard had torn up his last links with Charlotte. It was something he himself had not been able to do, and he hated them for forcing his hand.

As Larkin was checking the remaining rooms he heard a sound: the tell-tale creak of bodyweight on floorboard.

It came from the attic.

Fuelled by anger at the final desecration of Charlotte's memory and not stopping to consider the consequences, Larkin grabbed the first thing to hand – a snapped-off chair-leg – and made for the stairs.

As he came through the doorway, he heard footsteps beginning a hurried descent from his room. Obviously he'd made too much noise; someone was now coming to silence him. He flattened himself against the wall inside the doorway, turned off the light, and waited, club in hand.

The figure reached the bottom of the attic stairs and crossed over the wide landing to the main flight of stairs, back turned to Larkin. Larkin just had time to take in the figure: average height, as darkly clothed as he himself had been earlier but complete with black ski-mask. What the well-dressed burglar about town was wearing this season, he thought.

Possessing the element of surprise, Larkin rushed forward, club raised, and brought it swinging down, aiming for the back of the intruder's head. Unfortunately, the figure span round just as the club descended, diverting Larkin's aim from his head, though Larkin was still able to land a solid and very nasty blow to the intruder's right shoulder.

"Jesus *fuck*!" the figure shouted and turned fully to face Larkin.

"Come here, you fucker!" screamed Larkin, and swung his club again.

The intruder side-stepped in time to miss the blow, but lost his footing at the top of the stairs. All it took was a judiciously placed kick under the ribs – with which Larkin obliged – and the man went tumbling, coming to rest in a broken heap on the curve of the stairs.

"You want some more? Eh?" shouted Larkin, rage and adrenalin winning out over terror.

He took one step down the stairs towards the prone body. Then he felt a sudden sharp weight in his back that threw him off-balance and propelled him down towards the intruder.

As he landed on top of the man, chair-leg flying from his hands, Larkin turned to see a similarly black-garbed figure start quickly down the stairs towards him. He just had time to stick out his right hand in an effort to block the kick that the second man aimed at his head. It connected: the pain, like an electric shock, coursed through the tender skin of his palm, bringing with it an unpleasant reminder of an old injury. Larkin immediately retracted his hand.

The second intruder aimed another kick; Larkin was expecting it this time. He made a grab for the kicker's leg – using both hands – and didn't let go.

The man tried to shake him off, but Larkin held on, grabbing his shin in one hand and booted foot in the other. The man reached down, first to remove Larkin's hands then, when he found they wouldn't budge, gripping Larkin round the throat and squeezing as hard as possible. Larkin felt his windpipe contract as air abruptly ceased to enter his body. He knew his brain was losing oxygen; he started to blink. It was no good; he couldn't blink away the gathering patches of darkness that clouded his vision, like black ink dropped on his eyes in thickening quantities. There was only one thing he could do. He gathered all his remaining strength, forced it into his hands, and gave the lower half of his strangler's leg a vicious, prolonged twist.

Suddenly, Larkin felt the grip round his throat begin to slacken. He heard a sound like a ratchet being tightened and knew that he had done some damage to the man's knee; the scream confirmed it. Larkin gave an almighty heave, and the man lost his balance and toppled down the stairs next to him.

The three of them lay, slumped, out of breath. Larkin massaged his neck, willing the circulation to return. He had to get up, fast. If either of them came back for more, Larkin, in his weakened state, would be dead meat. He felt movement on the stairs beside him; the first intruder was beginning to come round. Larkin looked round. The other intruder had crawled back to the foot of the stairs and was hunting for a weapon.

With an almighty effort, Larkin tried to get to his feet and go after him, but as he did so he felt a sudden sharp punch to the back of his left knee. As his leg gave way, a punch to his left kidney and the sharp pain that accompanied it made him lose his balance completely. A swift kick in the back and he felt his body pitching forward, arms bouncing off the rail, legs thudding against the wall as he tumbled to a halt on the polished boards of the hallway. His head struck the floor with such force that he blacked out for a few seconds.

Larkin struggled to keep his grip on consciousness. To survive. Through blurred double vision, he saw the first intruder stumble towards him, disorientated but still dangerous. As he passed Larkin, he flung a kick into his ribs that sent pain spasming round his body.

"Leave it," the second intruder gasped painfully. "I got what we came for."

The first intruder bent down and stuck his masked face close to Larkin. "You wanna think yourself lucky. We'll make this a warnin'. Leave well alone, you cunt. You got that?" He stood up, nursing his injured shoulder, and Larkin felt another stab of pain in his ribs.

"Come on," the second intruder said, and made for the door.

"Stay where you are," the first intruder sneered to Larkin. "We'll be back."

After a few minutes Larkin hauled himself painfully to his feet. He gave himself a mental inventory: nothing life-threateningly serious, just battered to hell. He tried a few steps: nothing broken. At least he could walk.

What had they said? They'd be back? Did that threat have a specific timescale attached to it, or was it simply a cliché? He decided not to hang around and find out.

He quickly made his way to the attic; more than anything he wanted to find out what it was they had been after. He didn't own much, but what he had was in that room. And this was where the attack had been most fierce. Virtually nothing had survived intact. Bed, books, CDs, clothes, TV, VCR, stereo, laptop – all trashed. He sat down on what remained of the bed and surveyed the devastation, trying to find something still in one piece. There was nothing. It had been a methodical destruction.

He got down on his hands and knees and began to sift through the debris of his life, now littering the floor. He didn't even have time to mourn the passing of his painstakingly-collected Elvis

106

Costello and Tom Waits CD collections. He was looking for something. And he hadn't found it.

His computer disks.

He sat down again. At the moment he wasn't sufficiently *compos mentis* to work out why anyone would go to all this trouble for his disks. All they contained was stuff he'd written for the Agency. He didn't know what to do next. Call the police? That would be the logical option, if only from the insurance point of view. But that was for later. Right now, he had to get out.

On his way down the stairs he wondered: where he could go this time of night? Even Ruby's would be closed by now. As he reached the front door he stopped. What if they were sitting outside? Waiting for him? But he couldn't stay here – he'd be a sitting duck. The back way seemed safest.

He flicked the hall light off, plunging the ground floor into darkness. Once his eyes had become accustomed to the gloom he made his way to the rear of the house, found the key to the patio door in his pocket and slowly eased himself into the back garden.

The house backed on to another one and was bordered on all sides by sizeable gardens. He checked for the sturdiest fencing and, finding it on the right, climbed up and over, dropping like a stone into his next door neighbour's flowerbed. He looked around. All the houses were in darkness; the warm night had a tranquil calmness about it. In different circumstances this leafy suburb would be a pleasant place to be at this time of night. But not now.

He made his way over the next garden fence, then the three after that, almost dropping with exhaustion as he scaled the last one. The fence ended in a steep sloping embankment that led down to the Metro line. Larkin scrambled down on to the track. He knew he didn't have to worry too much about trains – it was too late, or too early for them to be running, unless they were doing some emergency track work – but all the same he hurried.

He ran all the way down the line until the tracks entered a tunnel, heading for the underground part of the line in the city centre. There Larkin climbed up the side of the cutting, pulling himself up by clumps of grass and tree roots until he reached the top. Checking for people and cars, he hauled himself over the mesh barrier and on to the pavement.

He stood light-headed, completely alone, the spire of Jesmond church, off to his right, darkly etched against the now lightening sky. He looked at his watch: nearly five. The one thing to be thankful for was having had too much to drink at Ruby's; he'd left the Golf near the drinking club at the back of Gallowgate bus station. Assuming the car hadn't been done over too, he would at least have somewhere to sleep for the rest of the night. And perhaps the alcohol had helped to dull the pain he knew he'd soon feel. He let out a huge sigh – of weariness or relief, he didn't know – and headed for the city centre.

14: Sunday Morning Coming Down

The day hit Larkin hard. The long-postponed hangover, the lack of sleep, the injuries, the fear – woke him up aching and empty. The early-morning sun had created a greenhouse effect in the cramped Golf, ensuring that the sleep Larkin had managed to get had been as disturbed as possible.

He opened the door and swung his body out slowly, allowing the blood to feed his crumpled muscles. He checked the time: seven forty-five. As far as he could see, there was not a soul around in this backstreet off Gallowgate. Good: at least he hadn't been followed.

Larkin bent down to climb back into the car – and suddenly felt a hand on his shoulder.

He froze. He turned, slowly, his hands balling automatically into fists. When he saw who it was he breathed out, let his hands drop. Ezz.

"What the fuck are you doing, creeping up on people? You could have given me a fuckin' heart attack!"

Ezz shrugged nonchalantly.

"What are you doing here? How did you find me?"

"You're not that hard to find. If you know where to look," Ezz replied in his expressionless monotone.

Larkin leaned against the car, suddenly too tired to stand upright. "You been following me?"

Ezz shrugged again.

"You just happaned to be passing, is that it?" said Larkin. "I could have done with you last night. Where were you then?" He told Ezz what had happened.

"Amateurs," Ezz said after a long pause.

"I don't think so," said Larkin. "I think they wanted to do as much damage as possible so I'd assume it was just kids. They seemed pretty well-organised when I caught them at it. Any idea who they might be?''

Ezz shook his head. ''But you must be treadin' on someone's toes.''

''That's what I reckoned.''

''This bloke from last night,'' Ezz asked, abruptly changing the subject, ''what you doin' about him?''

''I've already reported him to this copper I know. He won't get away.''

''Kiddie rapers usually do.'' The words were chilling, matter-of-fact. ''We'll have to make sure he doesn't.''

''He won't. And anyway,'' said Larkin, ''you're taking a lot of interest in this. Not like you. I thought you liked to stay detached.''

Ezz stared at him for a long, menacing second. ''I'll be in touch.'' And he turned and walked towards the city centre, not once looking back.

Larkin shook his head. ''Weird fucker,'' he said under his breath – when he knew Ezz was safely out of earshot.

Nearly fifty minutes later the emptiness in Larkin's body had been filled by an enormous breakfast at a run-down twenty-four-hour cafe near Marlborough Crescent Bus Station. It had been fried in enough oil to lubricate a fleet of articulated lorries, but it was just what he'd needed: a patch-up job to keep him going. He'd also had time to sort out his thoughts. With return to his house an impossibility, he had worked through his options until he hit on what to do next. And he'd made his selection. Go to Scotswood.

''Hello, Mrs Howells – is your Jane coming out to play?''

Larkin had decided not to call ahead to warn of his arrival; the surprised look on Jane's face had been worth it. He had driven straight down to Scotswood, parked and walked round the estate until he found her flat. She was now standing in front of him in a terrycloth dressing-gown and slippers, and if she had been up and about her sleep-filled eyes told him it hadn't been for long.

''What the hell happened to you?''

''I look that bad, do I?'' asked Larkin, attempting as heartwarming a smile as he could manage at that moment. ''It's a long story but I won't tell you it out here. Can I come in?''

"Yeah . . ." Jane stepped back, allowed Larkin to enter. "What time is it?'' she asked blearily.

"Nineish,'' said Larkin, moving into the flat.

He was impressed. The grey concrete and crumbling brickwork outside gave no indication of the interior. The hall led to a panelled pine door opening into the living room, where a hard-wearing, neutral-coloured carpet was covered by a large Oriental rug. Against one wall ran some pine bookshelves filled with classics – mostly by women, he noted – manuals on childcare, political history and videos, predominantly Disney. Alison's taste, he hoped. A stack of CDs and tapes was piled at one end beside an old but serviceable midi system; a TV and VCR sat next to it. A shabby but comfortable-looking blood-red leather Chesterfield had an Indian throw over it; a couple of mismatching but inviting armchairs occupied the corners. A huge, dark antique mirror hung on the opposite wall to the bookshelves, along with a couple of Modigliani prints. Dried grasses were stuck in a couple of vases and on all available shelves and spaces were interesting little objects, items collected and loved over the years, together with pictures of Jane and her daughter. The young girl had made her presence felt; dotted around the room, poking out from behind chairs, were numerous toys. It was a room crammed with life, with hope for the future.

"What a great place,'' said Larkin, admiration in his voice.

"You think because I live in a towerblock it has to be a dump?''

"No . . . I — ''

Jane smiled. "Wait till you see this.'' She flung open the curtains; Larkin saw immediately that the view was stunning. The Tyne curved all the way down, past the bridges and on to Tynemouth; he could see both banks, pick out all the familiar buildings. She clearly sensed what he was thinking. She moved up behind him and said: "When I first moved in here I used to do nothin' but complain about how miserable the area was. Then a friend of mine said, 'Aye, it might be shite down there – but what a view!' Tea or coffee?''

Larkin asked for coffee.

"What about breakfast?'' she shouted from the kitchen.

"I've eaten, thanks,'' Larkin replied, trying not to remember the grease. He sat on the sofa, gratefully.

"Coffee's on its way. Then I want to know how you ended up in this state.''

"Yeah . . ." He found the room's lived-in feel engulfing him and he started to relax. Distantly, he heard Jane's voice asking a question, but found he didn't have the strength to answer.

The next thing he knew, a small pair of hands was gently shaking his shoulders. He gave a start. Immediately he wished he hadn't; his sudden movement caused the little girl in front of him to jump back, alarmed. It took a moment to orientate himself and realise where he was.

"Hello," he said. "Is your name Alison?"

The little girl gave a quick nod then ran back to where her mother sat in one of the armchairs. Larkin stretched, yawned.

"Must have nodded off."

"You did. Your coffee's stone cold."

Larkin looked at the little girl. She was about three, with mousy bobbed hair and a pretty, intelligent face. She wasn't a deadringer for her mother but they shared some similar qualities. She was treating him with a healthy degree of suspicion which he found reassuring from her point of view and slightly saddening from his own.

Jane pointed to his mug. "Want me to heat this up?"

"No, I'm fine."

She laughed. "You look terrible."

"Had a busy night."

"Wanna tell us about it?"

Larkin glanced at Alison. "I don't think — "

"No problem," said Jane. She crossed to the TV and inserted a Disney tape in the VCR. Alison's face lit up as she saw Winnie the Pooh's features fill the screen, and she happily deposited herself in front of it.

"Come on into the kitchen," Jane said to Larkin. "You've got twenty minutes to tell me everything."

Fifteen minutes and one cup of coffee each later, Larkin stopped talking. He had told Jane virtually everything – the arcade, Andy's task, the break-in, the ransacking of his house – the only part he edited out was his drinking session with Moir. When he'd finished, he leaned back against the workbench and waited for Jane to speak.

"Shit," was her first comment.

"I agree," said Larkin. "The thing is, what do we do next?"

Jane sighed. "I'll have to talk to Lorraine and Trevor Carr – about Daniel."

"Have they got no inkling of what's been going on?"

"It was Lorraine who brought Daniel's behaviour to my attention. She knew something was wrong – she just didn't know what."

"What about her husband?"

Jane gave half a smile. "He'll probably try to snap the bastard in two. And I can't say that I blame him."

"Me neither. Want me to come with you?"

Jane gave him a wry grin. "You'll have to. Just in case Trevor wants to take it out on the messenger. . ."

Alison was left in the care of the neighbour who'd taken her to the park the day before. The neighbour's boyfriend loaned Larkin a T-shirt and jeans to replace his own filthy, bloodstained clothes that Jane had put in the wash. Although Larkin was grateful, it was with some reluctance he put them on, as the logo on the T-shirt turned him into a walking advert for Jimmy Nail's latest album.

Larkin and Jane then made their way over to the Carrs' house in a modern, redbrick council estate, built as an architectural apology for the earlier towerblocks.

Lorraine Carr was sitting on the sofa, coffee in one hand, fag in the other, reading the *News of the World*. Blonde, in her mid-twenties, her former attractiveness ground down to plainness, just as real life had ground down her dreams. She welcomed Jane with slight hesitation, gave a diffident nod to Larkin. They both refused her offer of coffee and sat beside her.

The room was cheaply but tastefully furnished and immaculately kept. Somehow, their desperate respectability made the situation worse. Jane was the first to speak.

"You know why I'm here?"

Lorraine nodded, resigned.

"It's what we were talkin' about. With Daniel. D'you want Trevor to hear this as well?"

"I reckon 'e'd better," said Lorraine, and went off to find him.

Left alone, Larkin and Jane exchanged anxious glances. The worst was still to come. "Trevor was made redundant from Siemens not so long ago," she told him. "He took it hard. Lorraine works part time at Kwik Save. They're good people." She shook her head.

"Where's Daniel?" asked Larkin.

"Out playing, I expect. Just as well."

Trevor Carr chose that moment to appear, his wife following at a discreet distance. He was in his late twenties, wearing the male uniform of T-shirt and tracksuit bottoms; he had the beginnings of a beer gut, and Larkin recognised from personal experience the look of a man fighting a losing battle with a hangover. He carried a barely concealed air of suspicion with the threat of violence not far behind it. It wasn't anything personal, Larkin knew; it was simply the natural defensiveness of a man attempting to halt the erosion of his pride and self-respect. He gave a barely perceptible nod and sat down on an armchair, Lorraine perched uncomfortably on the arm next to him. Despite the heat outside, the room had suddenly become frosty.

Trevor and Lorraine had obviously discussed their son's behaviour, but Larkin doubted they – particularly Trevor – had had any idea as to the extremity of the situation. The dawning horror in Trevor's face told him that. Jane discussed her suspicions and Larkin's involvement. She told them what Larkin had discovered – omitting any mention of his unorthodox methods. In short, she confirmed their worst fears.

Larkin sat silent throughout, occasionally nodding to corroborate Jane's words. He kept his eye on Trevor; the man's rage was visibly growing with every sentence he heard.

"So what we'll do now," Jane was drawing to a conclusion, "is call in Social Services. And the police."

"I don't want either o' them round here," said Trevor menacingly.

"They'll have to come," said Jane; her conviction and firmness quelled him. "Daniel will have to be given a full medical examination – and some counselling. So will you. Social Services will then place him on the 'At Risk' register — "

"*At risk* – from who? It's not us that's been doin' this!" Trevor exploded, jumping to his feet.

"They know that," Larkin's voice was reassuring, measured. "They'll have enough to put Noble away, don't worry."

Trevor began to pace the room, a feral animal trapped in its cage. "Bastard! Fuckin' bastard!" He moved towards Larkin. "They'd better have enough on 'im, otherwise I'll take the cunt out mesel'!"

An oppressive, heart-thudding silence fell on the room as the implications of what was being said sunk in. Trevor's anger had reached a momentary pitch; he sat back in his chair, shaking, fumbled a Silk Cut from the packet, fired it up, drew the smoke down deep. It seemed to calm him.

"But," began Lorraine, tremulously, scared of re-igniting the rage, "isn't it difficult to prosecute cases like this?"

"Sometimes," said Larkin. "Depends how co-operative the offenders are." *And how good a lawyer they've got*, he thought. "I don't think we'll have any trouble over this." He prayed that was true.

Another heavy slab of silence descended.

"So what happens when he's on this register thing?" asked Lorraine.

"His behaviour'll be monitored for three months," Jane answered. "After that they'll have another conference. Don't worry – Noble'll be well out of the way by then. Everything'll be fine."

Lorraine started to nod, slowly at first, then building up a steady rhythm, her head rocking backwards and forwards, her features starting to redden and scrunch up. Then the tears began: ragged sobs of pure grief.

Trevor gently placed a consoling arm around her; the gesture seemed so alien to him that it looked like he was in danger of crushing her to death. He stared defiantly at Larkin and Jane; his hostility told them, in no uncertain terms, that they had no business intruding at such a moment.

Larkin and Jane took the hint.

"I hated having to do that," Jane said, dragging on a supportive Silk Cut as they walked back to her place.

"I'd have been surprised if you didn't."

"I mean – they've tried so hard to make a good life for Daniel. And it hasn't worked out. Since Trevor lost his job 'e's been at a loose end, poor sod." She sighed. "Must really fuck you up, that. Redundant at twenty-six. Just – being defined by that word . . ."

Larkin nodded sympathetically.

"It must be enough of a struggle for them without this happenin'."

The sun, high now, glinted off nearby windows and buildings, giving the streets a harsh, unrelenting sheen. To their right a children's playground was surrounded by a chainlink fence, the swings, slides, roundabouts and climbing frames rusting and flaking on the concrete, like skeletal remains of long-extinct beasts. It seemed an appropriate metaphor for Daniel's damaged childhood.

"I mean, look at that place," said Jane, pointing angrily to something that resembled a grounded, low-budget spaceship. "Shopping centre. They redesigned it – but forgot to put any fuckin' shops there. Now pensioners have to get on a bus to cash their pensions and go to Kwik Save. Rebirth Of The Region? A fuckin' joke!"

She stomped ahead, indignant. Then she turned back to him.

"I mean — "

He cut her off. "You're right. You're absolutely right. I agree. It's a shithole – so let's not stay here."

She looked at him, questioning.

"Yeah," he said, "it's a sunny day, I've got money in my pocket – let's have a day out."

"OK," Jane said, slightly taken aback. "What d'you have in mind?"

"How d'you fancy Sunday at the seaside?"

15: In Absentia

In —
Curl —
Hold it . . .
Out —
Down.
And again.
In —
Curl —
Hold it . . .
Out —
Down.

The rhythm of the weights consumed Ezz's conscious mind. His hand, white-knuckled, gripped the barbell. Up to his shoulder – flex – down again. Face red, neck muscles taut, he changed hands and started the sequence with the other arm.

It was the reappearance of the face that had driven him to the gym. He'd returned to his flat from his night's work with Larkin and felt . . . strange. Somehow changed. His hands had started shaking and, with a shudder of realisation, he had known what that meant: he was going to lose control. The pressure and anxiety had begun to build up inside him, and he had only one chance of containing it. So he had pulled on his running shorts and gone.

Over the town moor he went, breath tearing at his chest, legs close to buckling, feeling like half his bodyweight was melting away as sweat. He kept driving on. His lungs begged him to stop; pain shot up his arms, increasing their weight and uselessness. The midnight darkness of the town moor was blotted out by the negative-

117

image sunbursts exploding behind his retinas. He ran faster.

But he knew it was no use. The problem was in his mind, not his body. He would outrun the face, lose it for minutes at a time while the mechanics of breathing occupied his body. But whenever he regained control of his physical equilibrium the face would reappear, reminding him that respite was only temporary. He kept on running.

Eventually his legs fell away beneath him; with sight gone and lungs burnt out, he collapsed, panting in a heap, pooled in his own sweat, his mind slipping in and out of oblivion. He couldn't see the face. He couldn't see anything.

After lying on the moor for what could have been hours, he slowly pulled himself to his feet and began to make his painful way back towards town. To his immense relief, the face hadn't reappeared. Yet. But Ezz knew there was plenty of time.

Not wanting to return home, in case the face haunted his dreams as it had in the past, he walked round aimlessly. The next time he looked up he realised he had arrived at Larkin's house. He didn't question what had drawn him there; he accepted that some inner voice, working on a subconscious level too deep and serious to be ignored, was working inside him, directing his actions.

He turned up at the house just as a car was drawing away. Whoever was inside it – two men, it appeared – were in a hurry to leave. Ezz didn't want an unnecessary confrontation, not the way he was feeling, so he concealed himself in the shadowy doorway of an off-licence opposite as the car sped by. Once it had gone he crossed the street and looked into the house through the hall window.

The first thing he saw through the gloom was the devastation. As his eyes adjusted, however, he could just make out a night-shrouded figure stumbling towards the back of the house. Larkin. As Ezz listened, he heard a door slam shut, heard the sound of a man hauling himself painfully over the garden fence. He decided to follow.

Years of clandestine surveillance had given Ezz an instinct for predicting human flight behaviour. He anticipated Larkin's route down the Metro line, correctly estimating the probable site of his reappearance further down, by the church at Jesmond. Ezz shadowed him all the way to his car. Once he saw Larkin was safely settled in for the night, he returned home.

But he couldn't sleep. Didn't want to sleep. The face was drifting at the corners of his mind. He dressed, took a couple of capsules that he kept for such occasions as these, and went to see Larkin.

After that he found his hands were beginning to shake again; more worrying, his breathing showed signs of convulsing into the spasms of a panic attack. Fearful of what might be about to happen, he headed for the gym, and the possibility of escape.

The gym he frequented was on the first floor of an old warehouse, opposite a strip joint off Westgate Road. It was a place where career hard men went to become even harder. A place where Ezz wasn't just known – he was respected. And it was there that he had worked his muscles until his limbs had turned to granite.

He put the free weights down and stood stock still, trying to quieten his body. He knew, objectively, that it was no accident the face had reappeared after working over Noble's flat. He knew what he had found there was directly to blame. He also knew that Larkin was, in some way, on his side. Perhaps the only way to get some peace would be to stick to Larkin, follow this thing through with him. Shadow him. He closed his eyes, breathing shallow, and —

It was coming back. Shaking – panic – it had started all over again. He knew then that he would never be free of it; no matter how far he went, what he did, the face, and the terrible memories it summoned, would always be with him. No matter how hard he tried, he could never kill it. If he hadn't gone beyond such things, he would have cried.

There was only one thing for it. He pulled on the gloves and stepped up to the bag. The few people using the gym parted to let him pass, perhaps recognising the urgency of his need. He positioned himself in front of the bag and gave it a few practice hits. It felt good. Steadying. Suddenly —

There was the face again. Etched on the bag. He focused, swung at it, gave it a roundhouse with his right, and the face disintegrated into a thousand tiny particles. It was gone. He couldn't believe it. He'd defeated it!

But as he watched, fear clutching his insides, the face slowly reformed, assumed the same position. Sneering: belittling him, mocking him. He hit it again, harder this time. The same result.

So he hit it again. And again, harder. And again. And again, and again, and again . . .

*　　　*　　　*

119

Twenty-seven minutes later he was pulled from the bag, his body unable to take any more punishment, his mind far out of reach. They had to prise his arms from the bag, so tightly had he clasped it.

As he was laid out on the floor, his arms started to flail. He was still punching: still fighting. Trying to defeat an adversary only he could see. And he wouldn't stop. He wouldn't give up. He couldn't.

The Strawberry opposite St James's Park was doing only minimal trade. The height of summer: no students, no football, just sad solo drinkers who had stumbled into the city centre on a Sunday afternoon. Lost, lonely; virtually all men. None of them talking, but silently acknowledging the others' presence. The brotherhood of the bottle, drinking away the seventh day of the week – the ghost of the other six.

Moir sat alone in a corner, nursing his third pint. He had woken up at home, sprawled on the sofa. For the first few seconds of waking he hadn't known who or where he was, had been able to breathe easily. But slowly, identity had oozed back into his empty mind, replacing the temporary comfort of alcoholic amnesia with a full, painful, realisation of just what sort of man he was.

Trying to stand induced the maximum effects of his hangover and he rushed to the toilet. Stomach empty, he felt more human, but the physical purging of his body didn't extend to his mind. He replayed the events of the previous night, and found that he could remember it all. His good memory, even when drunk, was sometimes a blessing – but in this instance nothing but a curse.

He showered, hoping the scalding water would sweat the remaining booze out of his skin. Then he dressed and quickly left the house. More and more he was finding that he couldn't bear to be in the place for longer than was absolutely necessary.

Moir headed for his den on Stowell Street, where he arranged all the updated reports on the discovery of Jason's body carefully on his desk. He'd photocopied them and dropped them off the previous evening before going to Ruby's, knowing that he would be here again today. He had nowhere else to go – and the gloom of his private office was, for him, a more conducive working atmosphere than the strip-lit, flush-doored, sterile CID incident room.

He stared hard at the photographs, the written reports and statements, though he already knew them all by heart. He was looking for clues, connections; something hidden which would suddenly reveal itself. But nothing came. He sat there for quite some time, but he knew that ultimately his forensic meditation wouldn't uncover the truth. His team was working on it – there was nothing for him to do.

The pictures of Jason, alive and dead, began to blur into one until Moir no longer knew which was which. Slowly the images began to dance before him, metamorphosing into a different face, a face he knew and loved.

Moir left his den and started walking. He ended up at The Strawberry, where he ordered the first of his afternoon's drinks. Although he wouldn't admit it to himself, he was drinking because he needed to, not because he wanted to. He never took pleasure in it, and only sometimes found comfort. But those times were enough.

He sat himself opposite the payphone: staring at it, seeing Karen's face in his mind. He willed himself to stand up, walk across the pub, put the money in, pick up the receiver and dial. He'd rehearsed the conversation over and over again; going through every possible permutation, every possible outcome.

He would do it. He would phone.

He looked at his near-empty glass on the table. He thought of Jason. Nothing he could do for him now. Karen. Yes, he thought, he would phone her. He drained his glass and stood up.

But he'd have just one more pint first.

Feet, legs and arms were all abused and aching. But Ezz didn't care.

When he'd been pulled from the bag in the gym he was incoherent with rage and exhaustion. He had struggled upright, shrugged off offers of support and stumbled into the shower – water as hot as his skin could bear without blistering. Then he was off again, searching for some way to end the nightmare.

The face had disappeared. Only temporarily – Ezz knew that from bitter experience – but the frenzied workout had bought him time. He knew he could postpone the face's reappearance for longer still, even forever, but to do that he needed some sacrificial appeasement. Some action.

Ezz walked with no direction; legs propelling him, in-built radar guiding him as he moved unknowing through city streets populated by handfuls of strollers, the summer sun beating down on him. He was looking for something only he would recognise when he found it.

Gradually the shining city streets gave way to poorer residential ones. Shabby houses, rusting cars. Hot, dusty air choked with the smells of fried cooking and cheap lives. At the end of one such street Ezz saw a patch of green. He headed towards it. A vague tingling began to churn in the pit of his stomach. Perhaps this was it – his catharsis. His final reckoning.

The area was badly tended: overgrown grass burst through cracked paving stones, wrought iron benches and railings were eroded down to abstract, oxidised sculptures, sabotaged streetlights turned wildwood pathways into rapists' pleasure gardens. Dot-to-dot dogshit on the grass. An inner city park. Museum-grade perfect.

To the left was a fenced-off area: a children's playground. Constructed of old tyres, wooden trunks, chains and bolts, the slides, swings and climbing-frames sat stunted and dark, bedded down in wood shavings. Kids with cropped heads and baggy jeans were punishing the equipment; venting pent-up emotions on a strictly urban assault course. Boys and girls: genders matched in aggression.

A frisson ran through Ezz. There was a reason he'd turned up here. He knew it. Eyes coming back into focus, he walked towards the children, searching.

Suddenly, from the corner of his eye, he glimpsed movement. With an abrupt halt he turned to where his attention had been grabbed. Hidden by a thick, gnarled tree-trunk and an unkempt mane of hedge was a figure. A man, furtively watching the kids play, pulling back into the shadows whenever one of them chanced to look his way.

This was it, Ezz knew, the chance to cleanse himself, to seek release from his suffering. With a single-minded sense of purpose, he strode over the grass to where the man was hiding.

He was so engrossed in watching the children he didn't notice Ezz until the skinhead was upon him. Ezz's right arm shot out, pinning his target to the tree by his throat. His eyes bulged with surprise and fear as Ezz looked him over. Cheap denim jacket and jeans, old trainers, T-shirt barely containing an expanding beer gut. Thinning blond hair, badly cut. An ageing Friday-night pub fighter: no contest. Ezz wouldn't even break sweat.

"You have a good look first, get yourself turned on, is that it?" snarled Ezz, his emotionless voice, for once, curling at the edges.

The man didn't see the swift left fist that connected hard with his stomach, but he certainly felt it. Ezz let him go, watching him slump to his knees and vomit over his stonewashed thighs. A quick kick to the side of the jaw knocked the man over on his side.

"You won't be doin' anythin' now. Not ever again." Ezz landed the man a kick in the balls that curled him into an agonised foetal position.

"Wait," the man groaned, "I'm not — "

"You never are," said Ezz calmly, pulling back his leg to take another swing.

"Don't, *please* don't . . ." The man began to claw frantically at Ezz's foot; Ezz relaxed his leg and dropped down next to him.

"You goin' to beg?" Ezz asked, a note of polite inquiry in his voice belying the rage in his eyes.

"Beg for what?" spat the man through ragged, shattered gasps. "Who the fuckin' 'ell are you anyway, eh?"

"I protect children from scum like you."

The man looked over at the playground, confused; the children were abandoning their games, crossing towards the two men, curious about the commotion. Suddenly the penny dropped and the man gave a short, bitter laugh. "You think I'm a paedophile, is that it? You think that's why I was watchin' them play? You're fuckin' thick as well as sick, you know that?" The man gestured with his arm, anger giving him strength. "That's me *son* over there. Me bitch of an ex got the court to stop us goin' near 'im, 'cos I was late with me maintenance a couple of times. It's the only way I can get to see him, hangin' round 'ere. Got that? Understand?"

Ezz's heart turned over. He couldn't have been more stunned if the man had bested him, one to one. He opened his mouth to speak when, suddenly, he felt a sharp pain in his left calf. He looked down to see one of the boys from the playground. Dirt on his face; fury in his eyes.

"Me da! You hurt me da! You bastard!" Kick. "You hurt me da!"

Ezz felt a pain larger than the damage being inflicted would ever have allowed. He swallowed, turned his head from the boy to the father, searching for something to say, some words that would heal the situation. He found nothing.

The tension began to build inside Ezz again, forcing his heart to thump faster and his head to pound. Sharp tears of self-pity and

123

helpless rage began to stab him behind his eyes. He turned and blindly ran, oblivious to anything but despair. He didn't hear the accusatory shouts of the children and the man directed at his back, didn't even feel the thrown stones as they hit him.

He had tried to help others to help himself. He had only made things worse. He saw the face. Sneering, taunting, mocking.

Ezz ran harder.

Eventually darkness had fallen; Ezz's pain was still unresolved. He felt like a human pressure-cooker: body of sculpted metal constraining a hot, combustible, poisonous stew.

He had been standing since dusk, lost in the shadows of Heaton Park, waiting.The lights in the flat still weren't on; not that he had expected them to be. But he had patience because it was Sunday night and only a matter of time.

As he watched, he saw a car pull up in front of the flat and douse the headlights. A Fiesta, almost new. Ezz's stomach lurched as he watched Noble get out, take a bag from the back seat, lock the car and enter the flat. He watched the lights going on and the curtains being drawn.

Ezz counted off five minutes in his head and stepped out of the shadows. If the ache in his head hadn't been clouding his thought processes, he might have been able to see a trace of irony in the situation. He was back where he had started. Where his current bout of pain had been triggered. Full circle.

Heart beating, he walked along the pavement and up the path towards a hope of salvation.

Drive

The powerfully sleek automatic eased through the light Sunday morning traffic on the A1 into Northumberland, gliding like the tyres were oiled and the road was ice. Pavarotti was trilling from the Blaupunkt, the sun was shining, and two boys, young bodies brimful of pleasures, were waiting at the other end of the journey. The man sighed, allowing himself the ration of a small smile. The car throbbed with energy and the temperature-controlled interior was like a warm cocoon. He was in his own world: safe. Secure. What more could he possibly want?

The people he was going to visit weren't friends – he didn't have any. They were – barring his brother – the people he'd known longest and most intimately, but they were not friends.

He had been approached by the two of them while he was still at college. Colin and Alan had both been misfits, their lack of social skills marking them out as lepers in the closed environment of the university. At first the man thought they just wanted to be friends, bask in the reflected glory of his popularity. Then, with a shudder of recognition, he realised that he and they were the same; all they lacked were masks. His first reaction was to panic: how could they have recognised him?

He forced himself to think rationally. To turn the situation around. They were outsiders. He could teach them the skills of acceptance, of protective camouflage. He was ready to push his predilections further; perhaps this association could provide him with a way forward.

So he became their teacher, passing on all his little tricks. All the while keeping his dealings with them at arm's length, until they were truly ready to be integrated. On their own, the three of them

*swapped dark, obsessive fantasies fuelled by alcohol and porno-
graphy, the sessions usually culminated in mutual masturbation.*

*This fulfilled the man for a while, but he still wanted to go further.
He knew that wouldn't be possible while he was still a student, and
without real power, so he controlled his urges. Bided his time.*

*After college was a different matter. He married his girlfriend – a
woman either pitifully naive about his true inclinations, or, perhaps,
wilfully ignorant. She saw him as a provider of wealth and social
standing. She was a shallow, venal bitch. He had chosen her well.*

*By this time he was well-connected: that made it easier to glide
into a career revolving around power and status, his assumed persona convincingly passing the psychological tests that would otherwise have been a barrier to his promotion.*

*As the man took his personal route to ultimate satisfaction, Colin
and Alan chose careers based on close proximity to children.
Opportunities for procurement. The three of them still held their
clandestine meetings: swapping fantasies, watching videos, using
pornography. Waiting for the real thing.*

*Eventually, inevitably, it happened. One of the boarders at the
public school where Alan taught. He didn't quite fit in. He was
blond, beautiful – and very unhappy. So Alan befriended him,
breaking him in over a series of weeks, eventually taking him away
for a weekend that was supposed to be "character-building".*

*They all met at Colin's house and the boy was turned over to
them.*

*Many of the things the man had plotted and dreamed of for so
long came true that weekend. Since the boy didn't complain, the
man assumed he enjoyed it too. It was one of the most blissful week-
ends he had ever spent.*

*When it was over, and the boy had gone back to school, the man
fantasised about the experience, replaying it in his head. Imagining
how much more intense, more pleasurable it could have been. Wondering just how far he was prepared to go . . .*

*Over the following months and years, the blond boy became a
frequent visitor to Colin's house. Eventually he became too old to
be of use, but he was too much a part of their circle to be easily
discarded. The answer was simple: as Alan, and sometimes Colin,
procured new boys, the blonde boy joined the men in taking*

pleasure from them. And then there were four.

Through the years they fell into a pattern. Alan, Colin and, latterly, James acted as procurers; the man was the driving force behind them. He drilled secrecy into them, forcing them to choose only the right kind of boys. Boys who wouldn't rock the boat.

And there was something he became aware of as the years passed: the others were frightened of him. That could only be a good thing. There was, after all, no such thing as having too much power.

But nothing lasts forever. Eventually, Colin and Alan's masks fell away. Once exposed, they quietly slipped out of their respective professions, seeking deliberate obscurity. No matter. James was eminently reliable, a true professional, so they could carry on just as before.

The man indicated and turned onto a minor road. He was excited. This would be the first time since Jason. He hadn't yet planned what he would do with the two boys, but he doubted he would go to the exquisite lengths he had with Jason. Not quite yet, anyway.

16: One Fair Summer Evening

"She off?"

"Yeah," said Jane, smiling. "Spark out. Hasn't had so much exercise in weeks. Not to mention the sea air, of course."

Larkin smiled and sipped his wine. He was sitting on the floor of Jane's living room, back against the sofa, legs crossed, wearing an old, oversized terrycloth robe of Jane's as his own clothes had been washed and hung to dry on the balcony. He had had a long bath to soak his battered body, during which he'd checked the progress of his bruises. They were coming along nicely, the only visible one being a purplish lump on the right of his forehead. He took another pull of wine. The room was having a calming effect on him, making him feel safe. Or maybe it was the fact that that no one knew where he was. Whatever, he'd managed to put the destruction of his home and his possessions right out of his mind.

Bamburgh was a small town on the coast of Northumberland. An old castle, a beautiful stretch of beach and some lovely, old stone architecture made the village very picturesque but, on a Sunday, rather uneventful. Nevertheless, it turned out to be just what they all needed. They'd set out, the roof of Larkin's Golf down, Alison in the back on a borrowed booster seat. Straight up the A1 to Northumberland, an old Crash Test Dummies tape blaring out, Larkin making the two of them laugh with his attempts at singing along to it. It set the mood perfectly: the further away the city got, the more relaxed they all became.

When they arrived at Bamburgh they headed straight for the dunes – Alison immediately rolling down them and getting covered in sand.

"She's enjoying herself," Larkin said.

"We don't get out of the city much," Jane replied, her face turned away.

After walking along the beach – shoes off for Larkin and Jane, Alison collecting stones and seashells as they went – they drove to Seahouses, a nearby fishing village, for a fish-and-chip lunch.

Larkin was unsurprised to find the place had altered. Unsurprised – but disappointed. They settled in the fish-and-chip restaurant at a plastic table with attached, moulded chairs just beside the fruit machine. Jane looked at Larkin with fond exasperation. 'Oi – what's the matter, misery guts?"

"This has all changed." Through the window they could see the main street; a half-hearted attempt at gaudy modernity had been superimposed over the old-style charm of the town. It hadn't worked.

"Everything does, you old fart," Jane remarked, teasing. "When were you last here?"

"Used to come here as a kid for summer holidays with my folks and sister. I remember it as somewhere I was happy. That's why I suggested it today."

Jane's smile broadened. "What – you were happy in Seahouses, or happy in the false security of your childhood nostalgia?"

Larkin felt his face reddening. "Aw, shuddup," he said, grinning wryly. The smile extended to his eyes and they locked with Jane's. Something zapped between them: something that had nothing to do with Seahouses or childhood nostalgia.

After lunch they walked round the harbour, Alison fascinated by the fishing trawlers docked at the sides, bobbing and unmanned, surrounded by floating seagulls feasting on the remnants of discarded fish guts. There were piles of lobster traps by the harbour wall and the whole area reeked, unsurprisingly, of fish. It was an unexceptional scene in many respects, but Larkin doubted Alison had ever seen anything like it in real life.

They found a pub with a play area for a mid-afternoon drink. Alison was happy amusing herself on the swings and slides, yelling to Jane and Larkin to watch her as she performed some feat she was particularly proud of. Other children quickly gravitated towards her, and they soon became friends, in a way that only children of that age can.

"She seems very contented," said Larkin, sipping his drink. "Very confident."

"She is," Jane replied. "Very happy, very bright. Makes friends easily." She sighed. "I just hope she doesn't change."

Larkin nodded. "Start running with a bad crowd, you mean."

"You've seen where I live. I can't afford to move. I just have to try me best, do me damnedest for her."

Larkin drank his pint. He knew what a fight Jane had on her hands.

Eventually the weather changed, and tiredness crept over Alison. They took that as a signal; it was time to leave. They had had fun: a good, life-affirming experience. Neither Jane nor Larkin could remember the last time they'd enjoyed that kind of day.

They returned to Newcastle with Alison asleep in the back of the car. As they approached the city and saw the sun slowly sinking behind the towerblocks, Larkin felt his heart ebb with the fading light. No matter how pleasant the day had been, he knew there were problems he had to face; for every escape, there was a return. By the time they'd reached Scotswood that feeling had lodged firmly inside him, but with it he'd forced a determinist attitude; the things that were to be dealt with were Monday-morning things. They could be postponed until then. Because first there was Sunday night.

Jane entered the living room, slapped a Teenage Fanclub CD in the player, poured a glass of wine, made herself comfortable in an armchair. Relaxed. As the abrasive but beautiful music started to cascade from the speakers, she looked at Larkin and smiled, almost shyly.

"So you don't mind if I stay over, then?"

"'Course not," Jane replied, then looked down to her wine, quickly adding, "That sofa's pretty serviceable. Besides," she looked up, cheekily, "I couldn't let you run round the West End of Newcastle dressed like that, could I?"

Larkin laughed. Sipped his wine.

"So," he said eventually, "what's a nice girl like you doing in a place like this?"

"I presume you mean Scotswood, not me lovely flat."

"I do."

Jane sighed, sat back in the armchair. "Where do I start?"

"At the beginning. We've got all night."

So, with a few glasses of wine for fuel, she started to tell him her life story.

She had been brought up in a council flat in Longbenton. Her father worked at Vickers; her mother was a cleaner. She had a younger brother, "And me dad used to let him get away with owt. He was one of the most troublesome little bastards on the estate. Honestly, it was like livin' with The Simpsons."

"With you as Lisa?" asked Larkin, amused.

"Too right," she replied. "Our Gary went round raisin' merry hell and I wasn't even allowed out. It was 'Study hard, do well for yourself' – all o' that. All me dad's doin'. If I went to a disco he was waitin' for us when it finished, he'd check me homework over – and boyfriends? I barely had any *friends*, never mind boyfriends. I think he was trainin' us to be a nun."

"I suppose he meant well."

"I suppose so," said Jane, taking a drink. "He thought he had me best interests at heart." She gave a half-smile. "Over-protective sexist old bastard."

"I take it you two don't get on?"

"Not any more," she said, her expression hardening.

"What happened?"

"I just had enough. He always said 'e wanted the best for us, that it was all for me own good an' that, but I think he was just a control freak. An' there's nothin' I hate more. I thought, 'Once I get to university I'll be shot of him', but I couldn't wait that long. So I rebelled. I would creep out at nights, go drinkin', partyin', whatever. I used to go to raves, get E-ed off me head, turn up home three days later, just to see the look on his face."

"And that made him madder?"

"Aye, did it, but he could see his control was slipping. He wouldn't raise a finger to me, but he was powerless to stop us. Then I got worse. I started knockin' around with Todd Gibbons an' that really annoyed him."

"Who?" asked Larkin, blankly.

"Todd Gibbons," Jane said with a laugh. Larkin noticed she was blushing. "Longbenton's self-styled teenage gangster Big Boss. Well, he was – he's inside now. Best place for him. Prick. I only started goin' out with him because he was the person who annoyed

132

Dad the most. I'd have gone out with Jeremy Beadle if it'd narked him more."

"It probably would have done," Larkin said, straight-faced. "But I think I can see what's coming next."

"Yeah," she said. "Predictable, aren't I? Todd got us knocked up while I was taking me A-levels. When he found out, I didn't see the twat for dust."

"And your dad?"

"Wanted to welcome me back with open arms. All in the past." She leaned forward, body involuntarily tensing as she immersed herself in old emotions. "On one condition. I had to have an abortion." She sighed. "He thought I'd done it to get back at him. Which I suppose I had. Anyway, I was goin' to have it done, but before I did, I weighed up the alternatives. If I went through with it, got rid of the baby, he'd have us where he wanted us, wouldn't he? I'd given in once – I'd do it again. I'd turn into me mother, an' that would be me life over. Then I thought of the baby. I knew it would be hard work bein' a mother, but I felt like I wanted to give it a go. Find somethin' to put all me love into, do somethin' positive for the future, make a child and bring it up with the right values. It was a challenge. That decided us. I told him to fuck off."

"And what did he do?"

"Threw us out of the house." She drained her glass and filled it to the brim again.

"So where was your mother while all this was going on?"

Jane gave a dismissive wave of her hand. "She disappeared years ago. At least, her personality did. She was just a ghost who cleaned the flat and made meals for me dad." Long-dammed anger seemed to be welling up inside her, spilling over into her words. "I've never seen either of them since I decided to go it alone. And I don't want to. As far as I'm concerned, they don't exist. I've got no family. Only Alison. She's me family now."

She stopped talking, took a couple of mouthfuls of wine, calming herself down. She continued. "So I got meself this council flat." She gave a bitter laugh. "Became the scourge of the tabloids – an unmarried, pregnant eighteen-year-old. Those bastards who bang on about scroungin' single mothers wanna come here an' see the conditions we have to bring kids up in. It's shockin'."

Larkin didn't contradict her.

"So then Alison was born. An' I was just so filled with love for

133

her. I made a vow always to do me best for her. Always be there for her. Make sure she grows up the best way she can."

Larkin smiled. "I'd say you were doing all right. And then came the daycare centre – is that right?"

"That's right."

"Very ambitious."

"Bollocks to that," she replied. "Pragmatic. Look around – it's gettin' worse. We've been all but abandoned by the council so it's up to the people who live here to change things. I didn't want Alison brought up in a war zone. Simple as that.

"I mean," she continued, warming to her theme, "some of the people round here are sub-human. No question. Hardly surprisin', though – you cage people up, you get animals. Simple as that. Some of them are beyond help, but the majority aren't. They've had bad schooling, bad housing, lack of jobs and opportunities, no doubtin' that. Politicians used to claim that there's no link between poverty and crime. Wankers. People round here aren't all criminals; they might become criminals, but they don't start out that way. They're just – impoverished."

Jane sat back, took a large swig of wine. They sat in thoughtful silence until she spoke again.

"Sorry," she said, "but you did ask. It's me pet subject. Gets us goin' every time."

"Your home," said Larkin, "you can say what you like."

"Right," she said, smiling. She put her glass down and leaned back in the chair, listening to the music, trying to regain some of her earlier peace. Suddenly she was sitting forward again, passionately animated. "You know what?"

"No. What?"

"You know what my dream is? My ambition?"

"Become Prime Minister?"

"Fuck off," she replied with a laugh, "that's not the way to get anythin' done. No, what I'd love to do is start up a refuge. A place where kids who've run away from home – from difficult or abusive families, whatever – somewhere for them to come to and feel safe. Instead of bein' on the streets, gettin' picked up by pimps and pushers. An easy-goin' kind of place where they could get help if they wanted it – counsellin', maybe – but with no pressure. No hassle. Kids like that now go into council homes and get treated like criminals, when all they've done is run away from a parent

134

who was abusin' them. I wanna give them somewhere they can feel sheltered, safe.'' She sat back in her chair again, her energy ignited by her project.

Larkin studied her, her black denim-clab legs tucked under her and her white T-shirt hanging loose. So much strength and determination in such a small person. He didn't doubt she would get her refuge. He didn't doubt she could do anything she set her mind to. Her no-bullshit attitude in fighting for what was necessary cast an interesting light on Larkin's nocturnal shakedown. Not for the first time was he having doubts about that. He felt like a self-aggrandising, twisted fraud who had come up against the real thing. He admired the hell out of her – but he also knew it was more than admiration he felt.

''What you thinkin'?'' Jane asked him.

''Oh,'' he said, ''miles away.'' He quickly took another gulp of wine. ''So,'' he began hesitantly, ''have you been involved with anyone since Alison was born?''

Jane smiled. ''I thought we'd get round to that eventually. No. Not really. One or two. Nothin' special.''

''Right.'' Larkin nodded. He knew what he should do next – but it had been so long . . .

''I think I've got the same problem you've got,'' she said suddenly, swinging her legs off the chair and coming to join Larkin on the floor.

''Which is?''

''Fear of gettin' involved. I mean, I can understand it in your case, I know how badly it ended the last time. How fucked up by it you were.''

Larkin nodded, relieved at her understanding.

''I feel the same. But sometimes . . .''

''You just have to take a leap of faith?'' finished Larkin.

''Exactly,'' she said.

They brought their lips together, and kissed.

Larkin couldn't sleep. He lay on the leather sofa, tossing and turning. Initially he had dozed, but some unexpected choral chanting of football anthems down below had forced him wide awake. He lay there, listening to the gangs roaming the estates, letting rip with occasional screams and howls, breaking bottles, overturning dumpsters. He heard the approach of sirens and the jeers that greeted their arrival. And, to get away from it all, he replayed the events of earlier that evening.

Locked in an embrace that was becoming more frantic by the second, Larkin and Jane's tongues were intertwined. They kissed fiercely, ferally; the pent-up need in both their bodies was released simultaneously. Their lips met, their teeth, biting and sucking, devouring. Their hands began to grab at each other's clothes; Jane pulled Larkin's robe off, he tore her T-shirt over her head. She undid her bra, he began to unfasten the buttons on her Levis. She arched her back, helping him to push them over her hips – and there they were, clasped together, completely naked.

Larkin pulled his mouth away from Jane's and began to work on her neck; kissing at first, then nibbling, then biting. She responded, moaning in time to his lips and teeth.

He ran his hands over her body, felt her small, firm breasts, the nipples immediately hardening to his touch; down over her flat stomach, to the soft, dark hair between her legs. He pushed a finger onto her clitoris and she groaned, pushing her pelvis forward to meet it, grinding herself onto him.

She reached down and grasped his cock, pulling the skin right back, squeezing hard. He sighed at her touch and she placed her mouth on his shoulder, sucking the skin. With one hand on her clitoris, he moved his other hand between her legs. She quickly parted them and he made to enter her.

Before he could, however, she reached for her jeans, pulling away from him. She produced a condom, snapped open the packet with her teeth, and rolled the rubber onto Larkin. All the time she kept eye contact with him; she looked like a wild animal, drunk on lust. Larkin imagined he must look pretty similar.

The condom in place, she began to move her hand up and down the shaft of his penis, squeezing as she went. Larkin pushed himself forward, into her, and she raised her hips, meeting him, finding a rhythm and rocking – deeply and violently.

Sweat ran down Larkin's body as Jane pulled him even closer, pushing him, matching him thrust for thrust. Suddenly her body stiffened beneath him and she flung her head back as orgasm coursed its way through her. He too could hold back no longer and came inside her; the intensity almost caused him to black out.

As they came down from their shared high, they gazed at each other, wondering, barely recognising in themselves the lust-fuelled creatures of a few moments ago. Larkin rolled off to the side of Jane and she snuggled into his chest. He threw his arm round her, keeping her close.

Larkin was perfectly, post-coitally, relaxed. And, although he fought against it, he couldn't help nodding off.

He was woken a short while later by Jane, gently trying to extricate herself from his embrace.

"Where you goin'?" he asked in a blurred voice.

She smiled. "I thought you were out for the night."

"C'mere."

Slowly she moved towards him. It was the first time he had really looked at her body. Small breasts, slim waist, rounded hips, shapely legs. She was beautiful. She lay down next to him again.

"I think we both needed that," she said.

"Yeah – we did."

"Stephen . . ."

"Yeah?"

She propped herself up on one elbow and looked at him, frowning slightly. "Don't take this the wrong way, but . . ."

Here we go, thought Larkin.

"Would you really mind sleeping on the sofa tonight?"

"Why?"

"Well, you might think I'm daft, but it's 'cos of Alison. If she wakes up in the middle of the night and comes in to me, I don't want her to be freaked out."

"Sure. No problem."

"You don't mind? Really? It's just that, I don't care what people say, somethin' like that can fuck your kid up for life."

"And you want to protect her."

"I do. I'd do anythin' to keep her safe."

Larkin smiled. "That's fine."

She kissed him on the lips. "Thank you for bein' so under-standin'." She made to stand up; Larkin held on to her hand, tight.

"Do that thing again," he said.

"What thing?"

"That kissing thing."

She knelt back down and planted her lips on his. He put his arm around her, and the kiss became more impassioned. Eventually, Larkin pulled away.

"So," he said, "you got any more condoms in those jeans of yours?"

They made love again. Slowly this time, more tenderly. They spent longer touching, exploring each other's bodies, finding the little idiosyncratic things that turned each other on. As their inhibitions were cast off, their pleasure increased. Finally they lay on the floor, satiated, until Jane got up to go to bed.

She gave him some sheets and a pillow, kissed him goodnight and left him alone.

And there he'd lain until the roaming gang had disturbed his rest. He had really enjoyed today, he thought; it had been the most fun he'd had in ages.

He was just dropping off again when he was woken up by a drunk, straggling along the landing outside, shouting a song whose meaning was known only to the singer, and dragging a broken bottle along the outside wall.

Larkin turned over, shoved the pillow over his ears. *What a fucking awful place to live*, he thought, thankful he didn't have to.

17: Back From Somewhere

It was the call Larkin had been waiting for.

Eight thirty on a Monday morning and he hadn't fully woken up yet. He was aware that Alison had left her own bed, gone into her mother's, forced Jane to wake. The child had managed to cajole a story out of her bleary-eyed mother and for the next twenty minutes or so, Larkin had been treated to the truncated, Disneyfied version of Peter Pan, Jane reading, Alison keeping up a constant barrage of often unanswerable questions such as, "But why does Captain Hook hate Peter?" and "Why don't The Lost Boys have mummies?" The two of them had then moved into the kitchen to have breakfast, walking on tiptoe so as not to wake him. Larkin didn't let on that he wasn't asleep – he was enjoying the warm doziness. He hadn't been in anything approaching a family set-up for years; after the untimely demise of his own, he had avoided parent-child situations. But spending the day and night with Jane and Alison brought it all back to him. It was both comforting and frightening at the same time.

His thoughts were abruptly interrupted by the insistent sonic bleating of his mobile. Larkin jumped up, grabbing it from the shelf he had left it on and pulling the discarded terry robe around himself in case Alison waltzed in.

"Yeah?" He knew who it would be.

"Mission accomplished, boss."

Andy.

"Where are you?"

"I don't know. Middle of fuckin' nowhere."

After much prompting – with Larkin naming practically every town in the north – he eventually managed to work out that Andy was in Northumberland, specifically Warkworth.

"You coming back down?" Larkin asked him.

"I reckon you should come 'ere." Andy seemed unusually grave.

Larkin, sensing the rare seriousness in his friend's voice, didn't push him for details over the phone. Instead, they made arrangements to meet in a tearoom-cum-craft shop in Warkworth in a couple of hours' time.

As Larkin was switching off his phone and hunting for his clothes, he heard a voice behind him.

"Mornin'."

Jane was standing against the doorway, kitted in black T-shirt and blue Levis, mug in her hand, smile on her face. Something about her stance gave Larkin a warm tingle inside. "I tried not to wake you." Her eyes, dancing with shared secrets, never left his as she spoke. "Wanna coffee? There's some made."

He returned her smile. "Yeah, ta."

She moved into the kitchen, hips swinging slightly more than usual, he noticed as he followed her. Then she turned to face him.

"How you feelin'?" she asked, without a trace of guilt or regret in her voice.

Larkin responded to her coded confidence. "Just fine."

"Good dreams?" she asked.

Larkin nodded. "But I don't know how you sleep with all that racket going on outside."

"Oh, that. You grow accustomed to it." She gave a half-laugh. "I'd probably miss it now if I moved."

They drank their coffee, making morning-after small talk. Larkin glanced down the hall to see if there was any sign of Alison before biting the bullet. "So," he said quietly, "was last night just a one-off?"

Jane looked up at him. "D'you want it to be?"

Larkin smiled, trying to mask the conflicting emotions running through him, not wanting to appear too eager, too vulnerable. "What d'you reckon? Leap of faith?"

Jane beamed. "We'll see how it goes."

As Larkin moved in to kiss her, Alison, with a child's impeccable timing, appeared in the kitchen. They moved apart, leaving the girl looking slightly puzzled; Jane took that as her cue to leave, before explanations became necessary.

"Say hello to James for me," Larkin said.

"Yeah, right," Jane replied sarcastically. "I won't say anything at all to him if I don't have to. I'll just wait and see what happens."

They gave each other a chaste kiss goodbye, with the promise of seeing each other later. Jane and Alison then left for the centre.

Larkin pulled on his T-shirt, Levis and boots, and went to meet Andy. He tried to put Jane out of his mind. He had work to do.

An hour and a half later, Larkin and Andy were drinking Earl Grey and eating passion cake in the tearoom at Warkworth. The village itself was pleasant enough – relatively unspoilt by contemporary standards, but still unable to escape the creeping gentrification of The British Heritage Theme Park plc. Andy steered Larkin to an outside table in a courtyard area with a fountain in the centre; they sat as far away from other customers as possible, aware that their conversation might cause any eavesdropping gentleladies to choke on their Lapsang Souchong.

"I feel like a member of the fuckin' WI," grumbled Andy, sipping his tea.

Larkin didn't rise to the bait. "So," he said, "how was your weekend?"

Andy's face took on a grim aspect. "I tell you, mate – we're onto somethin' big an' nasty here."

Then Andy told him.

On the Friday evening he had followed Noble and the two boys up into Northumberland. Noble hadn't noticed the tail: "Must've been too excited," Andy said.

Andy had followed them off the main road and onto some minor roads, careful to keep a discreet distance. Eventually, Noble had pulled up at a large, secluded house, well set back from the road. Andy drove past, stopped the Vitara at the first available place – a layby – and ran back over the fields at the side of the house, crouching low, camera equipment at the ready.

As he neared the house, he became aware of the security cameras mounted to the walls. He quickly judged their range and scope and safely set himself up behind a concealing patch of hedge.

He had trained his telephoto lens on the windows; thankfully, the occupants hadn't drawn the curtains. He could see three figures inside – two older, middle-aged men, and Noble. No sign of the two boys. "They must still be in there," Andy reckoned, "'cos I was sure neither of them had left. So I reckoned the best thing to do was get some snaps in and wait. So I kept watching until the lights went out, then went back to the jeep.''

"You slept there all night?'' asked Larkin incredulously; it wasn't like Andy to abandon his creature comforts.

"Yeah,'' said Andy, puffing his chest up with pride. "All three nights. SAS-trained, me. Survival expert.''

Larkin scrutinised his mate. Greasy hair, stubble, black-rimmed eyes and a funny smell emanating from his general direction. From the way he had polished off both his passion cake and half of Larkin's, Larkin reckoned Andy hadn't eaten since Friday. Or if he had, the Mars and Snickers wrappers and empty Pepsi cans that decorated the jeep's floor were a pretty good indication of his diet.

"Yeah, right,'' said Larkin, suppressing a grin. "Keep going.''

Andy had resumed his vigil on Saturday morning: same spot in the bushes. He could plainly see the three men moving about the house, the boys too. The men had been strolling around clad only in their swimming trunks.

"Pretty disgusting really,'' Andy elaborated. "I mean, these two old geezers had their best years behind them, know what I mean? You can do without all the wobbly-belly, droopy-tit stuff, can't you?''

"Your uncanny ability to paint vivid word pictures is beyond doubt,'' said Larkin, "but . . .''

"Oh yeah.''

Andy continued. All day Saturday the men and the boys stayed in and around the house. The boys were now wearing trunks too. Everyone seemed fine; laughing, happy, having a good time. Nothing untoward seemed to be going on. Andy began to think perhaps Larkin had been mistaken.

Then on Saturday night, the three men settled themselves in the sitting room. Beercans in hand, they sat facing the TV. One of the older men had put on a video and they got comfortable.

Whatever they were watching seemed to arouse them; Andy suspected they might have been masturbating. Once the tape finished, they had all left the room.

"Now the kids had disappeared at this point, I couldn't see them anywhere,'' Andy said, his face grave, "I reckoned they'd gone to bed. No lights went on in the rest of the house, so I didn't know what was goin' on. An' I hadn't seen anythin' I could call the cops about.''

The men never reappeared, so it was another night in the Vitara, with resumed surveillance on Sunday morning. Andy arrived back at the house just in time to see an expensive car pull up and an expensively-dressed, middle-aged man hurry from it and go inside. Andy had snapped away at the newcomer, but the man's features were obscured by bushes and trees. "It was like he was hidin' his face, just in case he was bein' watched. Know what I mean?"

"He must be pretty high-profile."

"I reckon so. I tried to get a shot of him once he was inside the house, but he just wouldn't come to the window."

Andy watched the house all day, with the next notable movement on Sunday night when Noble, all smiles, left the house with one of the middle-aged men. They had said their goodbyes to the others and piled into the Fiesta. Flash Harry came out later, alone, the darkness ruining Andy's shot, and drove off. The two boys never emerged.

"I thought I must've missed somethin'. Thought the kids had gone back to Newcastle when I wasn't lookin'. So I kipped in the Vitara, checked the place this mornin' – nothin' doin' – and then it clicked. These old houses must have big cellars, right?" continued Andy grimly. "So I put two an' two together. I reckon that's where they been all along."

"The cellar . . ." Something tightened in Larkin's stomach when he heard that. Something sickening, but unfocussed, ill-defined. There was a connection there, though it was just out of his mind's reach. He mentally put it aside. If it was important it would come to him. "Keep going."

"When I thought of that I phoned you. An' 'ere we are. What d'you reckon?" Andy sat back, looking pleased with himself.

"Well done," said Larkin, impressed. "I can see all those industrial espionage jobs have paid off."

"Not to mention the porn jobs I did before them."

"Well, you may get a chance to use those skills too, one day," said Larkin cynically. "But not today, sadly." Larkin shook his head. "I think you're right. This looks like something big and nasty."

"So what now? Take all this to the Old Bill?"

Larkin thought. He could feel the anger rising within him. "Fuck no!" he said in mock-outrage. "We've both got a fair idea of what's going on in that place. I reckon we ought to pay the owner-occupier a visit, Mr Brennan."

Andy's eyes lit up. "You think there'll be lots of gratuitous violence and plenty of aggro, Mr Larkin?"

"I fucking hope so, Mr Brennan. I fucking hope so."

18: The Righteous Red Mist

"I know what's happening in the cellar," Larkin said.

"I've got a pretty good idea myself," Andy replied, concentrating on the road. They were in the Vitara, Andy navigating by memory as he drove. Larkin was keyed up, eager for a fight; for once, he thought, there could be no doubt about whether his actions were justified. For once, the target of his anger would be an appropriate one.

"I mean, specifically," he said. "You aren't the only one who had a busy weekend, you know." He told Andy about the trip to Noble's house, and the discovery of his shrine: in particular the polaroids stuck round the mirror. Home-made, shot against a black-painted bare brick background.

"You reckon they were just for his own benefit, then? Him and his mates?" asked Andy.

"I did at first, but now – I don't know. All that advance planning, driving up to here and everything, it doesn't seem worth it if what they're after is just a quick fuck with an underage boy and a few snaps as mementoes. It's really risky to take a whole weekend over it, so why not stay in the city, where it's much more anonymous, and have somebody else take care of the organisation? There're plenty of people who'll find you a kid, no questions asked. I think there's more to it than that. What I figure is, they've got a nice little racket going. Those photos I saw had a professional feel. The kids looked posed. I think they pick up kids no one's going to miss for a few days, have sex with them – and make a few quid into the bargain by recording the occasion. Photos, videos — " He exhaled sharply, hissing air between his teeth. "Who knows, they probably take commissions."

"So it's some sort of paedophile ring?"

"Yeah. Either personal contacts or – well you know what the Internet's like."

"Bastards," spat Andy, nearly veering off the road. "So what happens to the kids? When they've served their purpose?"

Larkin looked at him, eyes miniature sunbursts of passion. "That's what we're going to find out."

Andy floored the accelerator as far as it would go.

The house looked pretty much as Andy had described it. Large, secluded, the charming country-manor atmosphere offset by the all-round security cameras. It managed to look both well-maintained and desolate. With no need now for secrecy, Andy pulled the jeep into the gravel driveway, screeching to a halt bang in front of the main entrance. The two men jumped out and began hammering on the door. No reply.

"Reckon he's out?" asked Andy.

"Let's look for another door."

They hurriedly made their way round the side of the house, peering in the windows as they went. Andy, palms cupping his eyes to the glass, saw a shadowy figure scurrying about inside.

"He's making' for the back door! Quick!"

Larkin ran round, reaching the back door just in time to see the figure run through the kitchen and reach the door, hands frantically fumbling the key into the lock. Larkin quickly grabbed the handle, put his shoulder to the wood and pushed as hard as he could. A loud thump, then the door gave and swung open. There, lying on the kitchen floor nursing his right hand, was one of the men Andy had described. Middle-aged, balding, spare tyre. Metal-framed glasses, cords and a checked shirt. Wholly unremarkable.

"I wanna word with you," said Larkin, catching his breath.

The man tried to shuffle his backside away from Larkin. "Get away from me!" he shouted. "I'll call the police!"

"Please do," Larkin replied, "it'll make our job a lot easier. Mind if we come in?"

The man stopped shuffling and crouched in a heap by a table leg, regarding them with circumspect sullenness. He didn't reply.

"Hear that, Andy? He hasn't said we can't come in, so we'll take

146

that as an invitation. OK? Just so – when he's in the dock – he can't say we forced our way in.''

The room Larkin and Andy stepped into was big and well-furnished with traditional country pine. But it was lacking in any kind of warmth, any cosy domesticity. Clean, ordered, it was functional, not friendly as most kitchens were.

The man, sensing no immediate physical threat, pulled himself up, and, flexing the wrist he had landed on, sat warily down at the table. ''Who are you and what d'you want?'' His voice, well-educated, had a nasal quality which Larkin knew was going to get on his nerves very rapidly.

''We've come to ask you some questions,'' said Larkin, pulling out a chair and sitting down opposite him. ''This your house, is it?''

''Yes.''

''Been doing a spot of entertaining over the weekend?''

''What business is that of yours?'' The nasal whine was more noticeable.

''Look,'' said Larkin, leaning forward menacingly, ''don't play the dumb fucker with us. We've been watching you. We saw Noble bring a couple of boys here, then two more men joined you. They left – but you and the boys didn't. So where are they?''

''I – I don't know what you — ''

''Cut the crap!'' Larkin stretched across the table and roughly grabbed the man's shirtfront. ''Where *are* they?''

The man, shocked by the unexpected violence of Larkin's move, began to hyperventilate so quickly it looked as if he were about to have a seizure. He dropped his head to his chest; gradually his shuddering breaths becoming weak whimpers.

Larkin looked up. ''Go search the house, Andy.''

Andy walked to the inside door.

''No, don't!'' The man jerked his head up, suddenly finding his voice; Andy stopped in his tracks. ''They're downstairs. In the cellar ...'' His voice trailed off.

Larkin stared at him with utter contempt. ''Let's go then, shall we?''

The cellar could apparently be reached by means of an old wooden staircase under the stairs. As they walked down the hall towards it, Larkin assessed the rest of the house. Like the kitchen it was conservatively, tastefully furnished: dark wooden furniture, expensive rugs over polished floors, framed hunting prints on the walls. Like the kitchen, it gave the impression of being lived in but of having no life.

As the man opened the door and switched on the light, Larkin immediately felt the cold from the cellar hit him. From the wooden steps, he could see the unshaded bulb illuminating the brick, black-painted walls. He hurried on down.

At the far end of the cellar, pushed against the wall, was an old, stained mattress. A tripod-mounted video camera in the centre of the room pointed directly at it. Behind it, towards the opposite wall, sat a couple of old easy chairs, and a playback monitor complete with attendant paraphernalia, cables and lights. To the side, chained to a radiator and lying naked on the floor, were two boys.

Larkin went over to them, knelt down, touched them. At first glance they seemed to be asleep: but they were so still, so cold his stomach suddenly knotted. Larkin gently pulled up one of the boys' eyelids – Kev, he thought it was – saw only the white of his eye, and let it drop.

"They're completely out of it," he said, turning to the man. "What have you given them?"

"Just . . . something to – to make them sleep," the man stammered.

Holding his rage in check, Larkin switched his attention to the boys. He touched Raymond's wrist: limp, cold, wasted, but there was a weak pulse. Kev's was the same. And the state of them: caked shit and dried blood had left jagged, dribbled tracks down the backs of their legs. Indiscriminate bruises covered their bodies, black rings underlined their eyes. The cockiness they'd shown in the arcade had belonged to two other boys. Now they resembled pieces of meat, chewed up and spat out.

Beside them was a bucket, clearly intended for use as a toilet but, judging by the state of the floor around them, whatever drug they'd been given had caused the boys to lose control over their bodily functions. Larkin, hands clenching into fists, stood up and turned to the man. He knew the boys were alive, that they weren't in need of urgent attention – now was the time for anger.

"You finished with them? You had your fun?"

The man turned his face away, refusing to meet Larkin's eyes.

Larkin crossed swiftly to him. "Well, we've not finished with *you*!'' he shouted, and swung his left fist straight into the man's face. The man's head snapped backwards, glasses flying; a bone cracked and he hit the floor, blood geysering from his smashed nose. He tried to cover it with his hands and lay there, moaning.

Andy nodded approvingly. ''The righteous red mist descended, did it? Nice one, mate.''

Larkin forced the blubbering, bloody wreck on the floor to unchain the boys; when the man was a little slower in responding than he could have been Larkin had to give his ribs a couple of hefty kicks, after which he was rather more compliant.

The man, escorted by Andy, brought the padlock key down to the cellar along with some blankets. And Larkin and Andy unchained Raymond and Kev, wrapped them up warmly and carried them upstairs, where the man showed them into a bedroom. The room, although fastidiously tidy, like the rest of the house, had a rancid, musky smell about it, as if the aroma of sweat and other bodily fluids outweighed fresh air by two to one. Larkin hoped it wouldn't evoke too many memories for the boys. Once they were lying in the relative comforts of the musty bedding, it was harder to remember what they had been through.

Larkin rounded on the man, who flinched at his gaze.

''Downstairs, you,'' Larkin said. ''We've got some talking to do.''

And talk he did. Resigned to the inevitability of his situation, he talked freely, spilling it all out, rehearsing his confession. While Andy did a recce of the house, Larkin and the man sat at the kitchen table and began the none too gentle process of fitting answers to questions. He told Larkin his name, mumbling it through the wreck of his broken face. Colin Harvey.

Larkin rifled through his memory. With a snap of his fingers, it came to him.

''What, *the* Colin Harvey?'' Larkin asked. ''The one who wrote that textbook about how children in care are just gagging for it?''

Harvey said nothing. He dabbed uselessly at his face with a handkerchief, twisted his smashed glasses in his fingers.

''So what happened? They chucked you out when they found you tried to put your theories into practice?''

"I took early retirement . . ." Harvey muttered.

Larkin laughed bitterly. "All quietly hushed up, was it? No scandal? No nasty court case? Oh, yeah, I know how councils look after their own." Larkin leaned in close again, a sardonic grin twisting the corners of his mouth. "No chance of keeping it quiet now."

Andy marched back in, sat next to Larkin at the pine table, ignoring Harvey as if he were something way down the food chain. "I've checked the house out. Professional video duplication systems in the attic – darkroom – the lot. Nice little set-up our friend here's got."

Larkin nodded. "He hasn't been idling away his retirement, that's for sure. So come on, Colin – tell all."

Harvey began to speak, haltingly at first, about his activities. Larkin's suspicions had, unfortunately, been correct. One of the four men, usually Noble, acted as procurer, picking up runaways, latchkey kids, kids from council-run homes – the kind of kids who wouldn't readily be missed. Kids who were vulnerable. The children would be brought back to the house; the men would drug them into passive compliancy, have sex with them, abuse them; all the while recording their degradation for posterity and for payment. What started out as a hobby had eventually – through contacts in Britain and abroad, and via the Internet – become a business. And a very lucrative one.

"And what happens to the boys after you've done with them?"

Harvey told them. Once the boys had out-grown their usefulness – once their voices had started to break – they were abandoned, left to pick up the pieces of their shattered lives alone. By this time they were too deadened to the abuse to complain to the authorities. Or – if they had retained some freshness, some attraction – they were taken to Amsterdam and sold into child prostitution.

Larkin's throat was dry when he spoke. "And how many times have you done this?"

"A few," Harvey replied, reckless now. "Alan takes care of all that."

"Who's Alan?" demanded Larkin.

"Alan Haining. He lives in Amsterdam, comes over here for our – get-togethers. He was here this weekend."

The man that Andy had seen leaving with Noble. Larkin pushed further. Alan Haining, he discovered, was an ex-teacher in a private boys' school: another one offered "early retirement". Another one who'd got away with it.

Larkin asked Harvey how they had met; Harvey replied that it had been at college. They had been drawn together by their common interest, vowing mutual self-protection throughout their lives.

"If that's the case," asked Larkin, "how did you meet Noble? He's an awful lot younger than you."

Harvey's head dropped. "He was . . . someone Alan and I have known for a long time."

Larkin and Andy exchanged glances. The implication behind Harvey's words was clear.

"One of yours or one of Haining's?" asked Larkin, spitting out his disgust.

"I . . . can't remember . . ."

"Tell me!"

"Alan knew him first," Harvey said, with some difficulty. "He was such a nice boy . . . a beautiful boy . . ." He looked up, his eyes misting over. When he spoke his voice was impassioned with lost, misplaced love. "His parents left him in that school. They didn't care what happened to him, they never visited . . . We . . . just gave him love . . ."

Larkin stood up, paced to the far side of the kitchen. "There's another way of looking at it, isn't there? He was left in the care of the school and Haining abused that trust, by fucking him!" Larkin walked back to the table, fists clenched, bent over Harvey. "In fact, Haining abused him so much, for so long, Noble became a child fucker himself!"

"It's not that simple!" Harvey cried, eyes shining with tears.

"Oh, you reckon, do you? Well, I've got news for you," shouted Larkin. "It fuckin' *is*!" He gave Harvey a vicious, left-handed slap; the man, emptied of all resistance now, was knocked from his chair. As soon as he hit the floor, Harvey curled up into a foetal ball, and lay there sobbing.

Larkin stared at him for a couple of seconds, his expression unreadable. Then he turned to Andy. "Come on – we've got a story to write."

"Ere, 'ang about," Andy said. "We haven't finished yet."

"No?"

"There's somethin' more he can tell us, isn't there? Give us a hand."

151

Together, Larkin and Andy pulled Harvey off the floor and placed him back in the chair. The slap had started his nosebleed again; he held the red-stained handkerchief to his face protectively, like a shield.

"So who's the third man?" asked Andy.

Harvey's eyes flashed an instant of fear. "I . . . don't know."

"You know fine well," said Larkin. "Who is he?"

"I . . . don't know!" Harvey dropped the handkerchief and reached across the table towards Larkin, beseeching. "Please . . . I never saw him before. He didn't give us his name. Please . . . you must believe me!"

"I don't think he wants to tell us," said Andy.

"He knows who he is," said Larkin. "He's just more scared of him than he is of us. Bad mistake. You've got one last chance, Harvey. Who is he?"

Harvey screwed his face up, pushed his hands so tightly into his face that his fingertips began to turn white from the pressure, and slow trickles of blood began to seep through the cracks between his fingers. A low whimpering, muffled by his fingers, started. And Harvey's body began to contract until his head was on the table and his elbows were tucked into his chest.

Larkin reached over and grabbed hold of Harvey's hands, attempting to prise them from his face. Harvey's whining increased in pitch but he held on, tenaciously.

"Give it *up*!" hissed Larkin. With one last surge of strength he forced Harvey's hands down. Harvey, face uncovered, began to cry, his body as limp as a ragdoll.

"Tell us his name," Larkin commanded, steel in his eyes.

Harvey threw his head back. "I'm *dead*! I'm *dead*!" he shouted, stamping his feet furiously, shaking his shoulders, all control gone. "I'm dead! I'm dead . . ." He repeated it over and over, like a mantra. As Larkin and Andy watched, Harvey began to wag his head to and fro as if it had become loose; his eyes took on a glassy, distant look.

"Reckon we've lost him," said Andy, sadly.

Larkin sighed. "Reckon you're right. Let's call the police."

"What the hell happened to him?" the uniformed constable asked Larkin when he saw the state Harvey was in.

152

"Fell down the stairs," Larkin replied.

"Pity he didn't fall a bit harder," the policeman said with a knowing smirk. "Will he be pressing charges, d'you think?"

"I doubt it very much," said Larkin.

"Good. Makes it easier to see who the villains are. Mind you," the constable leaned in conspiratorially, "once they get with their briefs it makes them brave."

Larkin glanced at Harvey. The man, still sitting on a kitchen chair, seemed to have passed into a persistent vegetative state. "I don't think this one's going to give you any trouble."

When the police had been mentioned, Harvey had freaked out. He had jumped up, made a pathetic, staggering run to the door, shouting the whole time. Larkin and Andy had grabbed hold of him; he had struggled, flailing his arms about like a madman. Larkin managed to pin the man's arms by his side while Andy rooted through the drawers and cupboards in the kitchen, eventually tugging a length of electrical flex from a lamp and binding his wrists together. Once bound, Harvey had become motionless, silent, as if the last remnants of his personality had been extinguished.

Larkin had initially tried to contact Moir, but was unable to reach the big man. He then dialled 999 and asked for police and an ambulance.

While waiting for the emergency services to arrive, Larkin and Andy checked out the tapes from the security cameras, hoping for clues as to the third man's identity. But when they shoved the tape in the machine, the screen filled with nothing but static. They tried a different tape: same thing.

"Fuckin' hell," said Andy in exasperation, "the bastard's wiped them. They don't take any chances this lot, do they?"

"Bollocks," said Larkin.

"Back to square one."

Larkin's eyes acquired a glint. "Maybe not."

Before Andy could inquire further, the two boys were stretchered out; no permanent physical damage, one of the paramedics said, but as for the effect on their psyches, who could tell? Larkin then gave the CID men an account of his involvement that was nothing if not creative: playing down Andy's surveillance, playing up the element of chance in finding the house. Larkin stressed the fact that they had been invited in, even threw Moir's name into the conversation to add credibility. CID took full statements, saying they would have

153

the rest of the "ring" – meaning Haining and Noble – in custody by that evening.

After Harvey's house had been securely locked and the police had left, Larkin turned to Andy. "We'd better get going – back to Newcastle."

"Hold on a moment," said Andy, puzzled.

Larkin, on his way to the car, stopped. "What?"

"I said this was a dead end, you said 'Maybe not'. What do you know?"

Larkin smiled. "I know enough, Andy. I know who the third man is."

19: The Batphone Rings

"So come on then," said Andy, at the wheel of the Vitara – they were travelling back to Warkworth to pick up the Golf. As soon as they were on the road and away from the ears of the police, Larkin had told Andy his suspicions about the third man's identity. "Who is 'e?"

"Swanson," said Larkin simply.

Andy laughed incredulously. "I thought it might be. You're determined to nail that geezer one way or the other, aren't you?"

"It makes perfect sense, Andy. I told you about the break-in, the computer disks going missing, the threat – all that. The only other thing apart from work I've been doing recently is shaking down councillors. And my partner in that little sideline is dead. So I'm either pissing off a politician, or a paedophile, or both. I'm starting to think the two things might be related, and Swanson makes the perfect link. He's got good connections to protect him; he's also got something significant to lose."

Andy looked thoughtful. "Yeah," he said at great length, "an' I suppose this mysterious Third Man fits that an' all. They've certainly done all they can to keep him under wraps." He nodded. "Ycah. You might be right there."

They drove for some time in silence, both lost in their own musings. Eventually Andy spoke.

"Of course," he said, brow furrowed, "there's always the chance you might be wrong."

"I won't be."

Andy gave a snort of a laugh. "Let's hope not," he said, "or we're both fucked."

*   *   *

Back in his own car, Larkin slipped an Aretha Franklin tape into the deck and tuned out the day's events. He tried to think of something positive and uplifting in his life; to blot out what he'd seen and heard at Harvey's house; his mind latched instinctively onto Jane and he actually found himself smiling. He was really looking forward to seeing her again. He liked her – probably more than he would allow himself to admit. And then, into his head, like a ghost, came Charlotte. He remembered how fond he had been of her – how much he had loved her – and look where it had got him. He was taking it slowly with Jane, not pushing it. Letting it come easy.

He eased back in his seat and drove back to Newcastle, while Aretha sang about the lover she still said prayers for.

Once in the office of The News Agents, the real work began. Larkin wrote up the morning's exploits, carefully skirting round what he couldn't legally say, since the case was a long way off coming to trial and was therefore still *sub judice*. All he printed was the facts, and they were damning enough. Andy did overtime in the office's photographic facilities, and the story was ready for the late editions of the *Chronicle* and the early editions of next morning's nationals.

Bolland, needless to say, was over the moon. Apart from anything else, the money the story represented in splashes and spreads provided by his agency was major. He took them over to the pub to celebrate – a unique event in itself. The Blackie Boy, near the bottom of the Bigg Market, had been refurbished a few years ago in dark wood and stained glass, in an attempt to give it some history and character. It now held several years of use, but instead of looking lived-in it just looked worn-out. The three men got their drinks – at Bolland's expense – and sat down at a window table.

"Well," toasted Bolland expansively, pint raised in the air, "here's to the successful conclusion of a job well done!" They clinked glasses, drank long and deep.

Then Larkin was assailed by a momentary mental image of the two boys lying in the cellar. He quickly blinked it – and the accompanying guilt for drinking a toast over their battered bodies – out of his head. "I wouldn't be so sure it's concluded," he said, setting his glass down. "There's still Noble, and this Haining guy to track down — "

"But the evidence!" enthused Bolland. "The two boys, the video

156

tapes, the photos . . . Harvey might have wiped the security tapes, but there's computer disks with customers' names and addresses. Once Harvey gives up the access codes the police'll be able to reap that little harvest. No," he continued, wagging a finger at Larkin and Andy, "mark my words, this is huge! Bigger than huge!" He reached across and enfolded Larkin in a bear hug, squeezing too tightly for comfort. *They must have taught him this at his male bonding class*, thought Larkin, raising his eyebrows at Andy over Bolland's shoulder.

"Love 'im! Love 'im!" Bolland, thankfully, released Larkin from his grasp. "What did I tell you, Steve? If there's an award winner in this agency, it's you!"

"Yeah, but," said Larkin, "there's still the court case."

"And then there's the Third Man," chimed in Andy.

"Oh, they'll find him," said Bolland with a dismissive wave of his hand. "Once they've got the others, it's inevitable. No, this is your moment of glory. You deserve it – bask in it!"

I might if you'd shut up and give me the chance, thought Larkin. But he said only, "Yeah. Right."

Bolland started to gibber excitedly once more, but his eulogies were cut short by the trilling of Larkin's mobile. He answered: it was Jane. No pleasantries – she came straight to the point.

"I've just had the police on the phone. It's Noble. He's dead."

That news was shocking enough, but what she told him next had Larkin grabbing Andy and running from the pub as fast as possible.

Bolland stared after them, taken aback. He shrugged and smiled to himself. "There you go," he said. "When the Batphone rings, the dynamic duo swing into action." He downed his drink and wondered where they were going. And how much money it was going to make him.

20: A Noble End

When the Vitara attempted to pull into Noble's street, Andy found the amount of people thronging the place made access almost impossible. Clearly the crowds had sensed something important was happening, something that would make the news. Carefully Andy steered the jeep through the crowds, only to stop short at the inevitable cordon. The police had used so much marker tape, they could have gift-wrapped the street for Christmas.

Larkin and Andy parked the vehicle where it had come to rest and hopped down. Already the TV news teams, both local and national, were hovering; cameras poised like electronic scalpels, waiting to rip open whatever story was there, spill its guts all over the public. Print journalists were also gathered; Larkin caught the predatory eye of Carrie Brewer. She didn't waste much time before heading in his direction.

"Thought dead children weren't your thing?" she said as unpleasantly as possible.

"Frightened someone else'll get your exclusive?" Larkin replied.

Andy's assessment of the situation was razor-sharp. "One exclusive in the day's quite enough, don't you think?" he said. Brewer recoiled as if she'd been slapped.

"Have you met Andy?" Larkin asked innocently. "I can tell the two of you are going to get along famously."

She attempted to recover her composure. "I don't know what you expect to find here. Even I can't get anything out of them."

"Really?" said Larkin, raising his eyebrows in mock-surprise. He pulled out his mobile, punched in a number. "I'm here," he said when it was answered and listened for the response. He hung up, pocketing the phone. Revenge was going to be very sweet.

Less than a minute later, a uniformed constable called his name. He made himself known, and the policeman allowed Andy and Larkin – who tried not to look too smug – under the tape. Carrie Brewer's jaw just about hit the ground. Larkin couldn't resist blowing her a kiss as he went.

"Bit of a childish victory," said Andy as they followed the policeman towards Noble's flat.

"I know," agreed Larkin, "but bloody satisfying, even under the circumstances."

"Now don't think I only brought you in here to give you an exclusive," Moir said, as soon as Larkin and Andy reached Noble's front door. "You're here as witnesses. I'll be wanting statements."

Larkin was shocked to see Moir: he looked terrible. Clothes more dishevelled even than usual, hair like greying straw, eyes bloodshot, black-rimmed. Most disturbing of all, the big man's hands had a nasty touch of the shakes. Larkin suspected he was tottering on the edge of burn-out.

After Jane's call in the pub, Larkin had phoned Moir; he'd been asked to come, with Andy, straight to Noble's flat. Moir's tone had told them to expect, not only the worst, but also a hard time.

At first glance Noble's flat looked much as Larkin had left it, leaving aside the white-suited hordes of SOCOs. "We'll talk in here," Moir said, and led them into the living room, where he sat heavily on one of the dining chairs, visibly glad to take the weight off his feet. He checked no one else was in earshot before he spoke. "Place look as you left it?"

"Pretty much," said Larkin. "So what happened?"

"Well, we began to make a routine enquiry into the abuse allegations brought about by your friend *Ms* Howells," Moir started, folding his hands into his lap, trying to conceal the shaking. "The uniforms were told Noble hadn't turned up for work today, so they came round here. No reply. Fearing he'd done a runner, they entered forcibly and found . . . I'd better show you."

Moir stood up and walked to the bathroom, Larkin and Andy close behind him. The tiny off-white tiled room was full of people; print-lifting, photographing, sample collecting. Noble was getting more attention dead than he had ever had when he was alive.

"Bit busy still – we'll have to watch it from here," said Moir.

159

Swallowing hard, Larkin looked in. He knew the naked body in the bath had once been Noble, but it was hard to imagine. The skin was soft-looking, blue-white, beginning to bloat. An arm hung limply over the side of the bath, vicious slashes visible at the inside of the wrist. Blood had stained the tiled walls in a collection of magnificently abstract arcs, trickling down the grouting, dying the carpet a coppery brown. The bath water was deep pink. Noble's head was thrown back, eyes staring, mouth gaping. Shit floated on the water, evidence of the moment when his muscles had finally given up the fight, the moment when he had died.

"Fuckin' 'ell . . ." said Andy, his face twisting at the stench.

"Want to take some pics?" asked Moir, cynically.

"No way," Andy said, shocked for once. "I doubt my usual publishers would touch this stuff. I hate to think who would wanna publish it."

"Fair enough," Moir replied. "Shame – the general public should see this. It would put them off Hollywood's idea of self-destruction."

"So this was definitely a suicide?" asked Larkin. "On the phone, you mentioned a note — "

Moir gave a cryptic smile. "Follow me," he said, and led them back to the living room.

"We found it on the screen," he said, pointing to the word processor. "Unsigned, of course. We printed a copy off." He produced a sheet of A4 paper from inside his coat, sealed in a plastic evidence bag. He laid it flat on the table. "Have a read," he said.

Larkin and Andy both bent over.

I admit I killed Jason Winship. I can't live with the guilt any more and have decided to end my life.

They straightened up. "Short and sweet," said Andy.

"And very convenient," added Larkin. "Does he know where Lord Lucan and Shergar are as well?"

Moir nodded. "My sentiments exactly. But until our investigations turn up anything else we'll have to go with it."

"What about his shrine? Have you seen that?" asked Larkin.

"You mean that little wank cupboard off the bedroom?" Moir replied. "Yeah – we found it."

"The polaroids round the mirror," said Larkin, "they were taken

160

in Harvey's cellar. Might be worth checking them out, trying to trace the kids involved.''

Moir looked confused. ''Polaroids? There weren't any polaroids.''

''Really,'' said Larkin. ''Then either Noble tidied them away to preserve his posthumous reputation, or some visitors with a line in self-protection have done it for him.''

''Fuck!'' spat Moir.

''Quite,'' said Larkin. Uneasy, he crossed to the window. The sky was rapidly darkening, and the spectators were beginning to drift off. Once they'd realised that nothing dramatic was going to happen, Eastenders had begun to look more attractive. Noble had had his fifteen minutes of notoriety.

As Larkin idly stared, trying to make sense of it all, the tape in the street was lifted by a couple of uniformed officers to allow the entrance of a car: a top-of-the-range Rover, sanctioned for official purposes. It purred to a halt outside the house, next to Noble's Fiesta. And from the back stepped Alan Swanson.

An unpleasant frisson ran the length of Larkin's spine. ''Andy – we've got company.''

Andy joined him at the window, and quickly did a double-take.

''I know exactly what you're thinking,'' said Larkin. ''Hey, Henry, how did that pisshead describe the bloke seen when Jason was abducted? Middle-aged, flash bloke, flash car? Come and look at this.''

Moir joined them at the window. Swanson was surveying first the dwindling crowd, then the house; his expression was grim. ''Swanson. Heard he was coming. He's going to talk to the media. High-profile case like this, specially where kids are involved . . .'' Moir trailed off, looked at Larkin. ''You're not thinkin' . . .''

''Why not? He fits the bill, doesn't he?''

Moir shook his head in disbelief. As the three men watched, McMahon emerged from the other side of the car; he too wore an expensive suit and a sombre expression. They came together on the pavement, exchanged words. Swanson shook his head, his face drawn.

''Look at the state of that,'' Moir said, referring to his boss. ''More like a politician than the politician. They could be brothers.''

''We all are, under the skin,'' said Andy.

The other two stared at him blankly.

161

"Apparently not," Andy said weakly.

McMahon and Swanson made their way to the front door of Noble's flat.

"I think we'd better make ourselves scarce," said Larkin. But before he and Andy could make a move, McMahon and Swanson were in the room.

"Henry!" McMahon moved over to Moir, enthusiastically pumped his hand. "Congratulations! Stroke of luck and we all get a result! Marvellous!" He stopped dead when he saw Larkin and Andy. "And who's this?" An icy coldness had entered his voice.

"Stephen Larkin and Andy Brennan. From The News Agents. They put us on to Noble." Moir glanced quickly at Larkin. "They've been giving us a statement."

McMahon regarded them as if they were insects, a cruel light in his eyes. Suddenly his mask of joviality was back in place. "The press. Well done, Henry! You've recruited them to our cause!" He crossed to Larkin, all smiles now. "I've heard of you. I like your attitude. You know, this is an unrivalled opportunity to write up a major story from an eyewitness point of view." He stared straight into Larkin's eyes, Larkin, unflinchingly, stared back. "I trust you know how to write it *properly*," McMahon said, a touch of frost back in his voice.

Yeah, thought Larkin, *the last thing you want me to do is upset your doctored crime clear-up figures.* "I know exactly what to write," he said.

McMahon clapped him on the back, everyone's favourite uncle. "Of *course* you do! You don't need me telling you how to do your job!" He gave a short burst of forced laughter then fell silent; Larkin knew an exit line when he heard one.

"We'll be off then," Larkin said. "Cheers, Henry – nice one. Think on what we said, though."

"I will," muttered Moir, clearly uncomfortable in McMahon's presence.

Larkin and Andy made their way out. In the doorway hovered Swanson, seemingly undecided whether or not to enter. Perhaps he thought that publicly entering a known paedophile's house would tarnish his image. Bring him a bit too close to reality for comfort.

Larkin nodded to him as he passed, then stopped, turned. "Mr Swanson?"

Swanson moved to face him. "Yes?"

162

"You don't know me. My name's Stephen Larkin, I'm a journalist. I was wondering if I could possibly have a word with you some time?"

"Of course," Swanson said readily. Larkin was taken aback. What was that look on his face? Anticipation? Resignation? Fear? He certainly hadn't expected Swanson to co-operate. What was his agenda?

"Call my office. We'll talk soon." Swanson caught Larkin's eye, held his gaze. A politician's honest sincerity. Then he took a deep breath and stepped inside Noble's house of horrors.

As they made their way back to the Vitara, Andy voiced his bewilderment. "That was fuckin' spooky, wasn't it? 'Im turnin' up, wantin' to talk an' all that – must 'ave a guilty conscience."

"Yeah," Larkin replied, a gleam in his eyes. "Still, we've got the bastard."

Near the Vitara, Larkin saw Carrie Brewer; she was standing at the barrier, doing her damnedest to flirt with a uniformed constable. The man – hardly more than a teenager – was beetroot with embarrassment, desperately trying to escape her attentions.

Larkin seized the opportunity. "Hey, Carrie – how's that dose of NSU you couldn't shift?"

Brewer turned to face him, glaring. Her hold broken, the policeman was able to scurry away. "Why don't you piss off?" she shouted.

"Gladly. Just off to write my leading article." He smiled winsomely.

"Arsehole!" She stomped off angrily.

"Wouldn't mind givin' 'er one," Andy said ruminatively.

"Who, Carrie Brewer?" Larkin was gobsmacked.

"Yeah, I know she's a bitch an' all that," Andy said, his brow furrowed as if he were wrestling with a particularly thorny philosophical problem, "but sometimes you can't beat a good vengeance fuck."

Larkin shook his head. "I hope you're a one-off."

"Naw," said Andy smiling, "I'm a clone. There's thousands — "
He broke off suddenly and stared. "Who the fuck's that standing in front of my jeep like he owns it?"

Larkin looked. He saw the figure of a skinhead, so still he seemed

163

to be on guard duty. "Don't worry – that's just Ezz. A friend of mine – sort of."

"Great," said Andy. "That makes me feel so much better."

Ezz didn't move; didn't even acknowledge their presence. As they reached the car, he came to life. "Is he dead?" Ezz asked.

"Yeah," said Larkin uneasily. "Ezz – that wasn't anything to do with you, was it?"

Ezz shrugged. "Dead," he said.

"Yeah," said Larkin. "That seems to be it. He's dead. And apparently he confessed to killing Jason Winship before he topped himself."

"No!" Ezz grabbed Larkin's arm, looked straight into his eyes; Larkin was more than a little surprised. He saw something in Ezz's eyes that he had never seen before. Emotion. Alarm? Anger? He couldn't tell. Ezz continued talking, his voice almost imploring. "It's not over yet. I can feel it — "

"You may well be right," said Larkin, "but I have to go now." He looked down at Ezz's hand, still gripping his arm; Ezz took the hint and immediately dropped it. Larkin opened the car door, swung inside.

"Let me know what happens," said Ezz. Was that really desperation Larkin detected in his voice?

"I will," said Larkin, and Andy started the engine.

As they pulled away, Larkin looked back over his shoulder. Ezz was still standing there. He looked lost, vulnerable. Like a boy who'd ventured far from home, and didn't know how to get back.

Safe

The Man was alone now, ensconced in his own private den. He sat back, stretching his legs under his desk, crossing his ankles. Taking his iced malt in small, measured sips. Safe.

His lucrative private enterprise was gone. Destroyed. No matter. Only money. And although his empire was presently being dismantled and closely examined, there was no part of it that could be traced back to him. He mentally patted himself on the back for that, and once again went over his plan for damage limitation, checking for flaws.

Power. There was no point in having it if one wasn't prepared to wield it. And he'd done that, all right. James had already been scapegoated; Colin would follow. And Alan? He was beyond reach. They were the three people he had known most intimately over the years. But they were expendable. If it came down to them or him, he would win, every time. This was self-preservation: he felt no remorse.

And the boys, all those boys . . . gone. All traces, all mementoes – destroyed. There would be others, but for the time being he would have to content himself with waiting. Planning.

Not even his brother could stop him now. Nor that do-gooding journalist, nor his bitch of a girlfriend. They would soon be taken care of. Permanently.

He smiled, feeling the crackle and buzz of power surround him like a magnetic field. Yes, he thought. Safe.

21: Casting Off

Back in the office, Larkin wrote his account of Noble's suicide. He stressed that Noble had confessed to Jason Winship's murder, but also intimated that there was still another person wanted in connection with the whole thing: someone who could blow the whole affair wide open. He said he expected the identity of the man to become known in the next few days – that the police were on his tail.

"Let's see if that counts as proper reporting," Larkin said to himself grimly as he put the piece to bed.

He let himself out of the office, drove to Scotswood and crashed on Jane's sofa. For the first time in ages his sleep was long and peaceful.

The next morning he was woken up by a newspaper, flung at his chest.

"Who's a star, then?" said a familiar female voice.

He pulled himself on to his elbows to see Jane smiling at him, mug of coffee in hand. She was silhouetted against the translucent curtains, her shape accentuated by the jeans and vest top she wore. Larkin began to feel a tingling sensation in his loins.

"Good sight to see first thing in the morning," he said.

She knelt down beside him, placing the coffee on the floor. "I know exactly what you're thinkin'," she said with a laugh, "and we haven't got time. Alison's in her room and I've got to go to work."

"And that's more important, is it?"

With a salacious smile slinking its way across her face, she pulled the material of her vest top to one side to expose her small, firm left breast, holding it up and massaging the nipple. Before Larkin

167

could do anything except get aroused, she rearranged her clothing, stood up, and fixed him with a mock-stern stare. "That's enough for now. You'll get the rest later."

Alison chose that moment to wander in, and she and Larkin exchanged morning greetings.

"Look," said Jane, "I've got to go. Well done on this." She pointed to the paper.

"Thanks. Everything all right at the centre?"

"Everythin's great. Social Services came to talk to Lorraine, Trevor and Daniel yesterday. Lorraine came to see me to say thanks. It'll be a struggle, but they reckon everythin's gonna be all right there. Wounds heal quicker at that age." She sighed. "Shame James had to end up the way he did, but . . ."

"Maybe it's better this way," Larkin concluded for her.

She nodded bleakly, lost for a moment in self-reflection. "Anyway," she said, "all we need is notification of our grant renewal, and we'll be up an' away."

"I'll see what I can do about that. Reckon I can pull a few strings."

She smiled, and her face lit up with genuine joy. "I think you've done more than enough already!" Her eyes twinkled mischievously. "And I'll see you later to give you a very special thank you." She kissed him and, taking Alison by the hand, left.

Alone, Larkin grinned to himself and picked up the paper. "Stop smirking, you daft bastard," he told himself. "You've got work to do." But as he read through his article, he couldn't stop the corners of his mouth twitching unconsciously upwards.

Once Larkin had dressed, he was hungry to go hunting. The Third Man was close – he could feel it. The first thing to do was collect Andy, so he headed down to the quayside, to the same beige aircraft hangar of a hotel that Larkin himself had stayed in on his return to Newcastle. He remembered enough of the layout to dodge the receptionist, and made his way up to Andy's room.

He gave an officious knuckle-rap on the door. "Room Service," he said briskly.

From deep inside the room he heard a grumbling voice and the reluctant creaking of bedsprings. The door opened and there stood Andy, towel round his waist, eyes barely open.

"Morning, Andy," said Larkin, brushing past him into the room. "Hands off cocks and on with socks, as my mother used to — " He stopped dead in his tracks, mouth gaping. There, in Andy's bed, was Carrie Brewer.

"Good morning, Stephen," she said, the sheet clasped over her breasts. She gave him a triumphant smile.

Larkin turned to Andy. "What's she doing here?" he attempted to hiss under his breath.

Andy held his head down, trying to hide his embarrassment. "Come 'ere," he said, and pulled Larkin into the bathroom, shutting the door behind them.

"Good vengeance fuck, was it?" Larkin asked once they were safely out of earshot.

Andy looked uncomfortable. "I know you won't believe me, but I didn't plan it this way. I just went back to Noble's place last night, tried to get some pictures an' that, right? An' she was still there. We got talkin', one thing led to another, and . . ." He shrugged.

"I thought you didn't like the woman?"

"You don't have to *like* them," Andy replied, as if stating the obvious. "Anyway, what can I do for you?"

Larkin looked at Andy, then at the door. There was no way he was going to talk about work with Carrie Brewer lying in the next room. "Nothing," he lied. "I just wondered if you fancied grabbing some breakfast, perhaps hitting a few bars later on."

"Yeah," said Andy, perking up. "That sounds cool."

"No, don't bother," said Larkin, jerking his head in the direction of the bedroom, "you're already tied up."

"Tied up? About the only fuckin' thing she hasn't done. Fuck me, she's made me work. I've lost two stone since you last saw me."

"Well," said Larkin, making for the door, "another time, yeah?"

"Smashin'," Andy replied.

Larkin let himself out, shaking his head at the perfidy of male sexuality, and went looking elsewhere for help.

It was approaching lunchtime by the time Larkin found himself walking up the rickety stairs to the first floor at the back of a Chinese restaurant on Stowell Street. He knocked on the door, and when it wasn't immediately answered he went on knocking. He wasn't about to take no for an answer.

Eventually, Moir opened up with a grunt and walked back inside, leaving the door swinging. Larkin followed, taking it for an invitation. Moir was in the process of redecorating. He was systematically pulling down from the walls and board all the information that had accrued on Jason Winship and neatly – by his standards – depositing it into half a dozen box files that lay open on the desk.

"Moving house?"

"Case closed, isn't it?" replied Moir gruffly. "Justice has not only been done, but has been seen to be done. No point in leaving all this lying around." He dropped a photocopied picture of the dead boy's face into a file and closed the lid. Looking weary, he sat down on the swivel chair; the springs screamed for mercy, but he wasn't giving any.

Larkin opened his mouth to speak.

"And before you say anything," Moir continued, "the results have come back from the path lab. The prints in the flat were all Noble's, the wounds on his body look to be self-inflicted and are consistent with suicide. None of his neighbours saw or heard anything or anyone suspicious. Including you. Admittedly, the folks round there are about as likely to help the police as they are to discuss their personal finances with the DSS."

Moir leaned forward, elbows on the desk. "And that's that. The end. Sometimes a bang, sometimes a whimper."

"But what about the Third Man?" asked Larkin. "Can't Harvey finger him?"

Moir straightened up. "You mean you haven't heard the news?"

"I'm taking a day off. Tell me."

Moir sat back expansively. "Harvey's dead."

Larkin took the news like a physical blow. "What?"

"Hanged himself in his cell at Clayton Street nick. Wasn't seen as a potential suicide – which I find hard to believe in the circumstances – but news of Noble's death must have tipped him over the edge. Reckon the Clayton Street lot thought it'd save the taxpayer the expense of a trial."

Larkin was in shock. He began pacing the room in disbelief, until a sudden recollection stopped him in his tracks. "Wait a minute," he said. "When I asked Harvey about the Third Man yesterday, he started shouting, saying 'I'm dead, I'm dead!' Perhaps it was the Third Man who killed him. And Noble. Or somehow had them killed." Larkin was warming to his theme. "Swanson, or one of his cronies, they could have crept in – I don't know, even persuaded someone on the force — " He broke off and looked at Moir. "What's the matter?"

Moir was sitting motionless at his desk. The shakes from the day before had disappeared, but the policeman seemed to have aged ten years in the last two days. He sat staring, as if he'd forgotten where he was.

"I said, are you all right?"

Moir's thoughts jerked back to the present. "Yeah, fine." He searched his memory for the thread of the most recent conversation. "Yeah, that sounds like a good theory. Look into it if you want to," he said, a marked lack of interest in his voice.

"You don't want to help?"

"My job's done," Moir said, in a tired voice. "Noble's dead, Harvey's dead, I doubt anyone will mourn their passing. The two boys are recovering nicely, it's all tied up. Bloody shame about little Jason, but — No, everything's fine."

"What about Haining? You found him?"

"Either gone to ground or gone back to Amsterdam. The latter, I expect. We'll get him eventually, now we know who he is."

Larkin was concerned. The longer Moir sat there, the more distant, the more strange, he seemed to become. Larkin perched on the edge of the desk. "Henry . . . are you really OK?"

Moir sighed, rubbed thick hands over his stubbly jaw. "This whole thing . . . It's unsettled me." He glanced up quickly, caught Larkin's eye, looked down again. "I've had enough. I'm . . . I'm tired. I might take some time off. I've got some . . . things to think through. Decisions to reach."

"Difficult ones?"

Moir gave a snort. "Are there any other kind?"

Larkin stood up. He had a fair idea of what Moir was getting at, and thought he was best left alone. "Let me know," he said, and left.

Alone. That's how it would have to be. Larkin sat in the car, mobile to his ear, pen and paper in hand, waiting for the phone to be answered. He knew there were plenty of other things he could be doing – assessing the full extent of the damage to his house, calling the insurance company – but that would have to wait. He was on

171

to something and he wouldn't – couldn't – let go.

He had spent the last hour and a half trying to get through to Swanson. The MP was either in a meeting, or not taking calls. So Larkin was trying yet again, without much hope, on the direct line he'd been given for Swanson's office.

After three rings, it was answered by a female voice, dripping with bionic super-efficiency. Larkin explained who he was and why he was calling. Again he found himself on hold.

Suddenly, the bionic woman was back. "Mr Swanson says he's tied up in meetings all week during business hours, but he can see you at eight thirty tonight, at Milburns. How does that suit you?"

Larkin said that suited him just fine, and the woman broke the connection, but not before telling Larkin that Mr Swanson was looking forward to meeting him.

"I'll bet he is," said Larkin.

Larkin spent the rest of the afternoon stocking up on clothes to replace his destroyed wardrobe. He even bought himself a new suit and shirt for the evening's meeting, liking it so much he walked out of the shop wearing it, his old clothes bundled into a carrier bag. He was charged, hyped-up. He drove down to Jane's; partly to see her, tell her what was happening, but also to show off his new finery. He laughed to himself when he realised what he was doing. Strutting around like a peacock out to attract a new mate. Well, he thought, it was a long time since he'd had someone to impress.

He rang Jane's front-door bell. After a long pause a small voice hesitantly inquired, "Who is it?"

Odd he thought. Fear of unexpected callers wasn't Jane's style. "It's me – Stephen. Can I come in?"

The door was pulled open, but only as far as the chain would allow. A pair of weary, red-rimmed eyes looked out, confirmed it was him, and opened the door just long enough for him to squeeze past. Then the door was slammed shut, chained and locked.

Larkin looked at Jane. She was holding a viciously sharp kitchen knife in both hands and she was quaking with mortal terror.

"What's up?" asked Larkin, his arms going out to her, wanting to hold her close, reassure her.

She fell against him, her body collapsing into wracking sobs.

"What's happened?" Larkin knew there was nothing he could

do until her tears subsided. He'd wait for her to talk in her own time. Meanwhile, all he could do was, literally, provide a shoulder to cry on.

Gradually, her sobs quietened. Larkin steered her to the sofa and they sat down. Jane looked lost, bewildered, like a frightened child. He found a paper tissue in his pocket and handed it to her; she wiped her face and eyes and then blew her nose. When she looked up again, the anguish on her face was horrible to see.

"Tell me what's wrong," Larkin said, as gently as he could.

She took a deep breath. "I guh-guh-got a call. At work. Said . . . if you don't stop what you're doin', then . . ." She broke off as the tears returned.

"So what are you doing?" Larkin said, confused.

"Not *me*! *You*!"

Larkin was stunned. "*Me*? What?"

"If you don't stop what you're doin', then they'll huh-hurt Alison!" Her eyes were wide, frantic with fear.

Larkin was still uncomprehending. "Who said this? Who was it?"

"Dunno . . . just a phone call. What's happenin'?" She grabbed hold of him, her fingers gripping his arm painfully. "I thought it was all over. What's goin' on?"

He looked her straight in the eye. "Noble's dead – you know that. And, yes, he was a paedophile – but no, I don't think he murdered Jason Winship. I'm pretty sure I know who did, though. I'm going to confront him tonight, and he's not going to get away with it."

"But you *can't* go! You can't! Think of Alison!"

"Where is she?" asked Larkin.

"In her room – and that's where she's stayin'." Jane was back in control now, her voice curt. She straightened up. "You're not goin'?" It was more a statement than a question.

"Don't worry," said Larkin, taking her hands in his. "That phone call was just a bluff. And a pretty desperate one at that. The guy knows I'm on to him, and he's trying to scare me off – that's all. Look, if you're really worried, I'll get someone round. Moir, or another policeman. You'll be protected."

She pulled her hands away. "You're actually goin'?" she said, her voice full of disbelief.

"I've got no choice," replied Larkin, as calmly as he could.

"Don't worry," he said again "It's probably just a bluff, as I said. He knows he's being watched."

Jane stood up. "Probably?" she shouted, her anger rising, "probably? What if it isn't? So what if you go tonight and nothin' happens? There's tomorrow, then the next day, then the day after that. Do me and Alison have to live our lives wonderin' if today's the day we're gonna get that knock on the door? Eh?"

"It won't be like that!" Larkin was exasperated. "Look, I know how you must feel — "

"No you don't! You haven't a fuckin' clue!" She paced furiously to the far end of the room, turning back to Larkin like she wanted to hit him. "Why do you have to go and play the hero? And drag everyone else down with you?"

Larkin couldn't answer that. "I don't know," he said, quietly. "I just have to. I have to know."

Jane's voice dropped ominously. She walked back, stood directly over him. "Well, you go and find out. On your own. Walk out that door, and that's it. I never wanna see you again. I never want you where you can harm me or my family."

He looked up. He could do it, he thought. He could stay here, try to forget his curiosity, erase that part of himself. Give in. Be happy. But ... Her eyes were boring directly into his, demanding an answer. "I'm sorry ..." he said. "I've — "

"Get out," she said, her voice low, deadly.

"Will you be OK?" he asked feebly.

"Fuck d'you care?" she spat back, then turned away.

Larkin was desperately searching for something to say, some magic combination of words that would put everything right between them. But he knew he would never find them.

He walked to the door, unfastened it, stepped out, and closed it silently. He stood on the balcony, looking down. In the quadrant below, some feral-looking kids were using a burnt-out transit van and an old sofa as an adventure playground. As he absently watched them whoop and shout surrounded by dogshit and toxic garbage, he could feel the weight of his heart in his chest: as heavy as a brick. He turned and walked towards the stairs, past Jane's window, hearing the wrenching sobs coming from within, the sound of her heart breaking.

22: Face Off

Milburn's. The name meant many things. Named after the late Jackie Milburn – arguably the greatest footballer Newcastle United has ever seen – the bar's title gave it both an air of nostalgia and a sense of history that was totally at odds with its stark modernity. Naming it after a footballer had also given an added boost, capturing an immediate sense of new-lad faddishness. From that point of view Milburn's was the perfect name: the bar couldn't be called MacDonald's for obvious reasons, it couldn't be called Davies's because no one remembered him – and it couldn't be called Mirandinha's because no one could spell it. So – Milburn's.

It was situated on the quayside; a watering hole for those who desperately wanted to associate themselves with the Rebirth Of The Region gentrification process. What you drank and ate there were considered to be bold statements about who you were and only marginally less important than how you looked. The crowd were young and so self-consciously hip that an original idea would have been more out of place than a Jehovah's Witness at a Satanist orgy.

As Larkin entered the ultra-modern, minimalist surroundings he immediately felt dozens of eyes giving him a less than surreptitious once over. Clearly they approved of his new suit because the bright young things quickly went back to their conversations; regurgitating film reviews and magazine articles, telling anecdotes that made them look good, greeting each quip with avalanches of false laughter.

Larkin moved to the bar and ordered a pint. His head was whirling with mixed emotions. The scene with Jane had been shocking, agonising even, and yet he understood her point of view totally. He didn't doubt the fact that she never wanted to see him again; in

175

all honesty he couldn't blame her. During the drive to Milburn's he had played the scene over and over in his head, each time saying what she wanted to hear. He'd drop it. Give it all up. Stay with her. But he knew, in reality, that was never an option. "Why do you have to go and play the hero?" she had asked him. And he didn't know. There were some things he couldn't explain, and some that he didn't want to explain. Especially not to himself.

He sipped his pint, scoping the bar, looking for Swanson. That was it – that was the answer. He wanted Swanson to be guilty – *needed* him to be – because then Larkin's prejudices would be confirmed. His hatred and mistrust of the Establishment, of people in power, and the subsequent actions he had taken against some of them, would be vindicated. There was a confession to be had tonight, Larkin thought; an admission of guilt. Swanson was ready to crack. And Larkin would be the one wielding the hammer.

As he downed his pint he noticed a man coming towards him. He wore an expensively tailored suit, had fine features and a smile with as much depth as a Steven Seagal movie. If it wasn't for the rippling muscles under his clothes, he could almost have been mistaken for a politician.

"Stephen Larkin?" the man asked in a tone of studied unctuousness.

"That's right."

"Follow me, please." He turned and graciously beckoned to Larkin, who grabbed his glass and went after him.

The man walked round to the side of the bar and up a stainless-steel spiral staircase. A sign at the top read CLOSED – PRIVATE PARTY. The man ignored it and walked straight past; Larkin did the same.

The top floor of the bar had a spectacular view the length of the Tyne. It was furnished by the same uncomfortably minimalist chairs and tables, all unoccupied bar one. Bang in the middle of the room sat Swanson, immaculately dressed, one leg casually crossed over the other, glass of orange juice on the table in front of him. In the muted light of the bar he was elegance itself, as if the only confession he was prepared to make was to being a subscriber to *GQ*. Behind him stood another employee from Urbane Goons R Us.

Swanson unfolded himself and stood up. "Mr Larkin," he said, giving a dazzling display of dentistry, "good to see you again." He stretched out his hand; Larkin took it and shook, firmly.

"And you," Larkin said, returning the smile, but not matching the dental work.

They sat down at opposite sides of the table. Swanson motioned to his two sidekicks. "Brett, Jonathan, take the rest of the night off. Mr Larkin and I have things to discuss."

The two bodyguards flashed concerned looks at each other. This obviously wasn't in the script.

"But Mr Swanson," Brett (or Jonathan) said, "can I remind you that our function is to remain here with you? Thus ensuring that dealings between yourself and Mr Larkin remain—" he looked knowingly at the two men in turn – "on message."

Despite the situation, Larkin had to stifle a laugh. On message? Minders that double as spin doctors, he thought – the ultimate New Labour accessory.

Swanson caught Larkin's eye, looked slightly embarrassed. "Don't worry, Jonathan." He patted his right hip. "I've got my pager, should Millbank desperately need me."

Clearly unhappy but disempowered, the two musclebound Mandys made a disgruntled exit.

Larkin and Swanson sat in silence while they clattered down the stairs, sipping their drinks. When they were sure they were alone, Swanson spoke. "I imagine you've been looking for me."

"You could say that," Larkin replied.

Swanson allowed a small smile to play at the corners of his lips. "And what is this in connection with?"

Larkin leaned forward, elbows on the table. "Let's not waste time. You know why I'm here."

"I do," said Swanson. "And I suppose the sooner we discuss it – and I apologise for using you – the better."

Larkin did a mental double-take. "Sorry? *Using* me?"

"Your activities with Mr Houchen." He shook his head sadly. "Very regrettable. Tragic. But at least you're still here. Where there's life and all that, eh?"

"Never mind that," said Larkin, struggling to clarify his thoughts, "what about Jason Winship? And the part you played in his death? Where there's life, eh?"

Swanson looked genuinely confused. "Jason Winship? My part? What am I supposed to have done?"

"Don't play the innocent with me. You know fine well what you did. You murdered him."

The shock and horror on Swanson's face seemed genuine. "*Me*? Is that what you think? That I killed him? Good God. I can assure you that – you are very much mistaken. But I know who did kill him. I thought that's what this meeting was for."

It was Larkin's turn to look confused. "What the fuck are you on about?"

Swanson gave an exasperated little sigh. "I think we've got off on the wrong foot. Perhaps I should explain." He sat back in his state-of-the-art chair. "It's a long story, so forgive me if this is taking up too much of your time—"

"I've got all night."

"Well. It begins with two brothers . . ."

And Swanson told Larkin the story of a family that appeared outwardly normal: a family that in fact was as dysfunctional as they come. The story of an unloving, absentee father, an alcoholic, sadistic mother: of her two sons, forced to perform unspeakable acts for her amusement. The story of how the shared nightmares of childhood had forced a bond between the two children – a bond that he had come to regret. Swanson's eyes were cold during the telling.

After their parents' deaths, the two boys had been split up and placed with adoptive families.

"I was lucky," Swanson said. "I was adopted by people who showed me just how solid, supportive and loving a family can be when it's working properly." He exhaled heavily. "My brother wasn't so lucky. For him the hell continued. Where he went . . . let's just say, he experienced things that no one should have to endure, let alone a child. By the time he was old enough to fight back, the damage was done.

"Fast forward a few years," Swanson continued. Larkin sat back and crossed his legs. He sensed that, in his head, Swanson had been rehearsing this speech for a long time. "I decide I want to help people. *Really* help people." He stood up, getting into his stride. "Of course, virtually everyone goes through a naive, saving-the-world phase, but I always knew mine was – more deeply felt. More strongly motivated."

"Fascinating though this is," said Larkin, "I've heard it all before. I covered your electoral campaign."

"Then you'll already know I mean what I say," Swanson snapped, back in politician mode. "Anyway," he crossed to the window, regained his grandiose sense of resolve, "I felt – fortunate.

178

My adoptive family saved me. Really saved my life. I wanted to give something back. Not just to them but to others less fortunate. So after college I decided to go into politics. Not the most obvious choice, I admit, but I wanted to work on the broadest canvas possible.

"And here I am. Swept in on the whim of a generous electorate, actually able to implement my grand scheme." He gestured out of the window, eyes shining. "The Rebirth Of The Region!" He paused, perhaps waiting for applause.

"Forgive me for saying so, but a few wine bars for the likes of that lot downstairs, some office blocks and car parks aren't exactly going to improve the quality of life for single mothers in Scotswood."

Swanson sat down again. "You're absolutely right, Mr Larkin. I agree. But one of the lessons I learnt early as a politician was work with what you have." He leaned back expansively. "Here's the part of the speech you've never heard before. You see, I also am under no illusions about my profession. Most politicians are corrupt, or at least in the pockets of the people who bankrolled their rise to prominence. Those are the people I have to work with. Self first, cronies second, voters way down the list. There was no point in me saying I was going to eradicate poverty, provide better housing, schools and hospitals, bridge the gap between rich and poor. For one thing, without complete redistribution of funds from Westminster I had no way of doing it. So what I've done is made a small start. The Rebirth Of The Region is a money maker. It will generate revenue for the whole of Newcastle. What I have to do is try and plough that revenue into projects that will make a tangible difference to everyone in this area, no matter who they are." He took a gulp of his juice, looking pleased with himself.

"Well that's all fine and dandy and peace and love," said Larkin, "but forgive me if I'm just a mite suspicious. All this sounds like so much bullshit to get you noticed at Westminster."

"Oh, I want to be noticed – make no mistake about that. But I want it to be for the right reasons."

"And what about your Minister for Youth ideas?" asked Larkin, feeling on familiar territory now that Swanson had admitted his actions were less than altruistic. Now he could go in hard. "Why make such a fuss over people too young to vote?"

Swanson's face became serious: his *Question Time* look. "Deride

179

my Rebirth schemes all you want. But don't doubt my sincerity on children's issues. I genuinely believe in the welfare of young people and children. They always get a raw deal. Remember – I have personal experience.'' He caught himself becoming solemn, allowed his face to rupture into a grin. ''And, yes, they'll grow up into voters. And when they see the opportunities that have been created for them – by my projects – they'll vote me in again. And again. I've got a lot of work to do, Mr Larkin. I intend to be around for a very long time.'' He leaned forward to emphasise his words. ''Think about it. If you were in a plane that was about to crash, who would you trust to get you down? A captain who cared only about the passengers' safety and not his own, or one who himself had no intention of dying?''

Despite himself, Larkin was impressed by the man's honesty. ''So how do you propose to do this?''

''The first thing I needed was a committed staff. And the best way to get a committed staff is — '' He looked playful. ''What, Mr Larkin?''

''Give them decent incentives?'' replied Larkin.

''They already have those. Try again.''

''Make them share your vision?''

''Getting warmer,'' said Swanson, his eyes twinkling, ''try again.''

''Threaten them?''

''Bullseye, Mr Larkin! Best of all, a combination of all three. Focus my team's minds. Keep them in line. And for that I'd need associates.'' Swanson's smile grew.

The sub-text behind the politician's words slowly started to dawn on Larkin. ''You . . . conniving little bastard! You set me up!''

''And didn't you do the same?'' Swanson's expression was suddenly stern, business-like. ''I needed results, Mr Larkin. I needed loyalty. I didn't want any bad apples on our side. I'd known Ian Houchen for years. He'd done some investigating for me before and I knew I could trust him. He and I hatched the plot together. He was going to do it alone, but he decided he needed help to make the plan effective. He mentioned you. I knew of you by reputation and thought you sounded perfect for the job.''

''So you used me?''

''Don't get high-handed with me, Mr Larkin. It's exactly what you were doing, and for exactly the same reasons. Putting on a bit of moral pressure." He gave a mirthless laugh. "Not pleasant being on the receiving end, is it?"

Larkin could feel the anger welling up inside. He sat on his hands to stop himself from lashing out. "So what about Houchen? How did he die?"

Swanson's face lost its smile. "Ah. Well that's where our story takes a rather disturbing twist. Houchen was killed because he knew too much. And I would like to see his killers brought to justice. But, again, I can't do it alone. I need your help."

Larkin was becoming intrigued, despite his better instincts. "Go on."

"Right," said Swanson, "I'm taking a big risk in trusting you with this. But I think I can. I think you're on our side." His face was earnest, wholly sincere. "In the course of us setting up our – little exercise to keep the troops in line, a tape came into Ian's possession. A snuff tape. Extremely unpleasant. A recording of the death of Jason Winship."

Larkin's heart skipped a beat; his stomach turned over. "How?"

"You might not believe it, but Ian was a very good investigative journalist. One of the best. I paid him well, but he wasn't one of society's consumers, so I imagine his children will be well-provided for. He wasn't the moral crusader type, just a bloody good workman. And he had a God-given gift for nosing out a story.

"Well, he knew someone who knew someone who knew someone ... etcetera. You know how it is. The course of his investigations led him to a house in Northumberland which I believe you yourself are acquainted with."

"Yeah."

"Unfortunately, his spot of breaking and entering didn't go unnoticed. Ian was terrified. He came to me and I took the tape and put it in a safe place. The person who owned it wanted it back and sent out his two pet Rottweilers to retrieve it. Unfortunately their efforts were a little over-zealous. The fire was a convenient cover-up.

"That left me with a dilemma. I wanted to expose the murderer, but I didn't know how. You, on the other hand, were closing in on the paedophile who made the tape. So you were my best bet."

Larkin was stunned. "But why didn't you just go to the police?"

Swanson threw back his head and gave a bitter laugh that startled both of them. "You haven't got it yet, have you? The reason I can't go to the police is because Jason Winship's killer – the person you call the Third Man – is none other than Chief Inspector David McMahon.''

Larkin sat there in shock. He couldn't have been more surprised if he'd found out he'd done it himself. ''That's ridiculous! It *can't* be him!''

''Why not? Because child killers and child abusers are supposed to be sick little outsiders with no self-esteem? Oh, he's all of that. He's also very good at masking his true identity, and let's not forget how well-connected the man is.''

Larkin sat in silence, shaking his head in disbelief.

''You still don't believe me? Then try this. Remember the brother I told you about? The one who had the hellish childhood? Endured experiences that might send anyone a little crazy? Well, that's him. Look what a monster he's become. Conclusive proof of the nature-nurture argument, wouldn't you say?''

Larkin stumbled to his feet. ''This is the biggest load of bollocks I've heard in my life.''

Swanson stood also, his face deadly serious. ''Look, I've had to live with the knowledge of what my brother is for years. But I thought it was only theory with him. I thought whatever – tendencies – he had were controlled. I didn't think he'd take the risk, to be honest. I was wrong. And he's gone way too far this time. He's got to be stopped.'' Larkin began to walk away. ''What about the tape, Mr Larkin? If you saw that, would it change your mind?''

''It would certainly help,'' said Larkin.

''And when you saw I'd been telling the truth? Would you help me?''

''If all this checks out, I reckon I would.''

''Then let's go,'' said Swanson, heading for the stairs. But as he reached the top step he stiffened, began slowly to retreat back into the room.

''What's up?'' asked Larkin. Swanson's face was ashen.

''You might well ask,'' said a half-familiar voice, ascending the stairs.

A figure was making its laborious way up, one step at a time. It seemed to be having trouble with its right leg. Nothing wrong with its right arm, though – an automatic was firmly clenched in the figure's right fist. As the man reached the top of the stairs, Larkin

182

had no trouble identifying Umpleby. And the figure following close behind was none other than Grice.

"Remember the two Rottweilers I mentioned?" said Swanson, turning to Larkin, his voice shaking. "Well, here they are."

"Dead right," said Umpleby, a murderous gleam in his eye. "We've met your little friend before, Swanson. You mentioned something about going to get a tape. Not much point making two journeys. We'll all go, shall we?"

23: Showtime

Larkin and Swanson were marched, as inconspicuously as possible, down the spiral staircase and through the main bar of Milburn's. Larkin was tempted to shout out that someone had a gun against his back and make a dash for it, but the bar was now full to bursting, and it would be impossible to run from the line of fire.

The four men made it eventually to the front promenade overlooking the Tyne. Since it was a warm summer evening, drinkers were spilling all along the waterfront, gossiping, guffawing. The crowds were less sparse than inside, however; it would be easier to dodge through. As he walked, Larkin mentally worked out his escape plan. Unfortunately his thought processes must have shown in his features because suddenly Umpleby's twisted face was nose to nose with his.

"Don't even think about runnin', you piece of shit," Umpleby snarled.

Larkin looked at him, holding eye contact. "You're grimacing, Umpleby – what's the matter? That knee giving you a bit of gyp?"

Umpleby drew back as if to strike Larkin but, aware of the watching crowds, struggled to contain himself. "Funny fucker. You'll be laughin' on the other side of your face soon."

"My mother used to say that," said Larkin with as much cockiness as he could muster. "I never did work out what it meant."

"You'll find out soon enough. Now, go."

"Where?"

Umpleby gestured to Swanson who stood in front of Grice. The MP's earlier bravado had disappeared; he looked defeated, crushed. "Wherever he says."

"It's not far," mumbled Swanson resignedly.

They started walking, Swanson leading. Past the newly developed quayside area, all the way to where the completed buildings ran out and the skeletal husks of half-finished ones loomed. Frameworks of steel, surrounded by scaffolding and planking. Four main buildings, all to be interlinked, ten storeys high: the jewel in the Rebirth Of The Region crown. The area was surrounded by a barbed-wire-topped chainlink fence. The gates were, of course, locked.

"You got a key?" asked Grice insolently. "Or do we have to throw you over the fence?"

"I've got a key," said Swanson, fumbling in his pockets. He found it and began inserting it into the padlock. Before the gate could open, Umpleby placed his hand on top of Swanson's.

"There's no guard dogs here, is there?"

Swanson shook his head.

"No cameras? Night watchmen?"

Swanson pointed upwards. "Surveillance cameras," he said, turning the key, slipping the padlock from its chain and pushing the gate open. They entered the yard and stopped, waiting.

Swanson turned to them. "Look," he said, his voice trembling, "there's really no need for all this. I'm sure we can work something out."

Umpleby and Grice didn't reply; Swanson took that as his cue to continue. "I'm a very wealthy and influential man. This spot of bother could be sorted out quite amicably — "

He was silenced by Grice swinging his pistol butt, slamming it into the side of Swanson's face. He crumpled immediately to the ground, a spurt of blood flying from his mouth.

"Shuddup, man. We haven't got all night." Grice's eyes were shining, as if the sight of blood had excited him.

"We've got work to do," said Umpleby. He dispassionately regarded Swanson's prone form. "Now, where's the cameras controlled from?"

Swanson stumbled slowly to his feet. "Construction office. Over that way." He didn't look at Larkin, didn't raise his eyes. He was beaten.

"Get a move on, then."

The construction office consisted of two portakabins joined together. The first one was set up as a meeting and presentation room: whitewashed, chairs and a table, TV and VCR. The back room was clearly used as an on-site office; battered desks, phones, old, chipped mugs in a dirty sink. On an end table sat two monitors hooked up to a VCR. The surveillance system.

Umpleby motioned to Grice, who crossed to the monitors, switched them off and removed the tape, thrusting it into his jacket pocket. "I'll deal with that later," he said.

Swanson crossed to the far wall and crouched down. Larkin realised he was examining a floor safe, cemented and bricked in, raised from ground level to the cabin's floor.

"In here," Swanson said, spinning the dial and opening the door. He pulled out a seemingly innocuous VHS tape in an anonymous white card slipcase. He straightened up and passed the tape to Umpleby.

"This the right one?" Umpleby asked.

Swanson nodded, eyes downcast.

"I wanna take a look at it."

Swanson had expected Umpleby to say that. He moved through the other office and silently set up the TV and VCR. He took the tape from Umpleby and inserted it. The four men sat down in the dark to watch.

"Anybody got any popcorn?" asked Grice, sniggering.

Video static bounced off their faces. Then the tape began.

The first thing that appeared was a bare, brick wall, painted black. Larkin immediately recognised it: Harvey's cellar. The sound was fuzzy; although the cellar was empty and silent, the atmospherics picked up by the cheap mic gave it a boomy ambience.

Suddenly the camera panned down, jerkily focusing on a young boy, naked. He was lying on the stained mattress Larkin had seen in the cellar. Jason Winship. He seemed to be waking from a heavy sleep; perhaps whatever they had plied him with was wearing off. He looked bruised, wasted.

The camera lurched back, was locked off. Into the frame came a hooded, naked man, middle-aged but in good shape, sporting an erection. He bent over Jason, caressing the boy's cheek with the back of his hand. Jason's eyes began to open, and his lips parted slightly, as if he wanted to speak. But he didn't get the chance. His mouth was suddenly, and roughly, filled with the man's penis.

His choking screams and the man's coarse, rhythmic grunting forced Larkin to turn his head from the screen. He thought he might actually be sick. He looked towards Swanson. The politician's eyes were unfocused and his lips were moving in a silent conversation

186

with himself. Or his past, thought Larkin.

Larkin looked at their two captors. They were watching the screen impassively: eyes, faces, bodies motionless, like things of stone, guns still clenched in their fists. Impossible to tell if they were enjoying it, or if they too were repelled. Larkin knew, though, that if he made a bolt for the door they'd be on him like a collapsing brick wall.

Drawn by the sort of morbid interest that compels an onlooker to a road crash, Larkin's eyes reluctantly returned to the screen.

Jason was putting up quite a fight. He was scratching and clawing at the masked man, with all the strength his small form could muster. His tormenter had had enough. He took the boy firmly by his shoulders, fingernails biting deep enough to draw blood, and brutally smacked his head against the wall.

Immediately the lights went out in Jason's eyes. Free of the man's steadying hands, the boy slid down the wall, leaving a glistening slug-trail of blood just visible on the black brickwork.

The man, panting with excitement and exhaustion, pulled off his hood. DCI David McMahon. His eyes were lit by a dark light, and his lips were drawn back into a feral grimace. He carefully moved Jason back onto the mattress. Then, smiling, he knelt down and went to work.

What happened next was the most clinical and all-encompassing form of lust and brutality Larkin had ever witnessed. Jason was sadistically beaten, his fingers snapped, his bones broken. He was repeatedly buggered. One man's hatred and self-loathing was forced into and on the young boy's body. As the attacks built to a frenzied crescendo, Jason began to regain consciousness; McMahon, seeing this, put his hands round Jason's neck, squeezing hard, lips drawn tightly back over his teeth exposing white, blood-less gums. As the final sparks of life were leaving the boy, McMahon reached orgasm. Then the body fell, lifeless and limp, from the man's hands.

McMahon straightened up and made his way round the room, like a victorious athlete doing a lap of honour in the Bizarro Olympics. After that, he moved to the camera, leered into the lens, and switched it off.

The screen returned to static.

As Grice removed the tape, Larkin realised his face was wet with tears. Grice noticed this and turned on him.

"You fuckin' soft shite," Grice sneered. "Look at the state of you."

"I always cry at love stories," Larkin snarled back.

"You soft shite," Grice repeated contemptuously.

"Is that what your dad used to say to you when he was fucking you up the arse?" Larkin spat.

Grice landed Larkin a left-handed hook which connected with his cheekbone, knocking him off his chair and sending blinding flashes to his eyes. Larkin immediately sprang up and lunged for Grice's right arm, the one holding the automatic. Slow-witted, Grice didn't have the speed to defend himself successfully, and Larkin made a grab for the gun, yanking his wrist down hard, praying he could do some damage. Grice groaned, his hand went limp and he dropped the gun. Larkin swiftly fell to his hands and knees, reaching for it, but Grice countered with a vicious, booted kick that caught Larkin under his left collarbone and sent him sprawling.

He lay there on the floor, holding his injured shoulder. All he could see was the barrel of Umpleby's automatic, pointed straight at him, the black tunnel an unblinking eye watching his every movement.

"Finished your lovemaking have you, boys?" Umpleby jeered. He turned to Swanson, who was so still he could have been struck by paralysis. "Not much of a mate, are you? Where's your sense of loyalty?"

Swanson flinched; Larkin could tell that the politician was almost catatonic with fear.

"So this tape," said Larkin, pulling himself painfully to his feet, "is this what you were looking for at my place the other night?"

"Yes," replied Umpleby. "And we'll pay you back for what you did to us."

"What *I* did to *you*? You destroyed my CD collection. If anyone is entitled to revenge, it's me!"

"You're not in a position to do anything," said Umpleby smugly.

"I can set a few things straight," Larkin continued. "I didn't have a clue until tonight what was going on. I suppose I should be flattered by the attention."

"Be what you like," replied Umpleby, sneering.

"Why are you doing this?" asked Larkin.

Umpleby rounded on him. "Why d'you think? We get paid. You spend all your life being ambitious, working your bollocks off to get to CID, up to Special Crimes – because they're the tops, they're the best coppers there are," said Umpleby bitterly. "You specialise in murder cases because that's where the prestige is. And then you get there and you find . . . what? Nothing. You notice other cops have got nice little sidelines going; Drugs, Vice, Robbery . . . all on nice little earners. Chances to skim. But not us. We just get less money and the satisfaction of a job well done."

Umpleby sat down, seizing the opportunity for self-justification. "McMahon got wind of how we felt. And he made a proposition to us. Bit of looking the other way, bit of strongarm – that sort of thing."

"By strongarm, I take it you mean murdering Houchen? And Noble and Harvey?"

Umpleby looked, slightly, embarrassed. "Well . . . yeah. Houchen – that wasn't really meant to happen. And the other two – you can't tell me anyone'll miss them. We just – did a bit of tidying up. For McMahon."

"Doesn't it bother you?" asked Larkin. "Covering up for a child killer and a nonce?"

"Did at first. You get used to it," Umpleby's brow furrowed. "As I said, we get handsomely rewarded for it. And McMahon's takin' too many chances. He's not going to be around forever."

"I suppose you'll see to that."

Umpleby shrugged non-committally.

"You're telling me an awful lot," ventured Larkin, his heart sinking as he began to realise why.

Umpleby gave a cruel smile. "Thought I'd satisfy your curiosity. Wouldn't want you to die unfulfilled."

"May I ask what will happen to me?"

Umpleby pointed out the window. "That's where you're going – you and your chatty friend. Up there." He gestured to the ten-storey-high steel skeleton. "You're going midnight bungee jumping. Without a rope."

24: Cliffhanger

Before they left the site office for the long climb, Umpleby knelt down in front of Swanson.

"Wakey wakey," he said and slapped the man's face. Swanson's eyes were startled back into focus, his hand going instinctively to his reddening and stinging cheek; Umpleby held the tape up, directly in front of his eyes. "Any more at home like this?"

Swanson shook his head.

"You sure about that?" Grice asked.

Swanson nodded. "Yes." His voice was scratchy, as if speech were unfamiliar to him. "It's the only one. I couldn't copy it myself and I . . . I didn't know who to trust with it."

Umpleby nodded; that was the right answer. He motioned to Grice who took the videotape and laid it on the table before bringing the handle of his automatic down on it hard, shattering the case. He unspooled the tape from the casing, tore it up and dropped it together with the casing into a metal wastebin. Then he chucked the surveillance tape after it. He pulled a small can of lighter fluid from his jacket. After dousing the contents of the bin with the fluid and throwing the tin in for good measure, he struck a match, tossed it in, and stood back.

The whoosh of flame made everybody flinch. The excess fluid burnt off quickly and the bin's contents settled down to be consumed, to the accompaniment of acrid smoke and a stench that penetrated deep into the nose and lungs.

Once the tapes had reduced themselves to an unsalvageable, molten mess, Grice got a kettle of water from the sink in the office and doused the flames.

"Of course," said Umpleby, "we could have burnt this place down, left you inside — "

"But you've done that once before," interrupted Larkin, "and you'd hate to repeat yourself."

"Something like that," Umpleby replied. He wasn't in the mood for repartee. "Now get going. I don't want this to take longer than it has to."

At first the climb was relatively easy: metal and concrete flights of stairs in a half-finished stairwell made for a brisk walk. Even the constant prodding of Grice's gun in Larkin's back – and Umpleby's in Swanson's – wasn't too disconcerting. The worst thing was looking down; you were suddenly hit by a feeling of exposure, of isolation. However, halfway-up the stairwell ended abruptly and was replaced by a more temporary, flimsy arrangement: a set of wooden ladders leading to a platform consisting of heavy-duty planking secured onto tubular scaffolding bars. Another ladder on that platform led up to the next one. And so on, right to the top. If the feeling of emptiness and vulnerability on the stairwell was bad, on the ladders it was absolutely chilling.

Larkin began by keeping count of the floors as he made his way up, but exhaustion soon prevented him from keeping a tally. The fronts of his thighs and the backs of his calves were aching; his new suit and shirt were soaked through. The constant rapid upwards movement and the extreme height conspired to make him dizzy and lightheaded; his chest heaved. As his palms turned slick with sweat, his grip on the rungs became white-knuckled.

After reaching the top of one set of ladders, he stumbled onto his knees, sprawling over the wooden platform. Grice was right behind him.

"Get up, you lazy cunt," he said, shoving the toe of his boot into Larkin's ribs.

"Just a minute ..." Larkin replied, glancing over to where Swanson and Umpleby were emerging onto the platform. They both looked as bad as Larkin felt.

"I said, get *up*." Grice prodded Larkin a second time, harder. "Or — "

"Or what?" said Larkin. "You'll kill me?"

"I'm gonna kill you anyway," Grice replied, "when we get to the top."

"And you couldn't throw me off halfway up, could you?" Larkin got to his feet, defiant. "That would be like premature ejaculation."

Grice's eyes turned to steel and his finger tightened on the trigger.

"Save it!" shouted Umpleby. "We do this properly. No fuck-ups!"

Grice reluctantly lowered his gun. Larkin grabbed the ladder, ready to resume his climb. "Let's get it over with," he said.

Larkin put his hands and feet on the rungs and climbed, going onto automatic pilot. As he reached the top of the ladder and began to lever himself onto the next platform, he saw in front of him, just within his grasp, a full-length, steel spirit level.

Working on pure instinct, he pulled himself clear of the ladder, reached for the level with his left hand and swung it round blindly.

Larkin's arm was jarred to a sudden standstill by a dull thud. He looked round, down, as a harsh scream issued from Grice's lips. The spirit level had made contact just above his left eyebrow, the steel edge embedded in the skin. Blood was beginning to bubble down his face. Larkin took another swing, knocking him off balance.

Grice frantically stuck out an arm, managing to grab the ladder as he fell backwards, landing hard on the platform below rather than sailing past to the ground. Larkin wasted no time. He threw the spirit level at Grice's prone body on the floor below, and ran.

The planking to his right looked the safest bet, so off he went, as fast as he could; aware that if he took one wrong step he would plunge to his death. The boarding faded out after a while, leaving individual planks straddling odd sections of scaffolding. Larkin could hear voices behind him; he had no choice but to keep going forward.

He edged his way along a plank, conscious of the wind whipping his body, trying not to look down. No good: the more he tried not to, the more he wanted to. He did so, and immediately wished he hadn't. It was a long, long way to the ground. To his mind, he might as well be walking on a tightrope, without a safety-net.

Suddenly, his feet lost their grip; looking down had made him lose his balance. Quickly he sidled to the end of the plank, arms flailing wildly, desperate to keep himself from falling. He jumped the last couple of steps, landing on scaffolding and gripping the supporting upright so fiercely his fingers seemed in danger of gouging the metal.

Breathing hard, but refusing to give in, he swiftly worked out the odds. The scaffolding itself began to peter out in only a few metres; clearly, he couldn't go back. The only alternative was the building itself. At this level, it seemed nothing but a tower of oxidised girders riveted together. No steel reinforcement, no poured concrete, no glass, nothing. Still, he had to take his chance.

His deliberations were interrupted by a couple of popping sounds in quick succession, and two corresponding zings from the scaff bars behind him. That made up his mind for him. Kicking the plank he'd walked along away from the building to slow his pursuer, he immediately set out along the first girder.

Determined not to look down this time, he glanced over his shoulder, and saw a dark figure edging its slow and painstaking way along an outer girder towards him, its progress hindered by a leg injury and the fact that Larkin had disposed of the connecting plank. Larkin thought of shouting at Umpleby, trying to put him off balance, but the surprise might have had the opposite effect: focusing the policeman's mind, providing him with a target to shoot at.

Opting for caution, Larkin successfully negotiated the next girder, gratefully grabbing the upright that greeted him. But looking ahead he found he was out of girder and he faced nothing but a huge tunnel down to the ground. Lift shaft? Courtyard? He didn't know. He didn't care. There was no place to go but down.

Staying in the corner, where the upright met the horizontal beam, he lowered himself tentatively to a crouching position, and swung his legs over the side of the beam. Immediately, vertiginous pins and needles attacked his feet. Trying to concentrate on nothing but the task in hand, he forced his heavy breathing under control. He grasped the beam he was sitting on and slowly lowered his whole body down.

Curling his arms around the horizontal beam, he slowly swung his legs backwards to gain momentum, then brought them quickly forward, wrapping them tightly round the upright girder. Once in position, he shuffled his arms along until he was able to grab the upright with first one arm then the other, clinging on for dear life.

Muscles screaming, palms slippery with sweat, he inched his way down. Once on the girder below, he chanced a glance upwards; Umpleby was edging his way round the side of the building, too busy balancing to be waving his gun around. Good, thought Larkin. With any luck, the night and the shadows of the building would cover him. He looked round again. Of Grice there was no sign. Taking short deep breaths, he prepared himself for the next descent.

It wasn't quite so painful this time; he managed to establish a rhythm. Even so, it still wasn't something he would do from choice. Landing on the next level down, he looked around, checking he hadn't been followed. But he was still alone.

He realised that this method of descent was too tiring and painful for him to make it all the way to the ground. His best bet would be to slide along to the ladders at the side of the building. Taking a few seconds to collect himself, to focus, he set off.

It was slow, agonising going. He made the first support, then the second. Then the third. One more, and he would have reached his target. He looked upwards. No one, nothing. That was beyond luck. That was unsettling. Still, he set out for the ladders.

He reached them without incident, grabbing the scaffolding and pulling himself onto the relative safety of the boards. He looked down. Nothing. He looked up. As if on cue, he saw a body being thrown, feet first, from a platform above. Even from this distance he could make out the figure of Swanson.

Larkin's heart seemed to stop as he watched, waiting for the fall, knowing there would be nothing he could do to catch the body. But Swanson didn't fall. He jerked to a sudden halt, arms stretched above him. It didn't take Larkin long to work out that the politician had been tied to a scaffolding bar and left to hang there. Frantically thrashing, Swanson's struggles showed Larkin that he was still alive.

Larkin knew he couldn't leave him there. Even if he went to get help, Swanson would be dead when he returned. He was being used as bait, to entice Larkin upwards. Knowing he was walking into an ambush – but knowing also that there was nothing else he could do – he made his way grimly back up the ladders.

The nearer Larkin came to Swanson's hanging platform, the slower his progress became. He was listening, trying to work out where the attack would come from. He heard nothing.

Larkin reached the platform, where Swanson was hanging over the side, secured to a scaff bar by a pair of regulation handcuffs.

194

Larkin could see that the force of the throw had dislocated both his arms. He was moaning quietly, his rational mind hiding somewhere beyond pain.

Larkin crossed to him, wrapping his arms round Swanson's body, hauling him back onto the platform. Swanson's legs came up easily enough, and Larkin tenderly laid the man out on the planking, leaving his useless arms still handcuffed to the bar. He cradled the man's head. Swanson's eyes were wide, glassy and completely empty.

"Hey! Fuckhead!"

Larkin turned at the voice, just in time to see Grice's face peering through the hole leading to the platform above. In his hand he held his automatic, the barrel pointing towards Larkin, his finger squeezing tightly on the trigger —

Larkin quickly hurled his body out of the line of fire, rolling over, saved from toppling over the edge by a judiciously-placed scaffolding bar. There was a loud crack, and the side of Larkin's head was hit with warmth and wetness. The air smelt of offal. But there was no pain, so . . . He looked round. Half of Swanson's head was missing; he'd taken the bullet, full on. And Larkin was covered with Swanson's blood and brains. He threw up over the side of the platform.

"Missed you!" the laughter was loud, uncontrolled.

Larkin pulled himself to his knees. Grice, his face a red mask from the earlier injury, was making his way down from above, grinning from ear to ear.

"Just like in the fuckin' films! Fuckin' *great*!" Grice was wired; the killing had given him an all-time high. Larkin knew he would be hungry for more, so he swallowed his anger and fear, trying to calm himself down before he spoke, so he would choose the right words.

"You've got me now, Grice." Larkin held his arms up. "You gonna shoot me too?"

Grice pointed his gun at Larkin, but stopped just short of pulling the trigger. "Naw," he said, as a new thought struck him, "we've got unfinished business. Get climbing."

Larkin saw he had no option. He cast a long, sad look at what was once Swanson, and started to climb.

It soon settled into the same pattern as before: Larkin climbing,

Grice's gun sticking painfully into his spine at almost every step. They were nearing the top: one more set of ladders and they'd be there. Larkin resisted the temptation to look down.

"Where's Umpleby?" asked Larkin, attempting to take the madness out of Grice with rational conversation.

"He'll be here when he's needed," was Grice's curt reply.

They climbed in silence until Larkin, hoping to make a last-ditch appeal to Grice's conscience, spoke again. "So what about the children?"

"What children?"

"The ones whose photos you took out of Noble's place. The abused ones. The missing ones. You ever wonder what happened to them?"

"Not really," said Grice, disinterested. "Way I see it, they're all little bastards anyway. Crooks in the making. Nothing you could do to them would make them any worse. McMahon said some of them ended up in Amsterdam – bloody good riddance, if you ask me."

They carried on to the top platform. The view was magnificent, but Larkin wasn't inclined to admire it. He'd never liked heights at the best of times, and this was far from the best of times. His heart pounding, he grabbed a girder for support and held on as tightly as he could. Grice emerged from the ladder and stood facing him, grinning.

"Now all you have to do," Grice said with obvious glee, "is take three steps back. And then you'll be gone. Or would you rather turn round and see where you're goin'?"

Larkin remained silent, staring at Grice solemnly.

"You want my face to be the last thing you see?" Grice sounded like he hadn't had so much fun in ages. "Fine by me. No last words? Nothin' to be remembered by?"

Larkin kept staring. Suddenly, as he watched, a liquid shadow seemed to flow through the opening onto the platform behind Grice. It pulled itself up to its full height and Larkin was filled with unbelievable, wholly unexpected joy. Ezz. Larkin forced himself not to smile.

"I said," Grice shouted, "have you got any last words?"

"Yeah," said Larkin. "Look behind you."

Grice emitted a short snort of a laugh. "Pathetic! Can't you come up with someth — "

The words were choked off in his throat as Ezz placed Grice's

196

neck in an armlock. His other hand effortlessly relieved Grice of his gun.

"Do *you* have any last words?" he calmly asked Grice.

All Grice could manage were a few strangled expletives.

"Thought not," said Ezz, and snapped his neck. The lifeless body crumpled to a heap on the platform as Ezz let go.

"Here," said Ezz, throwing Grice's gun to Larkin, "let's make a quick exit."

Larkin stood still, shaking. "Is he *dead*?" he heard his voice ask, like a child.

"Yeah."

"You *killed* him!"

Ezz shrugged. "He killed that bloke downstairs. He killed Houchen an' all. An' Noble."

"I thought that was you."

"I know," Ezz replied. "An' it could have been me, I was all set to do it, but then they turned up an' saved me the trouble. Don't lose sleep over it. He was goin' to kill you if I hadn't got to him first."

"What are you doing here, anyway?" Larkin asked. "You just happened to be passing and you thought you'd drop in?"

"I've been followin' you all day. I was waiting for the right moment to make an appearance." Ezz almost smiled. "I can't leave you alone for five minutes, can I?"

Larkin laughed, more to release tension than anything else. "That was almost a joke. I never thought I'd hear you make a joke, Ezz."

"Yeah, well," said Ezz, his usual icy detachment returning, "we'll have to move. There's another one still around somewhere."

"Yeah. And we want him alive. He's the only one who can prove McMahon murdered Jason Winship."

"That policeman?" asked Ezz.

"Yeah. Come on – let's get the hell out of here."

They decided not to go straight down in case Umpleby was waiting for them; instead they made their tortuous way round the top of the building, searching for another set of ladders. As they were edging their way round, Larkin noticed the adjoining building. The two were due to be interconnected at some time during construction, and the space between them, at this point, was only about seven or eight feet.

"What d'you reckon, Ezz?" asked Larkin. "Put a plank across here and make it down the next one?"

Ezz stared at it, brow furrowed in concentration. "Might work. If we can find a plank long enough."

"Let's have a look."

They scrutinised the planking. It all seemed to be of uniform length; two inches thick with metal-tipped ends. They pulled one up and, taking the weight on either side, brought it down to cover the gap. It made a reverberating, slapping sound as it connected with a scaff bar on the other side. But it held.

"Done it!" said Larkin. "I reckon we've got two inches at either side. I'll hold it, you get across – you hold it, I'll come. OK?"

Ezz nodded. Larkin held the plank firmly in place and Ezz stepped onto it.

Suddenly there was a zinging sound next to Larkin's left ear, accompanied by a raising of dust and chips from the scaff pole. Larkin turned his head. Umpleby was making his way to where they were. He was throwing out his injured leg awkwardly as he walked, but there was no mistaking the gun held firmly in his hand.

"Hurry!" Larkin shouted. Ezz nonchalantly walked along the plank, not looking down, blithely indifferent, as if he were traversing someone's living room Axminster. He neatly stepped off the other end, then knelt down to steady the plank.

"Your turn."

Larkin gingerly stepped out, trying not to think of the space between him and the ground, or the armed maniac coming up behind him. His whole body was shivering with fear; his legs felt like they had diving boots attached.

"Come on," said Ezz in his monotone.

Larkin edged his way out. From the corner of his eye he saw Umpleby getting nearer. The shakes increased. He felt like he was going to faint.

"Hold it together." Ezz, trying to be reassuring.

Larkin shuffled his feet past the halfway point. His internal organs were flipping over so much, it felt as if they belonged to a family of circus acrobats.

Three quarters, then:

"Stay there, you bastard." Umpleby had reached them. His gun was trained on Larkin.

Larkin froze. "Ignore him. Keep moving." Ezz, more urgent now.

"I'll shoot!" shouted Umpleby.

"You're gonna shoot anyway," Larkin shouted back.

Umpleby gave a brutal laugh. "Then I'll have to make sure I get both of you." He stepped onto the plank which bowed and creaked under the added weight. "Your mate's not goin' to move while I'm on this, is he?"

Larkin was rooted to the spot by terror. He could see the ends of the plank warping upwards, pulled away from their resting place by the extra bulk. Even iron-muscled Ezz wouldn't be able to hold them in place. The slightest movement one way or the other – and it would be all over.

Larkin swallowed hard. If he stayed put, he was dead. If he walked he was dead. He had only one option.

He braced himself and locked his eyes on the scaff bar next to Ezz. Ezz gave a slight nod: he knew what Larkin was going to do.

Suddenly, taking a deep breath, Larkin tensed his legs and jumped.

As soon as Larkin bounced his weight off the plank, it spring-boarded in the air with him. Umpleby, taken by surprise, lost his balance. He tried desperately to remain upright, but his injured leg made him clumsy. Off he went. He dropped his gun, made one last, scrabbling attempt to reach the plank with his fingers. He failed. Plummeted. His face was a mask of terror and shock as he fell, emitting a shriek that dwindled the further he went. Eventually, it stopped altogether.

Larkin had a tentative hold on the protruding scaff bar, but the sweat on his fingers rendered the grip non-existent. He frantically scrambled to hold on, legs kicking furiously in the air, but it was no good. He felt himself start to follow Umpleby.

Then his arm was gripped firmly, pulled hard. And his whole body moved upwards as he was yanked over the edge onto the safety of the platform.

Larkin lay on his back, gasping in great lungfuls of air. He thought he'd never be able to move again. Ezz's face and body loomed into view.

"Cheers, mate," Larkin gasped, "I owe you one. In fact, I owe you fuckin' loads."

Ezz shrugged, but his lips almost twitched into a smile. "That's OK." He looked down. "There goes the last bit of evidence against McMahon. Shame about that."

"Yeah," gasped Larkin between ragged breaths, "bastard's gonna get away with it."

"We'll see," said Ezz vaguely. "There's more than one kind of justice." He looked down at Larkin, extended a hand. "Let's get goin'."

Larkin was tugged to his feet. He removed Grice's gun from his pocket, wiped it carefully, and threw it after Umpleby.

They they made their way down and away.

25: Memento Mori

Larkin sat in the small crematorium and stared at the coffin. The grim irony wasn't lost on him: a man who had burnt to death was about to be burned in death.

The coffin containing Houchen's already charred remains lay at the far end of the hall. Saltwell Crematorium wasn't a huge place, which was just as well, since there weren't that many mourners. Work colleagues made up the bulk, mostly seated towards the rear, with a smattering of family at the front. Larkin took a good look at Houchen's ex-wife: a hard-faced woman who seemed to possess no grief to express; and her two children, a boy and girl, who appeared to be depressed beyond the loss of their father. Larkin knew the divorce had been acrimonious, and seeing the ex-Mrs Houchen he could understand why. So many unhappy families, he thought; such brief, sad lives.

Larkin sat near the back, Andy next to him. Then Bolland. Joyce was pouring forth her funeral tears; the others wore suitably sombre expressions. At the opposite end sat Carrie Brewer. Larkin noticed that she and Andy said as little to each other as possible. They had no reason to; the need that had driven them together – lust, loneliness, anger – had been satisfied. Larkin thought that in many ways this was an enviable approach to relationships.

The taped organ music faded out, taking with it any further contemplation. A robed vicar that none of them – especially Houchen – had ever seen before walked to the front and the service began.

They stood up, sang a hymn, knelt (or at least sat forward with hunched shoulders and bowed heads), prayed, sat. The vicar began to talk with assumed sorrow about Houchen; an anonymous eulogy for a man he would never know. Larkin looked across at Bolland;

the man was itching to jump into the breach, show them how it should be done. At least the vicar's address would be shorter, Larkin thought.

Not that he was really listening. As the vicar droned on he tuned out, mulled over the many and varied events of the last week.

The dreams had started again. And this time, no amount of whisky could fight them off. Swanson's death, Raymond and Kev in the cellar, the recorded death of Jason Winship: the images jumbled and juxtaposed in Larkin's sleeping head; forming themselves with implacable dream logic into twisted wraiths, haunting his waking time. He knew the images were lodged in his consciousness forever. More ghosts.

He'd been hauled in by the police: he'd expected that, so he'd had time to work out a convincing story and stick to it. After the discovery of Swanson's body two detectives had sweated him in an interview room, firing question after question at him for hours: Swanson's bodyguards had recognised him from Milburn's. Where had he gone with Swanson? Nowhere. They'd talked, he'd gone home. What had the meeting been about? He'd met Swanson the night before, asked for an interview. What did they talk about? Nothing much. Who were the two men who turned up? Umpleby and Grice – two coppers. What did they want? You'd have to ask them. Larkin had left Milburn's before he could find out, leaving the three men alone. And so on.

He told them a story that was half-truth, half-invention; the truths gave the lies a veracity that made it impossible for the police to work out which was which. As long as he stuck to his version of the events, there was no one to contradict him. He had, apparently, done nothing wrong, so there was nothing they could charge him with. After Larkin had successfully led them up several blind alleys, the police reluctantly let him go.

Going back to the house had been painful too. The first couple of nights he'd left everything as it was, straightening only his bed and trying to blot his surroundings out with alcohol before lapsing into oblivion. But he couldn't go on forever like that.

He hired a skip, gathered up all the debris and dumped it. As he sifted through the wreckage he found that some things had survived the attack in better condition than he'd first thought. Once the mouldering food had been cleared away, the kitchen was virtually good as new. The sofa and chairs in the front room were, with some minor patch-up work, still pretty serviceable. On the whole it was the smaller things, the personal things – the more important things – that had been lost.

The books. The CDs. The memories. Gone. And Charlotte's old room had been gutted. When Larkin had finished his painful clearing, all trace of her had vanished. Umpleby and Grice's actions had at least been a purgative: the house was now a blank slate, a chance to start again. Small comfort, but perhaps something to be grateful for.

Larkin had met Moir for a drink. The big man seemed to be unravelling before his eyes. They had met at the Waterfront on the quayside, sitting at an outside table. The sun was high, the day was hot and the sky was blue, but all they could see was the grey, scummy river flowing endlessly through the city and out to the sea.

"It's fucked, isn't it?" Moir had said eventually.

Larkin nodded.

"You cut off the limbs," Moir said, the words twisting with bitterness and rage in his mouth, "but you can never stab the fuckin' heart."

They both knew what he was talking about.

Moir was off again. "He played me like a fuckin' guitar. Told me he put me in charge of the case because of my unique talents. Some talents. He knew my weaknesses. Thought I'd let my own feelin's get in the way of the job. Make me weak. Make me controllable. And he was fuckin' right." Moir took a large mouthful of beer. "But he didn't think I'd find out about him." He gave a bitter laugh. "For all the good it can do me. The words of a few men. No evidence. Fuck . . ."

They relapsed into silence.

"I've made my decision." Moir stared at the water.

"Yeah?"

"I'm takin' some time off. I've got it owin' and I've got things to do." Moir took a deep breath. "My daughter . . ."

"I know."

Moir looked away, but Larkin caught a brief flash of tears in his eyes. "It's time to talk," he said, painfully. "I've lost my faith in justice. Let's just hope I haven't lost it in everything else."

Larkin looked at his friend. Despite Larkin's companionship, he

203

was very much alone. Moir carried an aura that said he would be alone whoever he was with, wherever he went. Larkin drained his glass, stood up, placed his hand on the other man's shoulder in an empty gesture of comfort, and left him there.

A few metres along, Larkin turned back; Moir still sat, unmoving. Staring into his glass as if the answers he wanted were in the beer as the poisoned river slurped past.

He'd also paid a visit to his tame transvestite-loving councillor. The man had just emerged from a meeting at the Civic Centre when Larkin accosted him in the car park. He quickly dismissed his assistant, his face draining of colour at Larkin's approach.

"I want a word with you," Larkin said without any preamble.

They sat in the politician's car; Larkin outlined his demands. The man listened in silence. When Larkin had finished, the man spoke.

"And if I do that?"

"You'll never hear from me again. That's a promise."

"And the photographs?"

"I'll destroy them."

The man looked wary, wanting to believe him, not daring to. "How do I know you're not lying? You could — "

Larkin was losing patience. "Look, I don't give a fuck about those photos. I don't give a fuck about your precious career. I just want you to do the job you were elected to do. It's what you get paid for. Do what I tell you – the photos get destroyed. Simple as that."

The man swallowed hard. "What you're asking – it's not up to me."

"Then make sure you lick the right arses."

"Well, I'll see — "

'No. You won't see. You'll fuckin' *do* it." Larkin pushed open the car door and stepped out, slamming it behind him. As he walked away he knew: the man would do what he wanted. He had no other option.

The next appointment he'd had had been the most difficult. Jane. He had tried calling her at work a couple of times but found himself holding a dead phone each time he'd tried. Clearly, the only way to reach her was to turn up in person.

He found himself opening the doors to the centre exactly a week to the day after he'd last seen her. He was lucky; she was walking past as he entered.

"Jane."

She stopped, turned at his voice. When she saw him her features immediately hardened; when she spoke, her voice did likewise. "What." Uninflected, flat. Not wanting to make a connection.

"I need to talk to you." Larkin's heart was pounding.

"So talk."

"Can we go somewhere else?"

"No." She didn't move, didn't take her eyes off him. She seemed to have turned into stone.

Larkin moved towards her, his voice lowered. "I've got something to tell you. Your grant for this place – it's been renewed. In fact, it's been increased."

"I know. They phoned."

"Not only that," he continued, "but that other place you wanted to start up – that refuge for kids? They're giving that the go-ahead too."

"They said. Did you do that?"

Larkin nodded.

"You didn't have to. We'd have managed. But thanks. I hope you did it for the right reasons."

"I did."

"And not just to get back in with me."

Larkin's face fell.

"Thought so." Jane turned to go.

"Wait," said Larkin. She stopped. "Listen, I . . ." He couldn't find the words.

"Stephen," Jane said, taking a step in his direction, "it's over. I've got to protect me family. I thought you were someone you're not. I like you. But I don't think I could ever trust you again."

And she walked away. Larkin couldn't be sure, but before she went, he sensed that the stone was beginning to crumble.

Larkin had attended another funeral that week: Swanson's. It hadn't produced as big an outpouring of public grief as Princess Di's – or even Jackie Milburn's for that matter – but for an MP it was big enough. There was a public memorial service in the cathedral, screens outside. All manner of locally and nationally prominent people were there, with Tony Blair wringing his hands, talking of the loss "not only of a visionary, but a personal friend".

Larkin had stood at the back of the congregation, surveying the mourners with cynicism. Swanson's death had generated reams of paper, hours of TV footage, all focusing on the "towering achievements" that he had brought about, talking inevitably about the manner of his death. All the theories were speculative; none were near the truth. Larkin's contribution to the attendant media circus had been conspicuous by its absence.

As Larkin looked round the crowded cathedral, his eyes alighted on McMahon. He was wearing full dress uniform: erect posture, face firmly set. He caught Larkin's glare, flung it contemptuously back at him. The look managed to convey more to Larkin than words could. *I'm bulletproof*, the eyes said. *And you're only alive because you're powerless to do anything against me.*

And Ezz? Larkin had tried to contact him, but there was no sign of him. It was as if he had never existed.

The service commemorating Houchen's life ended and the mourners made their way outside, congregating in front of the sparse funeral flowers. Larkin wasn't in the mood for the usual small talk. He stuck close to Andy.

"So, you staying around this time? In Newcastle?"

"Might as well. Seem to be drawn inexorably to the place."

Larkin nodded.

"There's a bit of a do on back at the ex's place. You goin'?" asked Andy.

"No," he said slowly, "I think I'll be off."

Andy shrugged. "Suit yourself. See you around, then."

Larkin managed to walk down the path and through the crematorium gates without saying goodbye.

Larkin sat in the Nine Pins, the nearest pub to Saltwell Crematorium, nursing his pint and watching a middle-aged man with a beergut that seemed to have a life of its own feed coin after coin into a fruit machine. Every time the man stretched his arm out, his stomach fluttered and rippled: it looked like the only exercise he ever got.

Larkin hadn't been able to face the funeral reception. Brittle-crusted sandwiches and even more brittle conversation. And with the knowledge he had about the circumstances of Houchen's death, the trite platitudes expected of him would freeze in his mouth.

He took a large gulp of beer, his mind trying to make sense of recent events. He had tried to do something good, but had ended up being used by a man whose motives remained unclear. Had Swanson been genuine? Did he have principles? Did he want to expose his brother because he hated what McMahon had become, or because he thought it would make him look good in the eyes of the voters? These were hypothetical questions now. Larkin thought of the people who had lined the route of Swanson's funeral procession with grief-stricken faces: they had believed in Swanson. Or had wanted to. But deep down, Larkin didn't buy it, any of it. Larkin had seen a quotation once, he couldn't remember who had said it, but it went: ''I have seen the enemy and he is ours.'' Someone else had changed it to: ''I have seen the enemy and he is us.'' As long as the Establishment stayed the same, thought Larkin, the monsters would always be with us. For every Swanson, there was a McMahon. And there was no way of changing that.

The overweight gambler sat down to drink his beer. He had lost all his money; the machine wasn't going to pay out. His life wasn't about to be transformed by a lucky win, but he seemed to have accepted that his existence was something he had no control over. It was something to be endured, accepted. Perhaps it was time Larkin did the same thing. But even as he allowed the thought to form, he knew it would never happen. He knew he was destined to spend his life, as another writer had put it, raging into the dying of the light.

If he didn't ask so many questions – if he learned to differentiate between the things he could and couldn't change – he might have a happier life. Jane had offered him a glimpse of that life, and he had, half-reluctantly, refused. Instead of comfort he had chosen rage and truth. Now he had to trust the faith he'd placed in those two things would be enough to keep him warm.

He drained his glass and ordered a refill, hoping the alcohol would satisfy more than his physical thirst. He raised the pint to his lips. ''Cheers,'' he mumbled.

207

                        *   *   *

He sat in the pub, methodically drinking one pint after another until it was dark. Despite his best efforts, he was still, depressingly, sober.

From the other bar, the evening's karaoke was starting, people who had settled for comfort working out their mediocre fantasies. A shaky male voice began to murder Bryan Adams. Larkin drained his glass and headed for the door. Not that he didn't agree with the sentiment, but there'd been enough killing in his life recently.

Outside, the air was decidedly cool. Autumn had arrived. Soon winter would lay its frozen grip on the city, a layer of coldness jacketing everyone. Larkin drew his coat about him to hold in the warmth and began the long walk home.

. . . And Justice For All

The man struck the ball hard with his club, following its arc against the blue sky, watching it fall to earth exactly where he had intended it to. A fellow golfer on the fairway praised his precision and accuracy; the man assumed a self-effacing air, passing it off as a lucky shot.

But of course it wasn't. The whole game had been calculated and there was no such thing as luck. This wasn't relaxation: this was another exercise in control.

Over the past month, the man had lost many things: a fulfilling and lucrative hobby, his closest associates. His brother. Well, in all honesty, he'd lost his brother years ago. The main thing, however, was that his instinct for self-preservation was still functioning perfectly. He was still safe.

He walked down the fairway to continue his game. However, as he neared the spot where the ball had landed, he could find no trace of it. It was nowhere to be seen.

He took so long looking for it when it patently wasn't there that the other golfer had taken his shot and caught up with him. He made a lame joke, asked if he could play on in front of him. The man said that would be no trouble and forced himself to laugh, but inwardly he was furious. The shot, he knew, had been controlled perfectly. There was no way it could have landed anywhere but here. Was there? There was that nearby clump of trees . . . Mask of a smile in place, the man entered the densely wooded area.

Once inside, he found his task harder than he had imagined. He beat the bracken, uprooting it with his club, but there was no sign of his ball. He was fuming now, trying desperately to control his

209

swings, not to let his anger show, even here. He went further in.

No sign. If he didn't know better he would have sworn that some-one had taken it. He waded deep into the wood, so deep he couldn't see the fairway behind him. Bent double, eyes fixed on the ground, he didn't see the figure emerge from behind the tree in front of him. Not until it was too late to run.

"This what you're lookin' for?"

The man looked up. He was confronted by a skinhead: DMs, black Levis, green nylon bomber jacket. In his gloved right hand he held a golfball.

"Yes, thank you. Give me that." The man went to take it, but the skinhead moved the ball away from his grasp.

"Just a minute," said the skinhead. "You thought you'd got away with it, didn't you?" He took a menacing step forward.

The man was in no mood for this. He spoke with anger and exas-peration. "I'm not playing games with you. Give me that ball."

A chilling smile broke on the skinhead's face. "This isn't a game. This is serious. Deadly serious."

"You've had your fun. Now, give me my property." The man made a grab for the ball, but the skinhead deftly snatched it away. The skinhead's smile widened, which only served to increase the man's anger. "I'm warning you! You don't know who you're mess-ing with!"

The smile suddenly dropped from the skinhead's face, leaving an icy killer's stare in its place. "I do. I know exactly who you are. And I know exactly what you are." The skinhead's monotone was in direct contrast to his own raised voice, uneven with emotion.

A shiver of fear went down the man's spine. He immediately con-verted it to rage. "Give me my fucking ball!"

The skinhead looked at him; their eyes locked. With a flick of his wrist he threw to the ball the ground, at the man's feet. "There it is. Pick it up."

Breathing through his mouth, the man bent to pick up the ball. With sudden whiplash speed, the skinhead brought his right fist down on top of the man's head. It was a punch he had been saving up for years, and he did it with such force the man's face was smacked hard into the ground, breaking his nose. He was so sur-prised, he didn't even have time to scream.

The skinhead knelt down beside him, picked the ball up. "You thought you'd got away with murder, didn't you? But you didn't

reckon on me. I want you to pay for what you've done. For fuckin'
kids. For fuckin' up kids. You see, that happened to me when I was
little. Me dad." The skinhead's voice became more intense. "An' I
can still see his face everywhere I go. 'Cos I couldn't fight back
then. But I can now."

Although the man was bleeding, in pain, he refused to back down.
"Right, you little bastard, you've asked for it." He struggled to his
feet, while the skinhead watched.

"You wanna fight?" asked the skinhead. "Good – I like a fight.
Especially when I've got right on my side."

"I can still take the likes of you, you little shit." The man squared
up to the skinhead, ready to take a swing at him. But he didn't get
the chance; the skinhead swung his right fist – the one holding the
ball – with sudden and unexpected force, straight into the man's
face. The man's front teeth tore through his lips and his body
flopped backwards onto the ground, hands once again at his face.
He was moaning now.

The skinhead picked up the discarded golf club and swung it
viciously at the man's ribs. He heard at least two break as it connected. He swung again.

The man opened his smashed mouth to cry out. Immediately the
skinhead stuck the golf ball in his mouth, pushing it right the way
down his throat, ignoring the man's thrashing, choking him from
within.

Fighting for every breath, the man began frantically to claw at
his throat. The skinhead hefted the golf club over his head and
brought it smashing down on the remains of the man's mouth. And
again. And again.

The man's fingers lost their power to claw. They slowly fell away
from his neck. He knew he was dying. Soundlessly, he began to cry
out. And was both surprised and appalled to discover that the voice
shouting in his head – the last thing he would ever hear – was the
lonely snivelling of a small boy: a boy whose ghost had been left
hanging from a rope tied to an old oak tree, many years ago.

The skinhead watched silently as the imploring light went out in
the man's eyes, to be replaced by the milky stare of death.

The skinhead straightened up, threw the golf club on top of the
body, sighed. The face wouldn't haunt him any more. He knew that.

They wouldn't find him. He had left nothing incriminating. And
even if they did happen to pin anything on him, when the full story

211

came out he would be viewed in a different, more sympathetic light. But in a sense it didn't matter. None of it mattered. Justice had been done. That was the important thing.

"Cleansed," he said out loud. No one heard him.

He walked to the far edge of the woods and stepped out into the sunlight. After a while, to his own surprise, he found himself whistling. He laughed aloud when he realised what the song was: Louis Armstrong's "Wonderful World".

Shaking his head and smiling, the skinhead walked towards the sunshine.